MY WORD
AGAINST HIS

MY WORD AGAINST HIS

LAUREN NORTH

bookouture

Published by Bookouture in 2023

An imprint of Storyfire Ltd.
Carmelite House
50 Victoria Embankment
London EC4Y 0DZ

www.bookouture.com

ISBN: 978-1-83790-178-4
eBook ISBN: 978-1-83790-177-7

For Tommy

Today 18:40

Where are you?

Today 18:41

I need you.

Today 20:04

*Getting really
worried now!!!*

Today 20:27

Don't go to the police!

ONE

CELIA

The kitchen surfaces gleam with the shine of a damp cloth and spray. Clean. Not new. But I don't mind the tired white cupboards or the chips in the corners of the worktops, the old crack in the tile by the window where Martin threw the vase the day he told me he was leaving.

As long as it's clean, everything in its place, then I'm happy. I peel off the rubber gloves and peg them to the inside of the door under the sink before glancing at the time. It's 8.25 a.m. Everything is in order. Henry is up and packing his bag for college. He's already eaten his breakfast, wolfing down a bowl of Cheerios in the time it took me to boil the kettle for my cup of tea, barely sitting at the round pine table in the corner of the kitchen before springing up again.

I step into the hall and smooth out my blouse. Green today. A pale avocado paired with a darker green cardigan and black trousers, the shapeless kind that come in packs of two from M&S.

'Time to go, Henry,' I call up the stairs.

'Coming,' he shouts back in a voice that's deep and still a little unfamiliar despite it breaking four years ago. He appears a moment later at the top of the stairs, looking so very smart in his burgundy blazer and tie. The Head Boy badge is pinned to his lapel, glinting in the light.

Henry is still so much the nervous little boy I remember from before. The one who loved potatoes in the shape of smiling faces, and building Lego, and yet he is different too. Tall, for starters. Far taller than me. He's thin but not skinny. At seventeen, he's yet to broaden into the shape of the man he will one day be, but it's there – a shadow, a promise.

His hair is neat – wet-combed and gelled, the way he knows I like it. It's the same chestnut colour as my own, before the peppering of grey and the six-week ritual of the hair dye box that always leaves a tinge of orange no matter which brand I choose.

Henry's bag is slung over one shoulder. 'I'm ready,' he says, before I have the chance to ask.

'Good.' I check the time. It's 8.29 a.m. 'One minute.'

'I know,' he says with a smile I take to read as exasperated rather than annoyed. He knows the routines just as well as I do, after all. He doesn't need to be told.

I follow him into the kitchen and watch him place the glass in the dishwasher. 'Have you got your chemistry homework?' I ask.

He pauses for a second, thinks, then nods. 'You know I'm going to have to do this stuff on my own next year, right?' He flashes me another wide grin, showing me the teeth that cost a small fortune in braces when he was thirteen.

'And until then I'll ask.'

I watch a playful retort form on his lips but go no further. A sound of clattering from the garage jolts us both. We turn towards the white door in the corner of the kitchen that leads into the garage. The door I always keep locked, the key never far from my side.

My pulse quickens, darts of fear shooting through my veins. I swallow down the rising panic and will it to be silent.

'What was that?' Henry asks, raising his eyebrows as he turns to look at me.

I huff a laugh and roll my eyes. 'The starlings must have got back into the roof section. Looking for somewhere warm to hide out for the winter. I'll take a look on my day off on Friday.' I wonder if it's true. If birds can be blamed. Somehow I doubt it.

'Maybe we should look now.' He tilts his head and for a moment I feel like he's challenging me, testing me.

I push the thought aside. The fear is making me paranoid. Henry knows the garage is out of bounds. I told him years ago that there's asbestos in the roof and it isn't safe. I make a show of looking to the clock on the wall above the table. 'It's time to leave now. You don't want to be late for school. Besides, it's only old junk in there,' I lie. 'The birds can't do any harm.'

'Sure.' He looks at the screen of his phone, his eyes widening a fraction at something there. I want to ask what it is, who is messaging him, but he's already halfway across the kitchen, pecking me on the cheek before striding to the front door and shrugging on his winter coat. 'Bye, Mum. Love you.'

The words are automatic and sound a little wooden but I take them anyway, hold them close as my darling boy opens the front door and leaves for school. My reply dances on my lips. *One more huggy?* Three words, silly nonsense really, but filled to the brim with love.

He's gone in a flash and, the moment I'm alone, my eyes draw back to the garage. I have half a thought to open the door, but it's gone eight-thirty and I need to leave for work.

I give a final glance back at my clean kitchen, the order restoring my calm. My eyes linger on the meal planner on the fridge. Tuesday night is pasta night. Beside the planner is Henry's revision timetable, stuck to the fridge with magnets from our holidays – Malta last year, Greece the year before that.

Henry's mock exams are looming and the coloured boxes for each night of the week keep him on track. Red for chemistry. Blue for maths. Tonight is green – biology, his favourite.

The end is in sight now. It hovers around us like the smell of cut grass on spring days, a feeling of change in the air, of something ahead. Only six months until his final exams. Only ten months until he'll be studying medicine – his dream. The thought causes a giddy nervousness to spin and twist inside me. Henry is everything to me. He's all I have.

I try to imagine how I'll cope without him. How he'll cope without me. There are no answers to these imaginings, no peace, so I check my lunch is in my bag – four Ryvita crackers and an apple – and I hurry from the house.

It's only a ten-minute drive to the high street and Citizens Advice, where I've worked for the past twelve years. As soon as I'm parked in the staff car park at the back of the building, I pull out my phone and check the Find My app. Henry's icon is grey; his phone switched off now he's in class. His last location is showing at the school and so I breathe a little easier as I climb out of the car.

One more huggy?

The question lingers in my thoughts as I walk across the car park. It's leftover from the dozens of times a day we said it to each other when Henry was little. At school drop-off. At bath time, bedtime. Any time of day.

I don't say these words anymore; he's too big for them. And yet if I'd known how much everything would change in eight short hours, I'd have let the question out, shouted it loud. I'd have pulled Henry back towards me, held him close. But how could I have known? Whole weeks, months, years of my life have passed by unnoticeably. There was no clue, no sign or signal that today was the day everything would veer completely off-course. All because of Lucie.

PART I

TWO

CELIA

Hour one

Everything has gone wrong. It's the one thought that sticks as the rest of my mind jumbles – a kaleidoscope of panic. Lucie's words thrum in my mind. *'It's life or death, Celia.'*

I press my foot to the accelerator and watch the speedometer climb up and up with the racing of my heart. Twenty. Thirty. Forty. Still I keep pressing. The needle hovers between forty and fifty. I'm speeding now. I never speed.

Everything was fine. Even an hour ago, life was normal. My thoughts had been on the pasta I'd cook for dinner and Henry's biology revision. And then Lucie called me as I was leaving work at the end of the day and it all changed.

What the hell was she thinking? I want to shout and rage. Stupid girl! But my chest aches for her, for this night and what I'm now doing.

The wipers glide back and forth against the spatter of rain as the town rushes by my windows. It's only 6 p.m. but the November sky is pitch-black in that middle-of-winter way, when it feels almost indecent to be out. It's too dark, too cold, too wet.

The neon orange of a small Sainsbury's glows in the distance, reminding me with a sharp prod of where I should be right now – driving home to Henry. I picture the kitchen – the kitchen table strewn with textbooks, and Henry's body bent over, one hand pushed into his hair, the curls no longer gelled into place after a day of ruffling it.

Four-fifteen until six-thirty is always revision. He'll be finished soon. Hungry too, glancing at the clock, waiting for me.

A sob rushes up inside me. A burst of emotion I don't expect or want. I swallow hard, pushing it all down. I'll cry later when it's over, when I can breathe again, when Lucie is somewhere safe and I've driven home and cooked the dinner and held the quiz cards on evolution and ecosystems. When the dishes are dried and put away and the house is tidy and Henry is in bed. Then I will cry.

Oh, Lucie. I'm on my way. I will fix this.

Thirteen years of nothing. Silence. No Christmas card. No birthday text. I thought she'd forgotten about me. Little Lucie with her greasy roots and the spray of orange freckles across her nose. Those blue eyes that took everything in. I still catch the scent of her uniform sometimes; that musky smell of clothes that haven't dried properly. Lucie slipped into my office one lunchtime and asked for my help, back when Henry was still so little and I'd found a part-time role in a school as a careers adviser. Ditching my accountancy exams halfway through because really I wanted to help people. And returning to work alongside Martin was never an option.

Lucie slipped into my heart just as easily.

Thirteen years of silence but she remembered me when she was in trouble. She picked up the phone. She called and I answered on the first ring. Not a moment's hesitation.

I don't know a single thing about her now. Twenty-six years

old. A stranger. Nothing to me anymore. Until tonight. And suddenly she is everything again.

No apology. Just a hurried whisper of needing me, of trouble. My mind pulls to the boot of the car and what lies ahead of me. It feels film-like, surreal. Impossible. But only I can help. Only I can save us. I *will* save us. And it is *us*. The moment I answered the phone I was in as deep as Lucie.

I drive east along the river, past the big cinema and the row of chain restaurants. There are red and green Christmas lights hanging from the awnings of a pizza place. The lights flap in the wind, gaudy and up far too early. I turn off the main road, away from the traffic, from people, life, safety. The night closes in and I drive, ignoring the shake of my hands and the danger I'm driving towards. There are houses and parks and then a petrol station and a row of run-down shops – a kebab take-away and an off-licence, a bathroom showroom and a hair salon.

A gust of wind sprays rain against the windows. I shiver in the thickness of my winter coat and wish I was home. I don't like to leave Henry alone for too long. My mind pulls to the garage and the noise earlier. Birds, I said. I hoped. I don't like to think about what is hidden in there alongside Martin's old golf clubs and the crate of football magazines he used to collect as a boy. For a moment it feels like a madness might jump right out of my chest.

I bite down on the inside of my cheeks and picture the meal planner on the fridge. The routine of it. The order. I take a breath, reminding myself that Henry wouldn't snoop. He's such a good boy – a young man, really. Eighteen next month. Besides, the door to the garage is always locked. Always.

There are traffic lights ahead. The light shines a bright green – the colour of the Quality Street triangles that Martin used to love, until he told me he was leaving and I stopped buying them. The colour of Fire Exit signs and the promise of a way out. Then it's amber and I think about pushing forward anyway, but I remember Lucie's call. The need to help tugs at my insides. I can't risk an accident now.

My foot eases from the accelerator and presses the brake, the car rolling to a stop. The only sound is the hum of the engine and the squeaking of the wipers.

Staying still. Waiting. It feels all wrong.

'It's life or death, Celia.'

Not the First World life-or-death kind of problem bandied around by my co-workers – a broken heel on a night out, a bad outfit choice, a child with a mean friend. Not the missed mortgage payments or the dodgy builder who's run off without finishing the job – the problems of the people who queue in the neat line that winds out the door of Citizens Advice day after day after day. This is real. If I don't help, if I don't succeed, then it's all over. For Lucie, and for me too.

My reply was instant. 'Tell me what you need me to do.' This is Lucie. The precious girl who almost felt like mine, for a little while anyway.

The thoughts spin, propeller-like, in my head. The light remains red. The road empty.

And then it's not empty. There's movement in the corner of my eye. Footsteps. My breath catches in my throat. And before I have the chance to react, the unlocked passenger door is thrown open and there's someone beside me, something sharp digging into my side.

THREE

CELIA

Hour one

'Get out.' The words come out of me in a breathless exhale, a whisper when I wanted to scream. There is a man in my car. The thought is a pounding fist of panic hitting and hitting and even then a part of me is trying to explain it away. He's drunk. He's on a dare. Any second now he'll laugh and disappear and I'll breathe again.

'Get out.' I repeat the words, stronger this time, shrill.

'Drive,' he says, the one word as sharp as the knife I now see in his hand – a black handle, a long silver blade, like the carving knife I use on Sundays to slice the chicken. He shoves it closer until it's digging into my coat, pushing beyond the layers of my cardigan and my blouse and all the way to the skin an inch above my hip. The exact place where I draw the tape measure around myself every Friday morning. An old habit from my life with Martin that I've never been able to shake. 81.2 centimetres. 32 inches. The same measurements as my wedding day. Twenty-seven years old and completely in love. Utterly devoted

– deluded – but then Martin could be so charming when he wanted to be.

I suddenly wish for more, a thickness, a cushion of fat between the point of the knife and my vital organs.

'Please.' Another gasping whisper. A tremor takes over my body, and I try to move, to do what he's asked, but fear has me in the tightest of grasps.

'Drive.' It's a bark this time, an electric shock that makes my foot jerk onto the accelerator, jolting us forward. The knife moves, snagging on my coat, and he pulls it back, just a fraction.

The car picks up speed. Thirty then forty. The night blurs with the tears building in my eyes. I catch it then, the smell of him – Lynx Africa. It's oppressive, all-consuming, reminding me of Henry and the obsession he had with deodorant when he first started at the grammar school, before I got sick of the whole house stinking of it and moved him to roll-ons.

Henry. My darling boy. I glance at the clock on the dashboard. It's six-fifteen. He'll be expecting me home soon, setting the table, thinking of the little titbits of his day that he'll share with me.

My chest feels as though it's being squeezed. I have to do something. I can't be here.

'Please,' I say again. 'If this... if this is about Lucie—' My thoughts are stammering as much as my voice. The last few hours unravel in my head and it's no longer Henry I'm thinking of but Lucie. Her call and my destination tonight.

'What?' Surprise rings in his voice.

I move my head a fraction, taking in the profile of the figure beside me. He's not the monstrous man I first thought. He's barely out of his teens. Not much older than Henry. A shaved head beneath a black baseball cap, a small beak of a nose and fair stubble spattering his chin.

'Just drive.'

'Where are you taking me?'

'You don't need to know. Go left up here.' His accent is northern. He's not local then. He points with his free hand and I see a phone cupped in it, the blue line of Google Maps displayed on the screen. I picture woodlands. A deserted car park. A derelict building. My throat tightens as more images follow with all the things he will do to me.

I'm forty-six years old. This man must be half my age. But I know that counts for nothing. I know from watching enough crime dramas that this is about power, and right now he has it all.

The town disappears and we pass country lanes and the black emptiness of fields. There are no cars on the road, no one to witness what is happening to me.

Why is he doing this tonight of all nights? I wonder again if he knows Lucie. But how? And why has he jumped into my car like this? Here. Now. It doesn't make sense. The questions are suffocating – a pillow pressed to my face. What have I done? Why did I agree so quickly to meet her?

'If it's about Lucie,' I begin again, 'and the money, I—'

'I don't know what you're talking about, lady. I don't know no one called Lucie.' He lifts the hand with the phone in up to his mouth, gnawing on the stubby nail of his little finger.

Henry used to bite his nails like that. A nervous habit he picked up at three or four years old, picking up on the tension of a marriage in tatters despite how hard I tried to hide it from him. He was always nibbling and pulling, leaving a sprinkling of nail splinters wherever he went. I knew what to do. I bought him some of that foul-tasting clear nail varnish. I painted it on one Sunday evening, telling him all about the germs that live under nails and on fingers. He stopped quickly after that.

I wonder about this man's mother. If she ever tried to stop him from biting his nails. Somehow, I can't imagine it. What kind of person raises a man who jumps into someone's car and holds a woman at knifepoint?

His words sink in. He doesn't know Lucie? Do I believe him?

Think, I tell myself. Concentrate. If he did know Lucie, he'd be asking about her, asking about the money. If he knew what was going on, we wouldn't be driving out towards the arterial road that snakes across the upper edge of town.

'Go up there,' he says, nodding to the slip road that leads to the A12 Northbound. I do as I'm told and we join the steady flow of evening traffic, and all the while my thoughts stutter on Lucie like a scratched CD, jumping in that same spot.

If this man doesn't know Lucie, then what does he want from me? If this isn't about Lucie, then what will happen to her? I picture her again as she was, that freckled thirteen-year-old whose stomach rumbled all through our first chat. She didn't need my pity back then. She needed my help. And I so wanted to give it to her. Just like tonight.

But I can't help Lucie now. No one can. There's a madman in my car, a knife at my side. The panic returns, a fist squeezing my heart.

I can't save us.

FOUR

LUCIE

Then

Lucie throws a glance over her shoulder as she steps out of the bright spring sunshine and into the gloom of the empty school corridor. There's still twenty minutes left of lunch-break and everyone is outside enjoying a dry day after three days of rain and sitting in packed form rooms.

There is no one behind her. In the distance, at the far end of the field by the tree stump, she can make out the red blur of Candice's coat.

It's a beautiful coat. A parka style with a soft fleece lining and a fake fur trim around a huge hood. Lucie had tried it on in the cloakroom once. She'd run in from a PE lesson to use the toilet and it had just been hanging there – bright red in a sea of white shirts and navy cardigans. She'd wrapped the warmth around herself and stared at her reflection in the small mirror above the sink. It was too big and the colour clashed with her hair but she loved it anyway. Lucie had ached with the desire to take it home. She would've done, too, if she could've, but

Candice would've noticed straight away and bags would've been searched.

Lucie watches the group for another moment. Her friends. Or as close to friends as she can claim to have. They're still there, Lucie reassures herself – the gang. Candice and Philippa, Claire, Tasha and Claire S, and Rob and Carl who join the girls sometimes, when the football gets booted over the fence and there's nothing for them to do but flirt with Candice. Everyone flirts with Candice, and sometimes the others. But they never flirt with Lucie. They never steal her bag or flick her hair. They never even look at her. No one does really.

Lucie thinks about turning around and heading back towards Candice and the others. But going back now won't make her feel any less of a hanger-on. She's pretty sure if she disappeared one day, they wouldn't notice.

She hates this feeling of always being the outsider. Like now, having to lie to her friends so they don't take the piss out of her. She told Tasha she had a lunch detention with Mr Butcher for messing around in science. Tasha just shrugged.

Lucie turns onto the languages corridor. There are posters of France and Germany on the walls. Someone had drawn a penis on the German flag and it's been covered by photos of last year's foreign exchange trip to Munich that Lucie didn't go on because it cost £799. She didn't even ask her mum; she knew what the answer would be.

If Lucie stops and looks at the photos more closely, she'll see the girls with their arms slung around each other, Candice in the middle, all grinning at the camera. But she doesn't stop to look today, to feel that deadening pang of loneliness. Lucie turns the corner and passes the library where she goes after school sometimes when she knows her mum is out. It's nicer to be in the warmth of the library with the neat bookcases than it is to be inside the bare walls of the flat with its radiators that never work properly, and the little pockets of black on the walls that creep out of the corners no matter how many times she wipes them away.

The careers adviser's office is in a small room next to the library. It's more like a large cupboard than an office. No windows and crammed with shelves.

Last year, Lucie's class got sent in twos to look at job specifications and do multiple-choice quizzes that were supposed to say what job they'd be good at. Lucie got Personal Assistant, which is not what she wants to do. Since then, no one in Lucie's class has come back to talk to the careers adviser, even though she's here every Wednesday and Friday afternoon. Lucie doesn't know why they don't come. She doesn't know why it's uncool to talk about their futures. Maybe because no one at this school is expected to have much of a future. Most of them will end up in the big clothes factory at the edge of town where her mum works.

But Lucie wants to talk to someone. She's supposed to be choosing her GCSE subjects this month. It feels important. The first decision she's been given about her education. Up until now, every subject and every class has been dictated for her. Now she has something to choose, and she doesn't want to make the wrong choice.

She hesitates, her face growing hot as she takes a breath and knocks.

A moment later a woman calls, 'Come in.'

The woman's smile is bright as Lucie slips inside the room, like she's genuinely glad to see her. She pushes away a Tupperware box with sandwiches inside and brushes down her skirt. 'Hello,' she says. 'I'm Celia Watson. I'm not a teacher, so you can just call me Celia. What's your name?'

'Lucie Gilbert,' she replies, shyness snatching the volume from her voice.

Celia is older than Lucie's mum, but not really old like some of the teachers. Her face is narrow, her features angular. She's slim with brown hair tied back in a tight bun and her eyes are warm and twinkly as she ushers Lucie into a chair.

There's no desk in the room, just two of those low armchairs with the scratchy material that feels a bit like the brown carpet tiles in their flat. There's a low coffee table between the chairs, stacked with magazines on photography and computing. Behind Celia is a bookshelf filled with large A4 binders labelled with each letter of the alphabet. A nervous energy twists in Lucie's stomach as she looks at those binders. Is it D for doctor or M for medicine? C for crazy more like, she thinks, biting the inside of her lip. S for stupid. She doesn't belong with her friends on the field, but she doesn't belong here either.

'What brings you in today, Lucie?' There's an odd expression on Celia's face for a second, like she's trying to figure something out, but then she gives a small shake of her head and the bright smile returns.

'Er...' Lucie pulls her school cardigan sleeves over her hands and pokes her fingers into the holes where the navy fabric has frayed. In bed last night, Lucie had thought about what she'd say. She'd been full of confidence, imagining that she'd explain that she wanted to be a doctor to help people. But now she's here, Lucie's cheeks burn red. F for freak.

What is she doing? The moment she says the words out loud, this woman is going to laugh her head off and shove a beautician course leaflet at her. Girls like Lucie don't become doctors.

'I can see you're nervous, Lucie, but there's no need to be. I'm here to help.'

'I...' Lucie swallows and forces herself to speak. 'I wanted to ask a question please.'

'OK.' Celia smiles. Her voice is silky soft. 'Ask away.'

'I... I just wondered... well, I'm in year nine and I've got to choose my options and I want... I want to know what to pick.'

Celia nods, her smile widening. There's something mothering in the way she looks at Lucie that reminds her of Mrs Weasley in the Harry Potter books. 'It's a good idea to talk it through as you can't swap once you've made your decision. Have you had any thoughts about what you'd like to do after your GCSEs?'

'I know it sounds really stupid and you're probably going to laugh, but—' She takes a breath. It's now or never. 'I want to be a doctor.' The words blurt out and Lucie lifts her head, her face hot. 'I know it's a stupid idea.'

'It's not stupid at all,' Celia says. 'It's commendable, actually. I'm sure you know it's a lot of studying.'

Lucie nods. A fizzing is spreading through her. It's the first time she's admitted her dream out loud to anyone, and Celia isn't laughing at her. 'I'm in top set for science and maths.'

'That's an excellent start. Well, the important thing right now is to focus on the sciences and get the best grades you can. Let's have a look at some of the core skills, shall we?'

It's as Celia is twisting around to pull a folder from the shelf that Lucie's eyes drag to the Tupperware box on the table and the cheese salad sandwiches on thick-cut granary bread. Her mouth waters and her stomach rumbles, a loud echoing noise. Her cheeks flush again and she coughs, trying to mask the sound.

Celia turns back, placing the folder carefully on her lap. She looks from Lucie to her sandwiches, before sliding the box towards Lucie. 'Do you want these? They had donuts in the staff room this morning and I'm pretty full already. You'd be doing me a favour by eating them. I really shouldn't,' she adds, patting her slender waist.

Lucie looks carefully at Celia's face, searching for signs that maybe she's trying to trick her, but all she sees is kindness, and she really is so hungry. She's not had anything to eat since a single slice of toast at breakfast and it was double games this morning.

'Thanks,' Lucie says, scooping up one of the sandwiches. The bread is soft, the cheese tangy. It's chewy and delicious, and it's a fight not to stuff the whole triangle straight in her mouth after feeling so hungry all day. 'Lost my dinner money,' she adds after her second mouthful.

The lie rolls easily off her tongue. It's the same lie she told the girls yesterday when they were queueing for lunch, and Philippa bought her a bag of crisps. Today, she told them she was dieting as her excuse for not buying anything, which is ridiculous because she's stick-thin, but Candice looked impressed and now Lucie knows she'll use that lie again.

She normally uses her paper-round money for lunches when her mum doesn't give her any, which is most days. 'Got to start paying your way sometime,' her mum always says if Lucie ever asks for it. But Lucie spent this week's money on a new school bag. She'd had her old one since primary school – a big green backpack with thick straps. It was getting tatty, and, besides, all the girls have these cute leather tote bags they wear on one shoulder. Lucie got one in black and loves it so much, even though it makes her shoulder hurt from the weight of her books.

'So,' Celia says, picking up a black ballpoint pen from the table and clicking the top, 'let's look at making you a doctor, shall we?' She smiles at Lucie and it's so warm that Lucie feels it reach all the way inside her, right to her middle.

Celia Watson.

Celia.

Lucie rolls the name around in her thoughts and, for the first time in her whole life, she feels like someone is seeing potential in her.

Today 18:40

Where are you?

Today 18:41

I need you.

FIVE

CELIA

Hour one

The ping-ping of message alerts is a bullet of adrenaline that pulses through my body. My legs are shaking so badly that I'm jerking the accelerator, the engine revving in protest. My phone is in my handbag in the boot. Thrown in at the last moment. I was thoughtless. Stupid. Lucie was all I was thinking of, and sorting out the mess she was in.

'You have to help me.'

I check the time. It's 6.43 p.m.

Henry will be curious now but not worried. I've been late before. There is sometimes a case that drags on, sometimes traffic. He knows to get on with things and wait for dinner.

But Lucie? What will happen to her now? Hurt claws at my chest. My throat threatens to close and for a second it feels like I can't breathe. Lucie's life is over. My life is over. I can't... I can't think what to do, how to save us. My breath comes as a rattling wheeze. I can feel the eyes of the man on my face. Watching.

The headlights of a lorry shine bright in my rear-view

mirror. I glance up and catch my reflection. I'm ghostly in the gloom of the car. I can't see the crow's feet creeping from my eyes, the pinch of skin on my brow. Just wide eyes staring back.

Another wheezing breath. I need to calm down. Thinking about Lucie isn't helping her and it isn't helping me. I force myself to focus on the road instead – the black night, the stream of headlights that show the curve of tarmac and the way ahead.

Cars shoot by me in the outside lane, going too fast to notice me. And what will they see? A woman with shoulder-length hair pinned into a bun at the nape of my neck. A man sat beside her – a son or a boyfriend or a husband.

Martin elbows into my thoughts. The Martin after the wedding. The one who didn't speak to me for five days of the honeymoon in the Lake District because I'd laughed at a joke the registrar had made about us being the same height. It hadn't been a funny joke, but I'd been nervous and the giggle had slipped out.

How many times over the years did we sit side by side like this, Martin in the driver's seat, our faces betraying our emotions just like now? Fury and fear. No one noticed then.

The car feels suddenly too small, the silence menacing.

Nothing is going to plan. Nothing. Nothing. Nothing.

'Where are we going?' I ask again, just to fill the silence, to distract myself.

'Just drive.' His voice is gruff, but there's a tiredness to it. I wonder what made him jump into my car. Did he have a plan? Or was it a split-second thing? Is he regretting it? A junction appears ahead of us, lit with a long stretch of streetlights, illuminating the road and inside the car. I see more of him now as I glance back and forth from the road to him and back again. There's a bag at his feet. A large black rucksack. He could be mistaken for homeless, but I know better. I see so many home-less people queueing beside the women who clutch their handbags, the younger generation hunched over their phones, the men with papers gripped in tight fists. All of them needing help.

This man is not homeless. His clothes are lived in but not dirty with the detritus of the streets. There's a sheen of sweat glistening on his forehead and his leg is jiggling up and down as he looks at his phone. He lifts his cap an inch before repositioning it on his head then bites at another fingernail.

A sign appears before us. A blue P – parking in 100 yards. The urge to stop takes hold of me. My foot eases from the accelerator.

'I can pull over,' I say, desperation ringing in my voice. 'You can leave me on the side of the road and take my car. I won't call the police.'

'I can't drive.' It's the first piece of himself he's offered me.

'But it's an automatic' – my voice is teetering between pleading and exasperation – 'it's basically a go-kart. I can show you how to do it.'

'No. Don't slow down.' The knife moves a fraction closer, its point finding the fabric of my coat again.

'It would be easier if you told me where we were going.'

There's a pause and then, 'Leeds.'

'Leeds? That's... hundreds of miles away. It'll take us hours.' My voice falters, the desire to cry pushing up inside me. I can't do it. I can't.

My gaze moves to the petrol gauge, praying it will be near to empty, but I always top up the tank on Saturdays on the way back from my weekly shop. My journeys to and from Citizens Advice on the high street have barely made a dent.

'Three hours and nineteen minutes,' he says, looking down at the map on his phone.

'Why Leeds?' It's not one of the questions I really want to ask, the ones I'm too scared to hear the answers to. Why me? Why this car – a fifteen-year-old silver Ford that Martin bought from a dealer he knew, pleased as punch and not even bothering to tell me that he'd drained my savings account to pay for it? And the final question – the one that makes my pulse hammer in my ears: what will happen when we get there?

'Gotta do something.'

I glance down at his bag again. He notices me looking and moves his leg, trapping the bag against him. Is he delivering drugs? Surely drug mules get cars. It's a ludicrous thought. I know nothing about drugs or mules or distribution. I know it's out there though. I have been asked about drug rehabilitation enough times to know that dealers are a sought-after commodity, but it's so far away from our little house at the end of the dead-end road, my quiet life with my darling Henry.

Three hours in my car with this madman. What will happen to Lucie? She's always been so stubborn. I remember that first time I saw her after school, when Henry was only five, his clammy hand clutching mine, tired legs dragging behind. I'd been to collect him from the after-school club and we were walking home.

She didn't come for dinner the first time I asked, even though I was sure she wanted to. I knew it was crossing a line to invite her. Staff members couldn't invite pupils into their homes. It wasn't an unspoken rule but a written one – large bold lettering in a long list of don'ts the deputy head teacher took me through as part of a welcome-to-the-school talk the previous year. His expression had been apologetic as he'd read out the list, like he'd known it was a waste of time to go over the rules with someone like me – a sensible woman, a mother.

I told him I didn't mind. The rules are there to keep children safe. And rightly so. You couldn't have young girls being lured into the homes of near strangers. But it didn't feel wrong to ask. Lucie needed care and love; anyone could see that. She needed feeding by the looks of her. Wrong would have been turning a blind eye like all the other teachers and staff. And for a while there, I helped Lucie. For a while – six months or so – she was part of our family. Right up until Martin ruined everything.

SIX

LUCIE

Then

The sun is warm on the back of Lucie's neck as she plonks herself down on the edge of the pavement. School finished twenty minutes ago and the road outside the gates is quiet. The smell of cut grass lingers in the air, tickling her nose. God, she hates hay-fever season. As if having pale skin and bright-orange freckles wasn't bad enough, she gets to spend the next month with puffy eyes and a running nose.

Lucie rests her head on her knees and watches a line of ants march their way along the gutter before she pulls a biology book from her bag. The cover is torn and there are pages missing from the middle, but it was only 20p from the sale shelf at the library and she really wants to stay at the top of the class. Celia said it's never too early to start revising. Lucie smiles to herself thinking of her chat with Celia. The warm feeling returns. She'll read three pages from the revision guide and then she'll disappear into the John Grisham she got with her mum's library card.

It's nice being outside, but she feels like she's doing something wrong by sitting here. She sighs, wishing the school library didn't close early on Wednesdays. She knows she should go home, but the flat always seems so gloomy after a day of sunshine, and she'll have to walk by the group of older boys who hang out by the entrance block, calling her carrot top and ironing board. If she waits a bit longer and times it right, she can walk in with the first lot of adults coming home from work. The boys won't hassle her as much then.

Lucie used to go into town with the girls on Wednesdays, mooching around the shops, looking at clothes. She was the designated bag and coat holder while the others wriggled into dresses and tops and jeans. She didn't mind. They always strutted out of the changing room to show her. They didn't buy much, except Tasha, who seems to get a new top every week. Lucie always pretended not to notice when they huddled around each other in Boots, shoving bottles of nail varnish up their coat sleeves.

Until two weeks ago that is, when Candice slipped a lipstick into Lucie's pocket and she didn't know until they were walking home. 'It was just a joke,' Candice said through her gasping laughter. Lucie pretended to find it funny, but she hadn't slept that night. She doesn't think she'll ever be able to go into Boots again.

She doesn't get why they steal stuff. Even Tasha does it and she can buy whatever she wants. It's like they don't care if they get caught, but Lucie can't risk something like that happening to her. She can't risk her future.

A line of ants marches over her left shoe. She watches them fall off the edge by the hole where the stitching has gone and thinks of her mum and how she'd wanted to be a model when she was younger. She's seen the photos of her when she was Lucie's age. Blonde hair and big Bambi eyes. Sometimes the old women in the flats stop to talk to Lucie and say she looks just like her mum, but she thinks she must look more like her dad.

Her mum is always saying how she could've been a model – *would've* been a model – if she hadn't got pregnant at seventeen with Lucie. By that point her mum hadn't bothered with school, thinking her future was set. So she got a job in the clothes factory, catching the number 47 bus at 6.45 a.m. and getting back in the early evening. They used to let her work around Lucie's school hours, but her mum says they don't do that anymore. Lucie sometimes wonders if this is true, or if her mum thinks she's old enough to look after herself. Which she is. But it would still be nice to have her home more. Most days, her mum goes straight over to The Dog and Duck and picks up an evening shift too, saving for the weekend when she goes out with her friends.

'I'm still young, Luce,' she says most Saturday nights as she shimmies into her favourite short leather skirt, and Lucie sits on the bed watching her get ready, the smell of hair spray and Calvin Klein perfume heavy in the air. 'I deserve a life.'

Lucie doesn't remember ever saying to her mum that she doesn't deserve a life, but sometimes she wants to ask what *she* deserves. The question makes her feel bad, so she tries not to think about the answer. It's easier to focus on the future and not making the same mistakes her mum made.

A page in her book flaps in a gust of wind and Lucie smooths it back into place, losing herself to reproduction and gene expression for a bit. When she looks up again, the sun has dipped behind the school and she's in shade. From down the road, a woman walks towards her, a little boy holding her hand. Celia, Lucie realises, with a jolt of happiness as Celia waves.

'Hello, Lucie.' Celia smiles, stopping beside her.

'Hi,' she says, scrambling to her feet and allowing her hair to drop around her face. It's not quite the same as bumping into a teacher on a Saturday, but it's still awkward.

'What are you doing out here? You must be getting cold.'

'I'm waiting for someone.' Lucie mumbles the lie.

'Oh, I see. We're just on our way home, aren't we, Henry?' Celia says, looking down at the boy.

He looks too young to be wearing a school uniform but he nods and Lucie sees he has the same soft brown eyes as his mum. He has a spray of light freckles across the bridge of his nose. Not as many as Lucie has though. Lucie wonders if Celia used to have freckles too and whether they faded with age like Lucie hopes hers will one day.

Celia and Henry have the same hair colour too, but their faces are different. There is something softer about Henry's. It's round, and when he smiles at Lucie, two perfect dimples appear in his cheeks.

There's a pause, a moment where Lucie thinks Celia is going to walk on. Lucie wants to say something about their first meeting, about how much it meant to her, but she doesn't know how to without sounding stupid.

'We live just over there,' Celia says, pointing to the dead-end road opposite the school. 'We're having fish fingers for tea. Would you like to join us?'

'And Smiley Faces,' Henry says with a hopeful grin that makes Celia laugh.

'Yes. Fish fingers with potato Smiley Faces and peas. There's plenty.'

Lucie doesn't know what to say. Of course she wants to go to Celia's house and have someone cook dinner for her and fuss over her in the way she is sure Celia does for Henry. But it would be weird too. She's only met Celia the one time, and even though she's really nice and Lucie is thirteen and can look after herself, she isn't sure she should go to a teacher's house.

'Thank you,' Lucie mutters, 'but I'd better get home actually. My mum will be wondering where I am.'

'Of course.' Celia smiles. 'I'm sure it's for the best anyway. I wouldn't want you to get in any trouble, or for me to get in trouble for that matter. You should head home.'

Lucie nods, and, with a wave to Henry, she turns and strides away.

Five minutes later, the twenty-two storeys of Blackbrook Court come into view. There's another tower beside it – Alderwood Court – built in the same shitty brown. Lucie spots a woman with a shopping basket ahead of her walking towards the same entrance and hurries to catch up, cutting across the grass and dodging the piles of dog crap.

There are eight boys sitting on the railings by the entrance today. They've covered the footpath with a skateboard and a BMX. The woman has to pull her trolley onto the grass to go around them. She knows better than to say anything, and so does Lucie.

Lucie catches up with the woman and they walk in together. She breathes a sigh of relief that the boys are crowded round a phone, chatting to someone on speaker, the tinny voice blaring out for everyone to hear, and don't look up to notice her.

Inside, Lucie takes the stairs. The flat is five storeys up but the stairwell is open to the outside so the stink of urine isn't as strong as it is in the lift.

Her legs are aching by the time she makes it to the fifth floor. Lucie lets herself into the empty flat and drops her bag on the sofa. The smell hits her – damp clothes drying on the radiators. Lucie knows that smell will cling to her when she next leaves the flat no matter how much Vanilla Impulse she sprays over herself.

The kitchen is the usual mess of bowls and plates that her mum discards on the side, always with a, 'Can you tidy these up later, Luce? I'm running mad late.'

She twists the tap to let the water run to warm and opens the freezer. She pulls out one of the microwave meals her mum bought for her. There's only the yucky ones left – the lasagne with the meat that tastes weird and the white sauce that's too creamy and thick, and the stir fry with the soggy vegetables.

Lucie likes the chicken and rice ones best or the macaroni cheese.

She flicks on the TV to fill the silence and, once it's ready, she picks at the stir fry, not really eating, not really watching, not really anything. She wishes suddenly that she'd said yes to Celia. She'd be eating fish fingers now if she'd said yes. Another wish rises up. Lucie wishes she didn't always feel so alone; so different.

She pushes her tray away and opens her school bag, pulling out the shiny black ballpoint pen. Celia's pen. She clicks it on and off, on and off, before tucking it into the shoe box of treasures she keeps under her bed.

Today 19:20

Missed call

Today 19:22

Missed call

SEVEN

CELIA

Hour one

The familiar ring of an iPhone fills the silence. I remember Lucie's old phone. A Nokia thing with a bright-blue case and a different ringtone every week. She always turned it off when she came for tea. She was good like that. She'd walk through the door, unzip that layer of insecurity and be little Lucie who played Lego and hide and seek with Henry while I made the dinner.

'I have a son,' I say when the ringing stops and the silence feels like two hands wrapped around my throat, squeezing and squeezing. 'He's seventeen. His name is Henry. He'll be worried about me now. He's young for his age, you see. Still needs me at home to cook his dinner and help him with his studies. Inevitable, I suppose. A mummy's boy. He's an only child. My husband didn't want any more.' I'm rambling, but it's helping to keep the panic at bay.

He says nothing, just continues gnawing at that fingernail. I try not to think about the germs as I shift in the seat, feeling the discomfort of my bladder. Three hours in this car. The thought still feels impossible. Then what? There's a plummeting feeling in my stomach. Dread and terror hitting me again and again.

'What's your name?' I ask, needing to distract myself.

Silence.

'I'm Celia. I'm forty-six years old. I work at Citizens Advice on the high street. I used to work in a school as a careers adviser, but I needed more hours and they didn't have them, so I moved and help adults instead. Before that I did admin in an accountancy firm. I started taking the qualifications but then I met my husband and, well, I stopped. I work Monday to Thursday. Not Fridays.' I clamp my mouth shut before I can say any more about Fridays and those six hours Henry is at sixth form, when I unlock the garage door. 'We... we see all sorts of problems at Citizens Advice,' I continue a moment later. 'Like you wouldn't believe. What I'm trying to say is that I help people. I'm good at fixing problems. I can help you.'

'Drive,' is the only response, his tone hard.

Fear ignites inside me, but I can't lose my focus if I want to get out of this alive. I grit my teeth, fighting back the tears threatening to fall.

The traffic starts to ease. Cars blast by in the outside lane. The man checks something on his phone. Tapping away with two thumbs. He's sending a message. Is he telling someone about me? Will there be people waiting for us in Leeds? I'm not a big woman. Five foot seven, and a slim build. But this man isn't huge either. I can't be sure with us both sitting down, but I don't think he's much taller than me and he's certainly not broad beneath his puffy coat.

But if we pull up to a darkened alley with two men waiting for us – that's game over. I swallow down a wave of nausea.

The silence settles over us for another few minutes before he speaks. 'My name's Sam.'

The words hit with a punch. I thought I wanted to know his name. I thought we could build something from it. But a new terror is slinking through my veins. I know his name. I know what he looks like. He must realise that I'll go to the police the moment this is over. Unless... he plans to kill me.

I shiver and turn up the heat.

His phone buzzes in his hand. Whatever is in the message, it rattles him. Sam shifts in the seat and stares at the road ahead. 'Go faster.'

'I'm going at the speed limit. I'm assuming you don't want to be stopped by the police?'

'No police is gonna stop an old lady doing eighty. Go the fuck faster.' He moves the knife, jabbing it towards me.

'Don't swear!' The snap of my words is automatic. I clamp my mouth shut, wishing I could snatch them back. 'Sorry.' The apology comes in a breathless rush. I increase my speed to eighty-five and wait for the point of the knife to touch my side. It doesn't. 'I don't know why I said that. I just don't like swearing. I didn't mean—'

'Whatever,' he says, but he pulls the knife back a little like maybe he is sorry too.

Martin used to swear. It was always f-ing this and f-ing that. He did it to annoy me. I told him once how dumb it made him sound. Over a million words in the English dictionary and that was the best he could do. He called me self-righteous. Adding in several expletives just to prove his point. Flinging the insult at me while I crouched on the floor and collected the pieces of vase that had smashed against the wall.

'You're a self-righteous bitch, Celia. And do you know what? I've had enough of it.'

Perhaps I should've seen it coming. Henry was five and I couldn't remember the last time we'd done anything as a family. I couldn't remember the last time I'd laughed with Martin, the last time he'd shown any appreciation for the things I did for him, the last time he'd taken Henry to the park or the shops. And yet, I was still surprised. I never thought he'd leave. But after the surprise came the relief. Henry and I were so much happier when it was just the two of us, and three, when Lucie was there.

EIGHT

LUCIE

Then

Celia's house is the kind of house Lucie used to imagine her dad would have, back when she would daydream about her dad knocking on the door one day and taking her away to live with him. It's nothing fancy or grand. Just a normal-looking house with flower beds and grass and tall green bushes hiding a shiny red front door. Inside, there's a living room with a bay window that looks out onto the street, and a kitchen at the back with white cupboards and swirly marble-like countertops. There's a garden too, as neat as the front with tall fir trees growing on all three sides. Lucie doesn't know how many bedrooms it has, but she bets it's four, and she bets they're all bigger than her room at the flat.

Lucie cringes at the memory of her fantasies and how she'd lie in bed after turning out the light, thinking up stories about her dad. Her favourite was the one of him as a soldier in the army, fighting somewhere far away, and then coming back to rescue her.

He'd scoop her up into his big strong arms and carry her

away to a nice house just like this one, and he'd pick her up from school every day and cook all her favourite foods.

Lucie told her mum once about her dream, and she'd laughed. 'He's no soldier, Luce. He was a loser. I've told you that. He worked the dodgems at one of the travelling fairs that came to town in the summers. He didn't want anything to do with you. You're better off without him. We both are. You and me against the world.'

It had been a Saturday night and her mum was already wearing her heels and her coat. She'd dropped a kiss on the top of Lucie's head before turning out the bedside lamp. 'Go to sleep now and don't open the front door to anyone,' she'd said, leaving Lucie alone with lipstick on her cheek and the feeling that it wasn't them against the world, it was just Lucie. Alone. She'd stopped daydreaming about being rescued that night and started thinking instead about how she would grow up to become someone far away from this flat and this life.

'Shoes off please,' Celia says as she closes the front door. She turns to the mirror, patting a stray hair back into place and straightening out the white blouse and sunshine-yellow cardigan.

Henry is already sitting on his bottom, tugging at the Velcro on his shoes. Lucie slips off her ballet pumps and bends down to help him. He smiles back at her with a questioning smile as though he's asking Lucie why she's here. She doesn't really know.

The house is bright and fresh with creamy-white walls and surfaces that seem to gleam in a way that Lucie has only seen on TV. There's a diffuser in the hall that smells of something floral and familiar that reminds Lucie of when she used to visit her grandparents in Clacton over the summers. Her granny would always slip a fifty pence piece into Lucie's hand before tapping the side of her nose. Her mum hasn't taken her to Clacton for years. Lucie had asked about it once and her mum had started crying. 'Just leave it, Luce.' So she had. She misses them though.

'Let's get you both a snack,' Celia says.

'Can I have a biscuit please, Mummy?' Henry asks in a quiet voice as he pads in his socks towards the kitchen.

'No, cheeky boy. Carrots and celery. You can have a treat for pudding tonight though.' Celia smiles.

Lucie thinks of the time she'd bought a packet of chocolate Hobnobs from the corner shop on the way home from school. She'd sat in front of the TV and eaten them all. One after the other until the chocolate and oats had got stuck in her teeth and she'd felt sick. She remembers thinking how great it was that there was no one to tell her to stop. How grown-up and free she'd felt. But now she wonders if having someone to say no is better.

A small smile touches her lips as she trails behind them into the kitchen. All day she's wondered about sitting on that same bit of pavement and waiting to see if Celia would walk by again, wondering if the offer of tea would come, and knowing this time she would say yes. With the carpet soft and squishy beneath her feet and Celia's reassuring glances, Lucie is glad she did.

The kitchen is spotless. There's a wooden knife block on the side and a spider plant on the window ledge, but there is no clutter. No almost-empty cereal boxes that don't fit in the cupboards or empty cups to wash up.

Henry pulls out a chair at the round table in the corner, the legs scraping against the tiled floor. Celia picks up a cloth and spray bottle and rubs at the already gleaming worktop, leaving Lucie unsure what to do, so she slides into a chair beside Henry.

A ray of sun streams in through the window and something glints in the light, catching her eye. It's a silver catch on one of the cupboards. And hanging from it is a small silver padlock, the kind she once had on a diary her mum had bought her for Christmas and lost the keys for by Boxing Day.

Then Lucie spots another one on the fridge and a third on the cupboard by the sink. Three catches, three padlocks. Three locked cupboards.

What are they for? Lucie glances at Henry and wonders if they're for him. Child locks to stop him from getting at bleach and stuff like that. But they don't look like white plastic child locks, and they're on too many cupboards.

She looks again at the catches. The three locks. The fridge and two other cupboards. It hits her then. It's not chemicals they are keeping safe. It's food. All the food in this kitchen is locked away. Her heart starts to beat faster like she's run a race. There must be a reason because it can't be Henry – the cupboards are too high for him to reach anyway, but there must be something Lucie can't think of that would explain why. Celia is so kind and nice and perfect.

Her eyes dart from little Henry, legs swinging at the table, humming a tune to himself, to the padlocks, to Celia, who is standing by the window, frozen suddenly, looking back at Lucie with a look of realisation and something else on her face. Fear, Lucie thinks.

There's a shift in the air around them, a tension that wasn't there a moment before. Henry stops humming. The silence is broken a second later by Celia's tinkling laugh.

'Oh, ignore them,' she says, waving her hand in the direction of the locks like it's nothing at all. Her voice is still bright, but there's something else in the tone that Lucie can't place. 'They're my husband Martin's idea of a little joke. We're a family of snackers, you see. This way we can't sneak a hand in and steal a biscuit while no one else is looking.' Celia laughs again before placing carrot sticks and celery on the table.

Lucie nods, but it's the expression on Henry's face her eyes are now drawn to. The way he's biting down on his bottom lip, his eyes like two giant pools.

She nibbles on a carrot and wonders if she'd been wrong to

come, and yet Celia isn't upset about the locks, so why should she be?

'Tell me about your mum and dad, Lucie? What do they do?'

Lucie fidgets in the chair. She hates it when people ask her this. 'My mum works for Beatstop, the clothes factory, and I don't know about my dad. I've never met him.'

'Your mum didn't tell you anything about him?'

Lucie gives a small shake of her head. 'Just that he worked at the summer fair. It doesn't stop in Hallford anymore.'

'My daddy is an accountant,' Henry chirps, pushing away the empty plate. 'Lucie, will you play with me?'

'Sure,' she replies, glad to be escaping the conversation. She liked it better when Celia asked about her school stuff.

Henry pushes his small, hot hand into hers and pulls her into the living room. They sit on the floor and build a Lego house with a Lego mum and dad and a Lego daughter and a Lego son. Every few minutes, Henry looks up from the colourful bricks and she sees that same question pulling at the features of his face. *Why are you here?* But there is something else there too now – fear. Suddenly she wonders if it isn't a question he's thinking, but a warning. *Don't be here.*

'Are you OK, Lucie?' Celia says later as she clears away Henry's empty dinner plates. Celia didn't eat anything herself, and Lucie guesses she prefers to eat later with Henry's dad.

Lucie nods, swallowing the last mouthful of fish finger. She knows it's not gourmet. It's just freezer food. Celia hasn't had to open the fridge or cupboards to make it. But it's so delicious. Maybe she'll ask her mum if she can get some different foods and cook for herself. It can't be that hard.

'It's just you keep touching your hair. I thought maybe you might feel nervous.'

Lucie drops her hands to her lap. She hadn't realised she'd been doing it – smoothing out the strands around her face so they lay flat. A habit that drives her mum crazy. 'Sorry.'

'You don't have to apologise,' Celia says. 'You've not done anything wrong. I just wondered if there was a reason?'

'No, it's just... my ears stick out,' she admits, thinking of Candice's taunts from year seven. 'I like my hair to cover them.'

'Really? I've never noticed. Will you show me?'

Lucie tucks her hair behind her ears as a flush creeps up her face.

'Oh, Lucie, that looks so much better. Come with me.' She motions to the hall and Lucie stands, allowing herself to be guided to a mirror with a thick silver frame. She watches her reflection as Celia stands behind her and scoops Lucie's hair into a ponytail, fastening it with a hairband. She can smell the floral scent of Celia's perfume, the same smell she caught in the living room when she first walked into the house. It's subtle, not like the way her mum splashes on her Calvin Klein.

'Now look at that. Your hair is just like mine. It's so fine and can look limp when it's down. See how it looks thicker in a ponytail?'

Lucie swishes her head from side to side and smiles shyly at her reflection and Celia's beaming face.

'You keep that hairband. I've got plenty. Make sure to wear it like that more often, Lucie. It really suits you.' She gives Lucie's shoulder a squeeze.

'Thank you,' Lucie says, her face glowing again, but then Celia's eyes move to the clock and the moment is gone.

'Oh my,' Celia gasps. 'It's getting late. You should head home now, Lucie.'

Lucie follows Celia's gaze to the clock on the wall. It's only 6.20 p.m. Lucie is about to tell Celia that her mum won't be home for another few hours and it's fine for Lucie to stay a while, that she wants to stay, but Celia is already talking again. 'Henry's dad will be home soon.'

Celia stands back, her hand already on the front door latch.

Lucie frowns, unsure what's happening. Celia was happy a moment ago, but now she seems nervous.

'Henry, darling,' Celia calls. 'Come and say goodbye to Lucie. We best get you in the bath too.'

Henry appears a second later, walking calmly towards them, a crayon still in his hand. 'I need one more huggy,' he says, looking to Celia.

Lucie isn't sure what Henry means, but Celia smiles and pulls him close, holding him tight for a moment. 'Sorry, my sweet boy. We forgot, didn't we.'

Henry lifts his face away from Celia's side and smiles at Lucie. 'Bye, Lucie. Will you come again?'

'Er...' Lucie smiles, looking hopefully at Celia standing by the open front door, staring down the street, looking worried.

'That would be lovely,' Celia adds, her eyes back on the road as she pulls at her blouse, smoothing out a crease Lucie can't see. 'We would love for you to come for dinner again, Lucie. Anytime.'

Lucie ignores the strange atmosphere and instead allows a warmth to radiate through her as she slips on her shoes and picks up her school bag. These are good people. Nice people.

She says her thank yous and walks slowly down the road in the dusky evening light. As she reaches the end, a silver car pulls into the road, a man with a bald head behind the wheel. It drives slowly and Lucie feels his eyes on her. She drops her gaze as a shiver runs through her body and she hurries away.

Later, when Lucie is home, she pulls out the coaster from the pocket of her cardigan and places it on her bedside table. It's plain white with a drawing of a flock of birds on it. Lucie found it in Celia's living room – a stack of six that is now five.

Her stomach twists, the guilt an aching burn inside her. She just wanted a little something, a reminder of Celia's perfect house.

Lucie pulls the hairband out of her hair and places it carefully on the coaster before digging out the ballpoint pen from her treasure box and putting it with the other items.

Today 20:03

Missed call

Today 20:04

*Getting really
worried now!!!
Where are you?*

NINE

CELIA

Hour two

My stomach rumbles, reminding me of the four Ryvita crackers I nibbled over lunch and then, with a pang that hits me dead in the chest, how I should be cleaning away the dinner plates by now, quizzing Henry on his revision. Instead I'm in a car with a madman, my heart breaking for Lucie, for how desperately I wanted to save us.

Will Henry think to make himself something? I'm not sure. He was right this morning. He will have to look after himself next year when he goes to university. He should be better at it by now, but it's been just the two of us for so long and I like to take care of him. He likes to let me.

I wish I could tell him to eat something, not to wait for me. I picture the thought shooting out of my head, snaking back along the road, past the cars and the lights, into the town and to our little house, landing with a plonk into Henry's head.

Eat something, Henry darling. Make yourself the pasta. You've watched me cook it hundreds of times.

It's stupid to think that. I've never bought into that telepathic mumbo-jumbo. It won't kill either of us to go hungry. We've been without meals before. I don't think he remembers those shining padlocks on the cupboards and fridge. I remember, though. They were the first thing to go after Martin. All these years later it still feels like a treat to open a cupboard without waiting for the key and the pop of the lock. The screw holes are still in the cupboards. I used to think I'd fill them or save up for a whole new kitchen, but I've started to think I might like them. They're a reminder of how much better things are now.

Lucie noticed the locks the moment she stepped into the house on that first visit. I could see her mind whirring. That flicker of panic that maybe she'd made a mistake agreeing to come to dinner.

I told her to ignore them, over-explaining in my haste to lie. She said nothing, but I could tell she didn't believe me. She wanted to be a doctor back then. Same as Henry. I always wonder how much he remembers of Lucie. Nothing, I hope.

Of course, the other locks were harder to explain.

The road ahead changes. Two lanes become five, spreading out like fingers in different directions. Stretching across the road above us is a lane sign. Cambridge and Huntingdon on the left, Peterborough and The North on the right. And another sign – Services.

The pressure in my bladder builds. I need the toilet. The feeling is suddenly desperate. I clench my pelvic floor and stare at the Services sign. It's on the left of the road. We are on the right. My stomach cramps uncomfortably. But with it comes hope. He can't deny me this. It'll be my chance to escape. It has to be.

'I need the toilet,' I say.

'What?' Alarm rings in his voice, making me wonder if he's thought this through. 'You can't.'

'I do. I'm sorry.'

He sighs and stares at his phone. A minute passes. The
turning for the services is just ahead of us. Desperation claws at
me – a cat fighting to be free.

'I really do need the toilet,' I say.

'All right.' The two words are snapped and make me jolt.
The knife moves closer and I shrink away. 'I'm finding somewhere. Get past this junction. There'll be a lay-by or something
on the A1.'

The hope dies, curling in on itself like paper burning. What
did I really think? That we'd swoop into a bustling services with
people I could throw myself at and beg for help?

I drive on, the road curving round and merging onto the A1.
My bladder continues to press down, urging me to stop. There
are no streetlights now and the road ahead is pitch-black, lit
only by the distant rear-view lights of a car ahead. I glance in
my wing mirror. Headlights are approaching fast in the outside
lane. The road is not empty, I console myself, but it's not the
slow-moving traffic I need. Even if Sam lets me pull over and I
manage to step away from him for long enough to wave my
hands in the air and holler for help, it's too dark and the cars are
moving too fast to notice or stop.

I need a better plan, a way out. I can't drive all the way to
Leeds and hope he doesn't kill me. I must get back to Henry.
I've never left him alone for this long before. I know what
people think when they hear that. I see the mocking looks
from my co-workers. They think I'm too protective, too
mothering.

Maybe I am.

But Henry is all I have, and, after Martin, it's the only way I
know how to be.

Yet planning is not something that has come naturally to
me. I'm impulsive by nature, throwing myself into something
without thinking. It seems rather ridiculous now, considering
how much I like routines. But every now and again my impul-

siveness rears up. Like tonight with Lucie, that whispered phone call.

'It's me,' she said. Thirteen years and I still knew her voice.

'Lucie? Hi.' Did those two words sound desperate? Did they ring with hope that maybe she needed me again? Probably. I wasn't foolish enough to think that she was calling me after all this time so we could pick up where we left off with dinners and homework at the table. But even in that pregnant pause when I could hear her breath on the line, I pictured us sat at the Costa in the town centre, her hands cupped around a hot chocolate, mine a green tea; talking tentatively about her life. Would she admit she'd made a mistake cutting me out the way she did? I knew immediately that I'd forgive her. That's what mothers do, and even though Lucie wasn't my daughter, I liked to think there was a bond.

'I need to talk to you,' she said, and I didn't hesitate to agree.

There have been other times my impulsiveness has got the better of me. Like when Henry was three months old and Martin was hovering over me, watching my every move, waiting for me to make a mistake so he could pounce. I'd sat in the nursing chair in Henry's room, breathing in that glorious baby smell, and for the first time I saw the bleakness of an unhappy marriage stretching out before me. I knew I had to get out.

I threw a handful of clothes into a bag for both of us, scooped up Henry's changing bag and dashed to the car. I drove for hours, circling the town, thinking what to do.

I didn't have any family nearby. I wasn't close to my parents. They'd moved down to Devon a decade earlier and were in a nursing home at that point, Dad battling with his blood pressure, Mum with Alzheimer's. No siblings, cousins, uncles or aunts I could call on.

I realised on that drive how small my world had become since my marriage to Martin. I had no money, no support network, no one to help me. Henry woke up and cried and cried, and in the end, I slunk home, and Martin opened the door to us without a word. I could see it on his face that he knew where I'd been, what I'd wanted to do. His silence shot a fear through me much greater than every one of his brash insults put together. I knew then as I carried Henry up the stairs to bed that I needed a plan. A way out. It's the same feeling I have now.

Ahead of us on the road, my headlights illuminate a blue P sign, promising a place to pull over in three hundred yards. 'There?' I ask.

He nods before he speaks. 'If you try anything stupid, I'll kill you.'

His words hit with another bolt of terror. My stomach turns – rocks and then liquid – and any thought of escape evaporates.

TEN

LUCIE

Then

They're walking towards the lunch hall when Lucie spots Celia ahead of them, a beacon of bright yellow in a sea of navy uniform. Lucie hoped she'd see her today. She'd been planning to stop by the careers office after lunch, hoping for another invite to dinner.

A spark of joy unleashes inside her. She tucks a stray hair into her ponytail and feels herself light up.

Celia is wearing the same cardigan and skirt that she wore last Wednesday. Now Lucie thinks about it, she's pretty sure Celia was wearing the same outfit on the Wednesday Lucie went to the careers office too. She wonders if Celia knows she's worn the same outfit on the same day three weeks in a row. Probably not. And anyway, Lucie has worn the same jeans and black jumper every Saturday since her mum gave her them for Christmas.

A smile stretches across Celia's face as she spots Lucie at the back of the group, a step behind Tasha and Claire who are deep in conversation about how much they hate their maths teacher.

'Oh, Lucie, could I have a word?' Celia says, stepping to the side of the corridor and out of the throng of bodies.

Lucie nods and watches Celia give a furtive glance around her, like she's doing something wrong. It occurs to Lucie then that maybe Celia *is* doing something wrong. Is it against the rules to invite a pupil for tea? Lucie isn't sure but she wants to tell Celia not to worry. Lucie isn't going to say anything, and anyway, this isn't the kind of school where anyone cares what the students do. Celia's gaze travels across the sea of heads in the corridor.

The lunch bell only went five minutes ago and there are students everywhere, laughing and shouting and chatting. The smell of sausages carries from the lunch hall, making Lucie's stomach growl. She squeezes the one pound coin in her hand. They serve chips on Friday. A whole plate of hot greasy chips for one pound.

'Hi, Lucie.' Celia smiles, her focus now on Lucie.

'Hi,' she says, matching the smile. She wants to say, 'Hi, Celia,' but it still feels strange to call an adult by their first name in school.

'You have your hair tied back,' Celia says. 'It looks lovely.'

'Thanks.' Lucie beams. She runs a hand along the length of the ponytail, pulling the ends towards her. Candice said she liked it, but Philippa and Claire S did that scoffing-laugh thing and Lucie isn't sure if Candice was joking or being mean or if she really did like it. It is nice to tie it back though. It doesn't need washing so much, even though she misses hiding behind it.

'It really does suit you,' Celia continues. 'Although make sure you still brush it first or it will look bumpy at the back. Anyway, I'm sure you're desperate to get into lunch with your friends.' She glances towards the hall, her brows pinching as though she's expecting to see a group of girls waiting for Lucie.

'I just wanted to give you these books. I saw them in a charity shop yesterday and I thought you might like them.'

Lucie takes the carrier bag and peers inside. There are five books, all with shiny bright-green covers. Revision books, Lucie realises, a spark of pleasure igniting inside her. Science, English and maths. They look brand new and nothing like the second-hand book she'd found. Lucie can't wait to look through them properly.

'Thank you,' she blurts out, hugging the bag towards her to stop herself from hugging Celia. She can't believe Celia has done this for her. 'Um... I can give you some money—' The spark singes, replaced with a tight panic. Lucie really does want these books, but there's no way her mum will give her the money for them. Her mum doesn't give her money for anything to do with school, always launching into a rant about how she already pays tax, so the school should be sorting that stuff. Lucie understands, sort of. Her mum works really hard on minimum wage and she doesn't have a lot of spare money.

'No no.' Celia looks momentarily horrified and Lucie's stomach unknots. 'It's my treat. I know you'll put them to good use.'

Celia starts to step away, but then glances around at the emptying corridor and back to Lucie. 'Tuesday is pasta night. You will come next week, won't you? Henry has really taken a shine to you.'

'Yes,' she blurts out. 'Yes, please, I'd like that a lot. I have homework on Tuesdays though—'

'You can do it at the kitchen table after dinner if you like? Henry always has quiet time and won't disturb you.'

'Thank you.' Lucie grins, pushing away the flashing image of the kitchen cupboard padlocks that flies suddenly into her thoughts.

'Wonderful. Henry will be so pleased. Right, I'd best get back to my office, and you'd best catch up with your friends. I've got spare sandwiches again thanks to Delores and her cakes, if you... if you want to talk more about a course in medicine.' She gives a waggly finger kind of wave and turns away, leaving Lucie in the corridor. She hurries down to the design and technology department where her locker is, and stuffs the books inside before rushing back to the lunch hall.

The queue has almost gone and Lucie feels a whoosh of worry that maybe they've run out of chips. She spots the girls in the corner by the window, halfway through their food. Claire S looks up and then instantly ducks her head down, saying something to the others. None of them look round but there's something fake about the way they're talking to each other, studiously ignoring the rest of the lunch hall and Lucie.

She takes another step towards the lunch line and realises the problem. They're on the round table for five that sits in the corner where the year eight boys usually sit. Candice, Philippa, Claire, Tasha and Claire S. No seat for Lucie. On the other side of the hall is a long table with loads of spare seats, but they've not chosen that one.

The hunger in her stomach disappears and she turns away, fighting back hot tears she doesn't want to cry. She walks through the school until she gets to the toilets by the language corridor. They're always empty at lunchtimes. She slips into the nearest cubicle and locks the door. She leans her head against the cool wood and lets the tears drip from her eyes.

She'll tell the girls she wasn't hungry when they ask later where she got to. Not that they will. Lucie wipes her eyes and thinks of the books in her locker, and the library, which is always quiet at lunchtimes. Then she thinks of Celia's offer of sandwiches and talking about medicine, and something lifts inside her. She has always been the hanger-on with the gang. Five plus one. Never six. It doesn't matter how hard she tries, how much she studies their behaviours and mimics them, she has always been the odd one out. She's the only one in the top sets and the only one from the tower block. Lucie has always felt bad about being different, but maybe it's OK not to be like them, especially now Lucie has Celia. Celia and Henry.

She wipes her eyes, smooths out the bumps in her ponytail and heads in the direction of the careers office. At the door, she hesitates. She can hear the mumble of a voice. Just one. It's Celia. She must be on the phone, Lucie thinks.

Even from her position outside the door, Lucie can tell Celia is upset. She can't make out the words, but there is something in Celia's tone and the speed she's talking at that worries her.

She waits for a while. A minute or more. Only when Celia stops talking, and Lucie hears the scratchy zip of her handbag, does she knock. There's a pause and then the door flies open and Celia is before her, elegant and poised like always. But just before she smiles and makes everything all right, Lucie catches something else in her face – something guarded and drawn that makes Lucie think of the padlocks she saw on the kitchen cupboards. And in that one second before Celia beckons her in, Lucie feels a strange urge to run away.

———

Today 20:22

Why aren't you answering?

Today 20:27

Don't go to the police!

ELEVEN

CELIA

Hour two

'Go on then.'

We're standing by the passenger side of the car, shielded from the road as the cars and lorries roar by, furious and fast. The car keys are in Sam's jacket pocket and the knife is tucked by his side, hidden from view. For the first time I wonder if he's done this before – jumped into a woman's car and forced her to drive halfway across the country.

If he has done it before, it would've been in the news, surely? I'd have seen it. Only if he got caught though... only if she'd lived to tell the story, I realise with a sickening shudder.

'I thought you needed to go,' Sam says and I jump.

'I do.' Hot tears spill onto my cheeks. Everything I've worked so hard to build is slipping away from me with every passing mile.

He nods at the ground by our feet and I shake my head. 'I can't do it here.'

'So hold it then. Let's go.'

My bladder stretches painfully and I know holding it is not

an option. I either wet myself and sit in my own urine or I squat in front of him. My hands go to the button on my work trousers before I stop. 'Can you turn around?'

He shakes his head. 'No.'

There's a moment. A standoff between us. An idea worms its way into the back of my mind.

'Can you give me your jacket then so I can hold it over me and protect my dignity?' My heart thuds in my chest as I wait for his next refusal, but instead he sighs and shrugs it off. He's just passing it to me when he remembers the car keys, fishing them out and stuffing them into his jeans pocket.

I hold his coat over my legs and shimmy my trousers and knickers down my thighs, bunching them at my ankles as I squat, repositioning the coat over my lap. There's a moment when nothing happens, when I don't think I'll be able to relax enough, but then the pressure takes over and the sound of liquid pattering on the ground fills the night around us.

Sam shifts uncomfortably and then turns away, stuffing the knife in his back pocket and unzipping his jeans to relieve himself too, as though the sound of running liquid was enough to remind him of his own needs.

I see a chance then. His back is to me, the knife tucked away. I push out the last of the urine and stand quickly, pulling up my trousers. But Sam senses the movement and is already turning as I'm stepping away. There's no time to run. I've never been one for fitness. A brisk walk at the weekends and around the park in my lunch-break is as active as I get. Sam would be on me in seconds.

I step to the back of the car, my eyes scanning for passing vehicles. One blasts by us in the outside lane, and then nothing. No one to see me. No one to help. I open the boot fast. Nausea burns in the back of my throat.

'What are you doing?' Sam shouts out, already moving towards me.

There's no time to reach the car jack tucked in the spare wheel arch.

'I... I made a mess,' I call back, throwing my coat in. I stuff his jacket in too, before slamming the boot shut again, pretending that was always my intention.

Sam is by my side in an instant. 'Get back in the car.'

We walk to the driver's side together. The cold night air whips against my face. I suddenly wish I hadn't taken off my coat. Sam's grip is on my arm, the knife pressing into me. There's no longer that extra padding between the tip of the knife and my skin.

He pushes close to me, the knife digging into my back. I yelp but don't try to move.

'If you run, I will catch you and I'll... I'll slit your throat and then I'll find my way back to your son and I'll kill him too.' The words come out in a rush, his voice carrying a desperate edge.

He shoves me into the car, slamming the door. Three seconds later, he's beside me again, the knife at my hip and the car keys held out. No time to open the door and run. No time to think beyond the threat still ringing in my ears.

I should never have mentioned Henry. Never. Did I really think telling him I was a mother would help me? Tears threaten again, desperate, angry tears that burn behind my eyes. For a moment I feel as though I can't go on. The threat to Henry is one notch of terror too far. I think of breaking down; slumping forward in my seat, half dead, half gone. What would Sam do then?

No. I can't. I start the car and pull away, our speed building quickly. Forty, then sixty, then seventy.

Another hour passes. There's a twinge in my back and my bottom feels tingly with numbness. I shift in my seat, trying to remember when I'd last sat in a car for this long. It must have been the holiday to Cornwall when Henry was eight or nine. Henry had got used to his father not being around by then and I'd stopped expecting our lives to come crashing down at any moment.

We packed up the car on a Saturday morning in July and set off to a little cottage I'd found. It was a tiny place but close to the beach and a gorgeous little town. We spent a week building sandcastles and playing in the waves, eating fish and chips and ice creams. I couldn't remember ever feeling so free.

In the evenings when Henry was asleep, I sat in the evening sun, sipping a green tea, and thought about staying there forever. It was a silly holiday fantasy, and when our last day came, I packed up our things and we drove home. Our lives carried on, and I waited for the knock at the door to come.

TWELVE

LUCIE

Then

Lucie smiles, catching the familiar scent of flowers in the hall as Henry tugs her towards the stairs.

'I want to show you my bedroom,' he says, twisting around and smiling. Two of his adult teeth have come through over the summer and they look too big for his five-year-old mouth. His hand is warm and gripping Lucie's palm as though he thinks she'll pull away from him at any second.

'Only if Lucie doesn't mind,' Celia calls from the kitchen.

'I don't,' she says, allowing herself to be dragged along.

A warm feeling envelops her body. It's Henry and his joy at her presence. It's Celia and her gentle support of Lucie, like the little gifts she gives her each week – a shampoo five times more expensive than the one Lucie normally uses because it's better for fine hair. A new top because Celia thought it would suit Lucie. It does, even if it's baggier than the style she's taken to wearing this summer.

Lucie has finally stopped being as flat as a surfboard, and her favourite outfit to wear is a tight black T-shirt and a pair of her mum's old denim shorts. But wearing the clothes Celia has bought her when she visits is one way to show her gratitude. Celia is always so happy when she arrives wearing the clothes she's bought her and has her hair up. It's the least she can do – especially considering how many hours she spends in Celia's house. She isn't sure when it happened, but once a week became twice a week and now it's been five months and September is here and the summer holidays are nearly over. The more time Lucie spends with Celia and Henry, the more time she wants to spend with them.

It feels like they've pulled a part of her into the light, a part of herself she didn't know existed. It sounds stupid when she thinks about it like that, but it's how she feels.

The summer has felt so long and Lucie can't wait for school to start again. Visiting Celia and Henry for dinner has been the only thing to break up the monotony of the endless warm days. That and working for Mrs Banks at the newsagents, picking up as many paper rounds as she can, arriving early to sort the papers, staying later to restock the shelves.

It's nothing official. Lucie is thirteen and too young to get a proper job, but Mrs Banks always gives her extra cash in her weekly paper-round money. On Saturdays, Lucie walks straight to the bank to pay the money into the bank account Celia helped her apply for. She has over a hundred pounds saved already. And she's not going to waste it on stupid bags or clothes, or on hot food at lunchtimes either. Lucie has learned so much from Celia, like how it's cheaper and healthier to take in packed lunches each day than buy hot food.

Lucie doesn't know what she's saving for yet, just that she is. Her desire to be a doctor used to feel like a childish dream, but now, thanks to Celia, it feels bright and possible.

'Will you read me a story too?' Henry asks as they reach the top step.

'If you want me to,' she replies, realising how weird it is to be going upstairs in Celia's house after all the times she's wondered about it; lying awake at night and picturing peachy floral wallpaper in Celia's room and bright-blue walls in Henry's. This is the first time in all these months that she's been upstairs. Celia has a downstairs toilet and Henry's toys are all in neat boxes in the living room so there's never been a reason to come up before, even if she has really wanted to.

They've settled into a routine over the summer. Lucie will walk over at 3 p.m. and sit with Henry in the garden while they have a snack – usually carrot sticks and strawberries. Then Henry will drag her into whatever whispered make-believe game he's playing with his cars or his Lego. Then they'll sit and eat dinner at the table and Celia will ask Lucie questions about what she's been doing.

After dinner, Henry asks for his one more huggy from Celia, and Lucie too now, before he goes back to playing and Lucie chats while Celia cleans up the dinner things. Lucie always offers to help, but Celia always shakes her head. At 6.10 p.m., Celia announces that it's bath time for Henry, and Lucie slips on her shoes and waves goodbye. Sometimes, Lucie waits on the corner of the road, out of sight of the house, and watches for Martin to come home at six-thirty. They've never met and Celia rarely talks about him, but there are times when Lucie senses that same uneasiness from the first visit, as though lurking in a corner of the house somewhere, just out of sight, is something bad. It's the look in Henry's eyes sometimes, the way he asks for one more huggy, as though desperate to cling to his mother. Lucie tries not to think about it.

But now there is a reason to go upstairs. Celia has asked Lucie to babysit Henry on Wednesday next week while Celia attends a staff meeting at the school. It's only from six o'clock until seven-thirty, and Lucie would've done it for free, considering everything Celia has done for her, but Celia said she'll pay Lucie £10 and Lucie really wants that money.

Henry lets go of Lucie's hand and opens the first door on the left. The room is not how she imagined. It looks more like a spare room than a little boy's bedroom. The walls are soft blue but there are no posters or pictures, and the bedding is a dull stripe instead of a favourite character or show. The only sign that the room belongs to a little boy are the brightly coloured books on the shelf above the bed.

'And this is the bathroom,' Henry says, opening another door.

Lucie turns to follow and catches sight of something in the periphery of her vision that makes her falter first and then gasp. There, on the outside of Henry's door, right at the top out of reach, is a bolt. Like the kind in the toilets at school, a metal pole that pushes into the wood.

Lucie looks to Henry and then to the other doors. There are four of them. Three bedrooms and one bathroom, and they all have bolts on them.

Why would there be locks on the outside? Lucie doesn't have the answer.

'Lucie?' Henry's voice is far away. Too far to reach.

There is only one reason Lucie can think of for these bolts to be here, and that's to lock someone in.

That feeling of something out of place prickles at her skin again. She's tried so hard to ignore it, to believe everything in this family is perfect, but how can she ignore this?

Lucie thinks about Henry and how quietly he plays, how he never runs in the house, never raises his voice. She always thought his whispered play was cute, part of the game, but now she's not so sure.

Lucie knows what domestic violence looks like. It looks like the woman on the seventh floor with the swollen mouth and the black eye. It looks like that woman's boyfriend in the tight T-shirts with the tattoos on his arms. That world is not this world, with Celia and her kindness and her lovely neat house.

An icy chill begins to spread from her middle, pushing all the way to the tips of her toes and the hair at the nape of her neck. Lucie wishes she could rewind the last few minutes. Then she feels sadness. Sadness for Celia, and for herself and the perfect family she wanted to be part of that isn't perfect after all.

Another realisation hits Lucie. A question, really. What is she supposed to do now? Does she tell someone?

A hand grips her shoulder and she jumps, a yelp escaping her mouth. She spins around to find Celia at the top of the stairs, a pile of folded washing in her arms. 'Sorry,' she splutters. 'I was miles away.' And even though she tries really hard to keep her eyes on Celia, the bolts on Henry's door yank at her gaze.

Horror crosses Celia's face – just a flash, and then it's gone. 'Don't worry about them,' Celia says with a tinkling laugh that falls flat. 'Martin sleepwalks. When Henry was a toddler, he used to creep out of bed, and once he did it when Martin was sleepwalking and he nearly knocked poor Henry down the stairs. This way, he's safe in his room.'

Lucie nods, dropping her gaze so she doesn't have to see the look of pleading on Celia's face. 'Sure. Of course.'

Safe? Lucie wonders how safe it would be if there was a fire. And what if Henry needs the toilet or has a bad dream? Whatever is going on in this house, safe is not the word for it. The thought makes her want to run, to sprint back to the flat with its mould in the bathroom and stinking clothes, because at least she knows it's crap. There is no pretence or subterfuge there. But here, beneath the floral fragrances and the gleaming surfaces, is something rotten. Something bad.

Today 20:45

Missed call

Today 20:47

Missed call

Today 20:49

I can't wait much longer!!!
Where are you?

Today 20:50

I'm in so much trouble. I need you!

THIRTEEN

CELIA

Hour three

The muffled ringing of the iPhone stops then starts then stops again. I catch the ping of a message and think of my handbag, dumped without a thought in the boot. If only I had it with me, I might've been able to call for help.

The noise of the phone is a harsh reminder of the world outside this car, of what's happening inside it too. My mind returns to Lucie. Hurt balloons inside me and with it comes a guilt so sharp, it takes my breath away.

'I need to ask you something,' she said to me earlier. 'It's important. It's life or death, Celia.'

'Ask me anything,' I replied.

The words tumbled out of her, talk of money and debts that must be paid, and it was bad. So much worse than I could ever have imagined. She was in trouble. How could I not get pulled in? Even if it meant we were both in danger.

Out the corner of my eye, Sam taps his phone and opens the map. He sighs, a loud exhalation, before slapping his phone against his leg and leaning close, checking the dashboard.

Something has changed. He's nervous. Edgy. The feeling hovers around us, peppering into my skin and into my body until I'm jumpy too. Is he thinking about what he'll do to me when we get to Leeds?

'What's wrong?' I ask before I can stop myself.

'We've wasted too much time. Go faster.'

I don't protest this time. I press my foot to the pedal and the night flashes by us. I lean forward, staring intently as the black tarmac unfolds too fast in my headlights. I try not to think about what will happen to Henry if we crash and I die. To Lucie.

My breath comes in short gasps again. I have to get a hold of myself.

'Why didn't you learn to drive?' I ask, the words coming fast. I take a shuddering breath. I don't care about the answer; I don't care about this man beside me. I hope he rots in prison for the rest of his miserable life for what he's doing to me now, but at the same time, I need the distraction of talking.

'It cost money. I didn't have any money.' His reply makes me think of Lucie's mother. On charitable days, I think she did the best she could. On other days, anger burns inside me for how much she neglected that poor little girl. What kind of mother stocks a freezer with microwave meals for their child? She was never there either. Always working or with her friends. Lucie didn't have a proper childhood with toys and play dates and stories at bedtime; that's why she liked it at my house. That sense of family and belonging. Having someone who cared.

I wished I could've helped her more back then. If only I'd met Lucie after Martin was gone. Everything would've been different. She so desperately needed someone in her corner then, and I wanted it so badly to be me, but I failed. I think of what else I put in the boot alongside my coat and bag earlier. I think of my destination tonight before Sam and this madness, and I know I've failed Lucie again.

'What about your parents?' I ask, desperate to distract myself from Lucie and what will happen to her now.

'My dad wasn't around much and my mum... wasn't good for it. My big sister was helping me save up but then I got arrested and did time.'

'What's your sister's name?' I ask, trying not to think about what he was sent to prison for.

A pause, and then, 'Bee.'

'Short for Beatrice?'

'No. And I'm just Sam, short for nothing.'

We both fall silent. I'm acutely aware that every question I ask and every answer he gives is knowledge I have about him. Evidence I can give to the police. The more he tells me, the more likely it is that the police will find him, and the more likely it is that he'll never let me out of this car alive. The thought brings another wave of terror with it, and for a moment I think it might drown me. I can't catch my breath.

I have to keep talking. It's calming me, and him. Besides, I've seen his face. I know his name. If he's going to kill me, then talking more isn't going to change a thing.

'What did you want to be when you were little?' I ask.

'Dunno.'

'You must do. Everyone remembers what they wanted to be growing up.'

He pauses. Considering. 'A firefighter, I guess. I wanted to drive the fire engine.'

'Why didn't you?'

''Cause it was a stupid little-kid dream. What about you?'

'A teacher or a doctor.'

'Did you do it?'

'No. I... I didn't.' It's been a long time since I've felt the keen smart of that particular humiliation. I didn't have the same upbringing as Lucie or Sam, where money was tight day in, day out. My parents were actors. Sometimes we had money, lavish holidays, parties that went on through the night. I'd creep out of bed and peer through the banisters at the men in tuxedos and the women in glittering gowns. Other times, the car was sold, jewellery pawned. My childhood was a rollercoaster of highs and lows. It wasn't stable like the life I've created for Henry, and yet I was loved and fed and cared for. My parents were not to blame for me throwing my future away.

At least they'll both be spared the knowledge of what will become of me after tonight. The thought is selfish. I think of Henry, and how, without grandparents or uncles or aunts, he'll be so alone if I die tonight.

It was my impulsiveness that got me into trouble as a child, almost the same age as Lucie was when we met. I never thought through the consequences of my actions. I thought I knew everything in that way teenagers do when they believe they're invincible. It's why I've kept such a close eye on Henry these past few years. So when I saw Gina Thorogood and her friends bullying one of the younger kids by the bike sheds, a fury rose inside me. I walked straight up to Gina and shoved her away, smacked her round the face for good measure. I expected the three-day suspension, the letter home to my parents. What I didn't expect was the campaign of hate Gina and her friends launched against me from that moment forward. I couldn't walk down a school corridor without someone shoving me or spitting at me. Even the teachers kept their distance.

By the time my exams were over, I couldn't wait to leave school. I found a job in office administration in an accountancy firm and breathed a sigh of relief that the bullying was over.

I was halfway through my own accountancy qualification when I met Martin. When we married, he suggested I stopped work and even though I knew it was dated and wrong, I was flattered. I thought he wanted to take care of me.

But it wasn't care he wanted. It was reliance. And he wanted me out of the company so I couldn't see him flirt with the secretaries. I became trapped, a prisoner in a nice little house with a pretty garden.

Martin rarely wanted my mind or my thoughts, but there were times when he needed them. I didn't forget my studies or the experience I'd gained at the company, and I often helped Martin at the weekend when his workload was heavy. There was one weekend when he was in bed with flu that I did all the work for him. Nobody even knew.

'I did want to be an estate agent when I was a bit older,' Sam says, pulling me back from my thoughts. 'I like houses.'

I want to ask him why he didn't do that. I want to know what path led him to my car. To kidnap and whatever he has planned for me. 'You wouldn't have needed a lot of qualifications for that either,' I say instead, my voice soft. Years of training – of people watching, of helping – kicking in.

'Yeah, well—' Sam's phone buzzes and he snatches it up, the conversation forgotten. The tension returns to the car.

A sign for Leeds looms ahead of us. Fifty miles to go.

Panic is a steel vice. We're almost there and I only have a scrap of a plan forming in the back of my mind. I feel like all I can see is the two metres of the road ahead of me and I need to see so much more. There are so many things that could go wrong. I could die, I could be hurt. But no matter how many ways I figure it, how many combinations of what ifs I compile in my head, I know one thing – someone will be dead tonight.

FOURTEEN

LUCIE

Then

It's only when Celia shouts a cheery 'Bye' and the front door closes that Lucie starts to relax. Nothing has been the same since Lucie saw those bolts a few weeks ago. She's tried to forget, she's tried to believe Celia's explanation about Martin's sleepwalking, but she can't. They are all she thinks about, all she sees when she closes her eyes – the shiny silver, the thick cylinder. Sometimes she even thinks she can hear the noise of them sliding into place. A clunk. A thud.

It's like a curtain has been pulled back and Lucie is seeing everything differently. Like how nervous Celia gets after 6 p.m., how Lucie is always ushered out the door before Martin gets home. How Lucie has never met him in all these months.

'Bath time,' Henry announces, racing up the stairs ahead of her. 'And then I put my pyjamas on all by myself and then you read me four stories.'

'Your mum said two,' Lucie says, pretending to be stern.

'Three?' Henry gives a hopeful smile that Lucie knows she can't say no to.

'You're a hard negotiator, Henry. Three stories, but that's it.'

He giggles, muffling the sound behind his hand as though the noise of it is somehow forbidden. He does that a lot, she realises.

Upstairs, Lucie runs a warm bath, checking and double-checking it's not too hot, and Henry squeals with delight at how many bubbles there are, stripping off his clothes in two swift movements before clambering in.

Lucie kneels down beside the bath, lifting the top from the bubble mountain and dropping it on Henry's head. 'A hat for you.'

'And for you,' he says, shifting onto his knees and scooping bubbles onto Lucie's head, making her laugh as water trickles down her back.

Lucie doesn't see the bruises at first. They play with a green plastic frog, winding it up and letting it swim back and forth across the bath. Henry is squirming around, lifting the frog high in the air and dropping it in the water with a splash, absorbed in his play. But there on the underside of his left arm, only visible when his hand is in the air, are three dark circles that look to Lucie just like finger marks. They're high up, only a few centimetres from his armpit, and would be completely hidden beneath a T-shirt.

Her mouth turns dry and she wishes more than anything in the world that she had someone she could call right now. Her mobile is in her bag downstairs, but even if she had it in her hand, who would she call? Lucie knows what her mum would tell her: she'd say to mind her own business. She thinks of the girls she only sees in form room, passing with hellos and awkward glances. Would any of them answer if she called? She doubts it.

The only person who would help her, the only person she wants to call, is Celia, but her mind is racing over the last few months spent in this house and all the things she's seen that she's desperately tried to ignore. The fear in Henry's eyes, the way he always seems to be asking her a question in his expression. And Celia too – that nervous way she gets as the evening draws in and Martin is due home. Then there are the bolts and Celia's false laughter as she tries to explain them away.

No. Lucie can't talk to Celia about this because Henry isn't the only one that needs help. Celia does too.

'Henry?' Lucie says, her voice barely a whisper. She takes a breath and even as the words form in her thoughts, she doesn't know whether she should say them. There's a big part of her that wants to carry on pretending everything is fine, and if she asks this question and Henry tells her what she already suspects, then there is no going back. And yet, this is little Henry, who is sweet and kind and makes her feel adored. How can she not ask? 'Where did those bruises come from on your arm?'

Henry stops playing and pulls his arms around himself.

'It's OK,' she says. 'You can talk to me.' Lucie isn't sure it is OK, or what she'll do if Henry does tell her what she's already guessed, but there are people she can call, surely? Childline or the NSPCC. She wants to be a doctor so she can help people. She has to help Henry and Celia.

'I'm a good boy,' he says with a furtive nod.

'I know,' she replies.

'You're like me.' His voice drops to a whisper. 'You need to be extra good because you don't have any brothers or sisters either. It's down to us.'

'What do you mean?' she asks, unsure what Henry is trying to say.

The little boy shakes his head and in the silence that follows they both jump at the sound of the front door opening. Lucie glances at her watch. Celia is home early and Henry should've been out the bath ten minutes ago.

'You'd better get out,' she says, holding out the towel. Henry jumps up, almost slipping as he clambers out.

'Hello?' A voice travels up the stairs and she jumps again. The voice is deep and unfamiliar. Male.

'Daddy,' Henry whispers.

'Er... Hi,' Lucie calls back, her heart thumping in her ears. She's about to come face to face with a man who she is sure is abusing his family. The thought sends a bolt of adrenaline right through her.

A part of her wants to slide the lock across the bathroom door, wrap Henry in her arms and wait for Celia to come home, but she can't. She has to pretend everything is normal, doesn't she?

Her indecision costs her too much time and before she can decide, the bathroom door opens and he's standing there, a tall man with wide shoulders and a creased shirt.

He frowns as he looks from Henry to Lucie, staring at her with eyes that narrow and then widen. 'What are you doing here?'

'I'm... Er...'

'This is Lucie, Daddy. She's my friend.'

'I see. And why haven't you told me about Lucie before?'

The silence that follows crackles with fear.

'I think I can guess,' he says before looking at Lucie. 'I'm Martin. Henry's dad.'

'Celia asked me to babysit,' Lucie blurts out as she takes in the man standing before her. He has short dark hair, thin on top. Lucie can see his scalp shining beneath the bathroom light. His small eyes stare back at her with suspicion, and when he smiles a tight, unwelcoming smile, a shiver runs down her spine.

'I guessed. Well, Henry boy, you'd better get your PJs on before your mum gets home. You're welcome to leave, Lucie.'

Henry drops the towel and scurries to his bedroom, and it's just Lucie and Martin alone. She doesn't like the intensity in his gaze, those dark eyes watching her like he knows something she doesn't.

'Er...' She doesn't know what to say. Should she go? She wants to. She wants to sprint out the door and run and run and run until the wind is whipping her face, but Celia left her in charge of Henry. What if Martin hurts Henry while they're alone?

It's Henry that saves the moment. 'Lucie said she would read to me,' he shouts from his bedroom.

'I really don't mind,' Lucie jumps in.

'All right then,' Martin says with a shrug. 'I'll be downstairs.' He turns to leave and Lucie walks on jelly legs to Henry's room.

She spends as long as she can reading to Henry, acting out the noises in *Peace at Last* that make him giggle, and then a book about a cat called Mog she reads twice. But when his eyes grow heavy, she knows she has to say goodnight and face Martin.

The thud of her heart drums in her ears as she makes her way downstairs. Lucie finds Martin pacing in the kitchen. There's an agitation rippling from his body that makes her linger in the doorway.

He stops when he sees her. She expects anger or something sinister but all she sees in his face is anguish. They watch each other for a moment and then he moves – two urgent strides and he's on her, a firm hand gripping the top of her arm. He talks low and fast in Lucie's ear. Phrases like 'trust me' and 'you know nothing' stick in her head.

She shakes her head, a furious movement. She doesn't want to hear the words that hammer into her mind. He's lying. He's a bad man, she tells herself. His hand continues to squeeze her skin and tears are rolling down her face and the front door is opening and Celia is standing there, her mouth a perfect O.

'Lucie,' she gasps, and then to Martin, 'I thought you weren't home until eight.'

'The dinner got cancelled,' he replies, his hand slipping away from Lucie's shoulder.

Lucie moves fast, almost knocking into Celia as she pushes her feet into her shoes and rushes outside, running as fast as she can, not stopping until she's home, the door slamming shut behind her. But she can't run from the soft growl of Martin's voice still ringing in her ears, and the sick words implanted on her brain.

Today 21:07

Please reply!

Today 21:09

I don't know what to do!!!

FIFTEEN

CELIA

Hour three

Less than an hour to go now. I have to do something. Every minute feels like a lifetime and the longer I wait, the harder it is.

I took Henry to one of those tree-climbing places once for his tenth birthday. The ones with the obstacles way up high and the safety harness and clips that kept us tethered to thick metal wire. We climbed and climbed, hopping and wobbling, up and up until we reached a platform high in the canopies. There was an instructor waiting for us. He unclipped us from one wire and clipped us to another, and he pointed to the ground far below and told us to jump.

Henry went without a moment of hesitation, shouting a 'Yahoo!' as he zipped to the ground, landing on his feet before turning to wave at me. I knew I had to jump. Henry was alone. I knew it was safe. I knew the wires and the harness and all the safety measures would protect me. But still, an innate part of myself – the long-forgotten animalistic part of my genetic make-up that remembered caves and wild beasts and real danger – screamed at me not to jump.

I did it in the end. For Henry. He was wandering towards the exit and even from my position high up in the trees I could see how quickly he could get lost. So I blanked out that voice telling me not to jump and I leaped from the platform, landing with my bum and legs dragging on the ground.

That is what this moment feels like. The voice telling me not to do it. And knowing that I have to.

Sam is twitchy beside me, jabbing on his phone every few minutes. I'm sure he's planning something. He won't let me live.

'I'm never coming back. I don't want to see you ever again,' she'd said.

'Lucie, wait,' I'd called as she'd ran out of the house. 'You're making a mistake.' And then, 'I'll always be here for you,' I'd shouted after her. I didn't think she'd heard that last line – but I was wrong.

It's stupid to look back and wish things had been different. To wonder what life would be like if one little thing had changed. But I do. Even now, my insides squirm and I wish more than anything that Martin hadn't come home early that day. I swore to myself on the very first day Lucie came for tea that I wouldn't let Martin see her, and I was so careful, so cautious. But time passed and I started to relax. I got complacent, and when Martin said he had a client dinner, I thought it would be safe. It wasn't. Lucie never looked at me the same after that.

Another sign for Leeds comes into view. Forty miles. Time is running out. The hours of fear and panic build up inside me. It's almost over. Tears form in my eyes, blurring my vision. I don't try to fight it.

I've messed everything up.

My life is over.

I'm going to die.

I think of Henry and a heaving sob breaks loose. Then another and another.

'What are you doing?' Sam asks as though it isn't obvious. 'Stop it.' He lurches towards me, raising the knife, and I yelp. My hands leave the steering wheel and I cover my face and cry. I cry for everything that is happening to me, for Lucie who I couldn't help tonight, for Henry and what will become of our family of two. I cry with the terror of what will happen next. There are so many ways I could die tonight. So many ways my life could end one way or another.

'Hey, the road,' Sam shouts, grabbing the wheel with one hand. I sense his gaze flicking back and forth between the road and me. 'I'm not gonna kill ya, all right? I promise. Please, take the wheel back.'

I lower my shaking hands and move them back to ten and two. There's a moment when Sam's hand is still in place and our fingers touch. His skin is hot and clammy and I move my grip lower down the wheel, away from the place he touched.

The signs for Leeds are everywhere now. Time seems to race forward.

Thirty miles.

Twenty miles.

Ten miles.

And then Sam is telling me to take the next exit and we're driving into the outskirts of the city. I ease my foot from the accelerator as empty land becomes factories and then rows of low brown brick buildings, a petrol station, a corner shop, signs of life.

I can't wait much longer. I glance at Sam's phone screen and the map showing our route. My eyesight isn't what it used to be. The numbers at the bottom are a blur. Is that eight minutes or eighteen? Either way, it's nearly over.

'I'm sorry,' Sam says into the silence.

His words sink in. 'What are you going to do?'

He doesn't reply. Instead he stiffens, his gaze locked on something ahead, and I see it too – a police car coming towards us from the opposite direction.

SIXTEEN

LUCIE

Then

Lucie doesn't go to Celia's after school on Tuesday or Wednesday the following week. She wants to so badly but when she thinks of Henry and Celia and Martin her stomach aches and she doesn't know what to believe anymore. Hurt seems to radiate from her chest constantly. It feels like a part of her has been taken away and yet there is no one she can tell. She feels more alone now than she ever did before.

Lucie doesn't want to think anymore. She wants them out of her head, and so she spent the week studying, forcing herself to concentrate on her homework and extra revision late into the night until her eyes blurred and she couldn't stay awake anymore.

At school, Lucie avoids the library, taking her book outside and finding a corner of the field to hide herself away in. But on Friday Celia finds her by the lockers first thing. She steps forward and Lucie catches the scent of jasmine. The smell makes her long to be back in the warmth of Celia's house. But the image is quickly replaced by another – the looming figure of

Martin, the grip of his fingers pressing into her arm. And those words she still hears in her nightmares. Lucie wonders if the smell of jasmine and the memory are linked forever. If for the rest of her life she'll feel his grip anytime she smells it. The thought makes her feel sick.

'Lucie,' she says, her eyes darting back and forth. 'Can I have a word?'

'I've got form room,' Lucie mumbles, allowing her hair to drop down around her face.

There's a tsk from Celia. 'Your hair,' she says. 'You really should wear it back.'

Lucie's cheeks smart. 'I didn't want to.' She shifts her feet and forces herself not to scoop her hair back. There are questions she wants answers to, but there are words she cannot say, like why did you want to help me? Why did you bring me into your family? What do I do now?

'I wanted to say I'm sorry about Martin,' Celia says with a quiver to her voice. 'I'm so sorry. He's gone now. He left us. We've been having problems for years. The truth is that he threatened to walk out more times than I can count, but I never thought he'd do it.'

The news startles Lucie and she looks up, seeing the tears swimming in Celia's eyes.

'He was... not a nice person,' Celia continues. 'I think you guessed that. What did he tell you?'

Celia's gaze is fierce and Lucie finds herself looking away, wishing she could shrink herself down somehow. 'Nothing,' she lies. Her face is hot and there's sweat dampening the armpits of her shirt. She can't tell Celia the truth. She just can't.

'We miss you,' Celia says after a pause, her hand touching Lucie's arm. Lucie shrinks away, thinking again of Martin's touch. 'Henry misses you.'

'I miss him too,' Lucie says with an ache that spreads through her body for Henry and Celia and how much she wanted them to be her family. But they're not, Lucie reminds herself, gritting her teeth to stop herself from crying. She has a mum, and she might not be the best mum in the world, but she's at least always honest.

Celia's hand tightens around Lucie's arm and she steps closer. 'Please come back. I want to help you.'

'I... It's just that I have a lot of homework now.' Lucie moves her arm, but Celia keeps hold a moment longer.

'Please, Lucie. Come next Tuesday. You don't have to come for dinner, but to babysit. I have a meeting at the school and Henry really wants to see you. He doesn't understand why you've stopped coming and I don't know what to tell him. It's hard for him with his dad leaving too.'

Lucie thinks of sweet little Henry and how none of this is his fault. A final time babysitting would give her the chance to say goodbye to him properly. And Celia will be out anyway.

Lucie wishes more than anything that they could go back to how it used to be, but she doesn't think they can. Something has been broken and it can't be stuck back together.

'Please,' Celia says again.

'OK.' Lucie nods. 'I'll come just before six on Tuesday. Just to babysit.'

'Six is perfect,' she says. 'I'll only be out a few hours. Henry will be so pleased.'

And he is. He wraps his arms around her the moment she steps through the front door at 5.58 p.m. the following Tuesday.

'Be good for Lucie,' Celia says, kissing the top of Henry's head. Her gaze rests on Lucie and she mouths a *thank you*. There's something else in her eyes, a pleading, and Lucie wonders again if they can go back, and how nice that would be. Her homework is getting hard and she misses sitting at Celia's kitchen table, working through essay questions while Henry colours beside her. She misses Celia's kindness and guidance, always pointing her in the right direction. But then she thinks of

Martin and that hand on her shoulder and everything feels so... so wrong.

The moment Celia leaves and Henry pulls Lucie up the stairs for bath time, her eyes drag to the bolt on his bedroom door. Except this time, it's gone. All that's left is the outline where the bolt sat and the empty black screw holes. Something releases inside her – a tension that started with Martin's hand on her shoulder.

It's fun to be back with Henry. They play froggy chase in the bath and have a bubble fight. There are no bruises this time either. No finger marks or purple blotches, just his smooth skin and his boyish giggle, and Lucie feels herself relax again.

They read *What the Ladybird Heard* together, with Henry doing the animal noises and making Lucie laugh. And then she tucks him into bed and even though she knows she should say goodbye, she can't.

The scream comes half an hour later while Lucie is in the kitchen, running her hands over the holes in the cupboards where the locks used to be, staring into the garden at nothing in particular. The piercing sound echoes through the house, jolting her from her thoughts. She spins on her heels and races up the stairs.

'Henry.' Her voice is drowned out by a second scream.

She rushes into his bedroom. There is still daylight pushing in at the edges of the curtains, enough for Lucie to see him sitting bolt upright in bed, hair damp with sweat, tears wet on his face.

'Henry, I'm here,' Lucie soothes, rushing to the bed. He launches himself at her, hugging her tight.

'Henry,' she says, 'what's wrong? Did you have a bad dream?' Fear is clutching her body. She's had bad dreams before, but never like this.

'I... I saw... I saw Daddy,' he says, gasping out the words

between sobs. Her eyes flick to the empty doorway before she understands what Henry is saying.

'You saw your daddy in your dream?' Lucie rubs at his back as his head bobs up and down against her.

'Where is Daddy?' he asks with a gulping hiccup.

'I don't know, I'm sorry,' she says. Celia said Martin left but she didn't tell her what Henry has been told and now she doesn't know what to say. She wishes Celia would come home now. 'When did you last see him?' she asks.

'On the kitchen floor,' Henry says, his voice still watery.

'The kitchen floor?' He must mean in his dream, Lucie thinks. But still, she can't stop the shiver racing over her skin.

'Mummy said he was sleeping and then... and then she put him in the garage. She thought I was asleep but I wasn't, and later I saw her put him in the garden.'

A chill runs through Lucie's body, icy and sharp, and she stiffens. She tries to ignore the alarm bells roaring in her ears. 'That's just a bad dream, Henry,' she says, hoping her words sound more reassuring than they feel. 'I'm sure your daddy is fine and you'll see him soon.'

'It—' Henry stops talking. From downstairs, they hear the catch of the front door. Relief floods Lucie's body. Celia is home. She can comfort Henry. Except Henry turns rigid in her arms and then wriggles quickly down the bed.

'Don't tell Mummy I'm awake,' he whispers, scrunching his eyes shut and turning onto his side.

Lucie wants to tell him it's OK. She wants to tell him that Celia won't mind that he's awake. Everyone has bad dreams. But something stops her and she steps quietly from the room and closes the door.

'Everything all right?' Celia's voice is low and close, making Lucie jerk back. How long was she standing outside Henry's room? What did she hear?

'Er... Yes, Henry just had a nightmare but he's fine now. Fast asleep,' Lucie lies.

She follows Celia to the kitchen, sitting at the table while Celia makes a hot chocolate for her. She's tired and wants to go home now, but she also needs to talk to her about Henry. A burst of nerves pops inside her stomach, willing her to get up and go, but she forces herself to stay. For Henry.

Lucie waits until the cups are on the table and Celia is opposite her.

'How was the meeting?' she asks, wishing it didn't feel so awkward.

Celia smiles. 'Oh fine. It was nice to get out even for a few hours. How was Henry?'

'Fine. He's always so good. It was just...' Lucie's voice trails off. She doesn't know how to say it. 'He... had a bad dream about his dad.'

'Oh?' Celia's face is expressionless and yet Lucie thinks she hears a note of worry in that one word.

'He said he saw him sleeping on the kitchen floor and then you put him in the garage.'

There's a beat of silence before a peal of laughter escapes Celia's mouth – a high, shrill sound. 'Sorry,' she says, shaking her head. 'Poor Henry. I don't mean to laugh. I know it must be hard for him having Martin leave so suddenly. He's been having the same silly dream every night. I've no idea where it came from. I'm sorry, I should've warned you.'

Celia steers the topic on to Lucie and her coursework, suggesting angles for the history essay she's writing.

Lucie is only half listening. She knows what Celia is saying about Henry makes sense. He's a five-year-old boy with an active imagination. And yet she can't shake the feeling that something is wrong in this house.

Martin's voice hisses in her thoughts. *Listen. Listen to me.*

She's not what she seems. Trust me, you know nothing about her. She's crazy.'

Lucie didn't have time to ask what he meant, but little things pop into her mind now. How fast Henry moved in the bed, his whispered plea not to tell Celia he was awake. It's all the little things that on their own are nothing. Like how insistent Celia is about what Lucie wears and how she does her hair. Things that Lucie has blindly ignored because she's wanted so badly for this family to be her family, but together these things are something. Something twisted.

'She put him in the garage.'

Lucie stands suddenly and Celia stops mid-sentence.

'Lucie, are you all right?' she asks.

Lucie shakes her head and steps to the sink and the window that looks out over the back garden. The night is closing in and she stares into the gloom. She didn't register it before – the space at the back near the fence where a flower bed used to sit.

'What's that?' she asks, pointing into the darkness.

Celia stands and moves beside her. 'A concrete foundation for a summer house. They're fitting it next week. The garage has become too cluttered and we need somewhere to store the garden equipment. Lucie—'

Lucie staggers back, out of Celia's reach.

'She's not what she seems.'

'And later I saw her put him in the garden.'

Lucie gives a furious shake of her head, dispelling the voices she doesn't want to hear or believe, but they won't go away.

'Where's Martin?' Lucie asks, her voice sounding far away.

'Martin?' Celia bites her lower lip. 'I told you, he left us.'

Lucie watches Celia's face, waiting for her eyes to betray her, and they do. Just as Lucie's had moved to the bolt above Henry's door when she hadn't wanted them to, Celia's move to the garden.

Lucie staggers back again. She has to get out. She has to get away from this house. She was stupid to ever think she belonged here. She grabs her bag from the floor, almost dropping it again in her panic. 'Don't... don't contact me again,' she says, wishing she could stop the tremble that had entered her voice. 'I'm never coming back. I don't want to see you ever again.'

Celia's face contorts before her eyes. Disbelief, then sadness and then... Her eyes narrow and anger sets into her features. She steps forward, her arms out as though she's going to grab Lucie, but Lucie is too fast. She races to the door and is gone into the night.

Today 21:07

CALL ME NOW!!!

Today 21:09

What's going on?
I'm so worried.
I can't call the police.
You know that, right?

SEVENTEEN

CELIA

Hour Four

The police car is cruising slowly along the road, sirens off.

I'm here, I want to scream. *Help me, help me.*

'Don't do anything,' Sam barks, sitting back in his seat and making a show of staring straight ahead. As the point of the knife digs painfully into my side, I gasp.

My gaze flicks to the rear-view mirror. Another car is approaching from behind. Yellow pools of light from the lamp-posts illuminate the wet road, the empty pavements.

Time stands still. I'm frozen, unable to draw in my next breath. I blink and the police car is closer. I can see two officers sat side by side. They're talking, laughing, not looking my way. In another moment they'll be gone, and with them, my last chance to escape from whatever is in store for me. My last chance to save us.

I feel myself on that ledge up high in the trees again, that same conflict of body and mind. And then I stop thinking. I do what I know I have to do to survive this.

Every muscle in my body tenses and I grip the wheel,

bracing myself as I veer a sharp left, and we're no longer driving straight but careening off to the side of the road. I'm jolted by the movement, falling hard on the knife in Sam's hand as it slips through my skin and into my body.

Ice cold floods my abdomen, then burning pain. I think I cry out, but the noise is lost to Sam's yells.

He yanks the knife away, dropping it to the floor as he tries to grab the wheel, but it's too late. It all happens in seconds. I see the lamp-post looming in the headlights, I turn the wheel again, a sudden jerk, and then I'm being thrown forward and the airbags release, hitting my face like a punch.

For a moment there is nothing. No movement. No thoughts. No sound. Just a stunned silence and a ringing in my ears. My nose and eyes throb along with the racing of my heart. An ache takes over my body. My head is pounding and my blouse is sticky with blood.

I touch my side and the pain snatches the air out of my lungs.

I take shallow breaths and peel open my eyes. I don't know what I'm doing here, I don't know what happened. It's as though the impact has knocked all the thoughts right out of my head.

There's a groan and movement from the seat next to me and I gasp, my arms flying out to Henry, but it's not Henry. It's Sam. I turn my head and watch him push away the airbag. There's blood dripping out of his nose. His eyes are watering, his face grey.

It all comes back in a whoosh and I make a noise in the back of my throat, a little cry as I remember everything. Sam jumping into my car. The hours we've spent side by side, the knife at my hip. The police car. Lucie. Oh, my poor Lucie.

The need to be out of the car becomes a physical force. I fumble with shaking hands for the seatbelt clip and then the door handle. I half step, half fall into the freezing cold air.

I'm shivering all over as my knees land on the hard tarmac.

'Help.' My voice is a whisper.

No one comes to my side. I look up into the night. The street is empty, lit only by the dim orange of a streetlight. I can't see the police car.

Where are they?

Where is my help? My rescue?

My eyes dart back to the car. Sam is moving. His arms are up and he's holding his face. Any second now and he'll have that same lurching realisation and spur into movement. He'll come after me. He'll kill me.

Tears swim across my vision and I start to move. A shuffling crawl, a drag of my body that causes a sharp burn of pain to shoot out from my side. My hand is still clutching the place where the knife went in. It's sticky with blood now, some of it already drying between my fingers.

There's a flash of light. With my spinning head, I think it's me, that I'm going to faint, but it comes again and again – a strobing blue. A siren. The police are here. They saw the crash. I try to gather myself, but my thoughts are a cup of rice dropped to the floor, scattering into every corner.

My pulse quickens to a rapid fire. My wound throbs harder.

One of the officers reaches my side. 'Miss, are you OK?' And then to his colleague, 'There's a passenger.'

'The boot.' The words come out a sob, garbled and incoherent.

'Stay calm. An ambulance is on its way.'

'Open the boot,' I shout this time, forcing the words out. 'Open the boot. That... That man – he jumped in my car, he kidnapped me, made me drive here.' Tears roll down my face. 'Open the boot.'

The officer moves with painful slowness, unaware of the storm of panic and emotion raging inside me. He steps towards the rear of the car, fiddling for a moment before finding the catch and opening the boot.

'Oh, Jesus,' he says, leaping back. 'Jesus Christ. Paul, we've got a body here.'

'What?' The other officer steps up beside him, staring in for a second before turning away, hand clasped over his mouth.

Their voices carry through the night with the crackle of their radios, but it's hard to keep listening. I'm shaking all over. Cold to my core. I feel myself sink to the damp road and close my eyes. All I wanted was to save us – me and my darling Henry. He needs his mother.

PART II

EIGHTEEN

CELIA

There is movement all around me. Voices, authority. My thoughts are disorientated – drifting across my mind like the little pieces of glitter in the Christmas snow globe Henry used to love, digging it out of the decorations box the moment it was out while I went back to double-lock the garage door.

I've crashed my car. I've been in an accident.

I've been held at knifepoint for hours.

Stabbed. I've been stabbed.

Henry. Lucie. Henry again.

The desire to open my eyes itches just beneath my eyelids. I want to sit up, I want to take back control. I want to go home. But none of these things are possible. The pain in my abdomen is pinning me down. The police are here. There is nothing for me to do except lie on this cold road and be the victim.

Sirens wail in the distance. Two or three emergency vehicles. A cacophony.

Fear clutches at my chest. Thoughts no longer drift – they smack right into me. There is no going back now. No quiet escape, no dark overgrown ditch on a country lane to dump

Lucie's body in, keeping her safe from prying eyes for as long as possible. Suddenly the plan that wormed into my thoughts somewhere on the hellish drive with Sam seems flimsy – a tent pole to hold up a tower block.

Shouting pulls me back to the road. 'Stay where you are.' The voice is loud – a commanding force that punches the air from my lungs.

They know. They know what I did. I keep my eyes squeezed shut as footsteps smack on wet pavement.

'He's running,' another officer shouts.

Sam. They're not talking to me. They're talking to Sam. I breathe again – a ragged gasp that makes my stomach scream in pain.

Will they catch him? Even in my current state, I hope not. It's easier to tell a story when there's only one side, one version. And what a story I have to tell, but I'll worry about that later.

Somewhere in the distance of my thoughts, somewhere far away, emotions roil. Fury at Sam for forcing me here, fury at Lucie too. And betrayal and grief and guilt. The emotions are hidden under a thick layer of shock, bubble-wrapping me from reality.

I had to do it! The words tumble into my mind.

Poor Lucie. Such a silly girl.

She thought she knew everything. She was going to tell the police. About Martin. About me. She was going to destroy my life and, with it, destroy Henry's life too. Did she really think she could blackmail me?

I think of her at thirteen and the confidence that I alone coaxed out of her. She could have become anything, anyone, under my care. She could have been studying to be a doctor, all her dreams coming true. But she ran away from me, and now she's dead.

This isn't my fault. It's hers.

The rumble of an engine approaches. More feet. Someone is by my side. 'Miss? Can you hear me?'

I give a small nod and she continues. 'I'm Jules, I'm a paramedic. My colleague, Tim, is here beside me. Can you tell me your name?'

'Celia,' I say without opening my eyes. My voice is weak, pathetic. The perfect voice of a victim.

She carries on talking – a mellifluous tone, soothing and calm. I let them do their thing. I let them examine my wound and I answer their questions, but I'm not really here. The shock is keeping me snuggled up tight and I let it.

Conversations happen around me. 'The other ambulance is on its way,' Jules says to someone above my head.

'No rush,' one of the police officers replied. 'Poor thing. She looks young too.'

She is, I want to tell them. A whole life ahead of her. She threw it all away.

'Celia, I'm sorry to ask this, but do you know the name of the woman—' The officer doesn't say the rest. The woman in the boot. The body. He's trying to be gentle with me.

I give a small nod, tears falling easily. 'Lucie Gilbert. She... I was helping her, then she saw him get in my car and he... he killed her.' Lies, lies, lies. Can they tell?

There's radio static and voices. 'They've caught him,' the officer tells us, the excitement in his voice strengthening his Leeds accent. 'Just around the corner. They can add fleeing the scene of a crime to kidnap and murder.'

Murder.

The word is a tacky glue in my head.

They believe me. They believe Sam killed Lucie. The relief is a gust of cold wind pushing through me. My plan has worked and maybe, maybe it's better like this.

When Sam jumped into my car, I was on my way to the

back roads that connect the town to a scattering of villages. The kind of places with old houses and barn conversions surrounded by fields, places pretending to be in the middle of nowhere instead of nestled on the edges of a bustling town.

The lanes are twisty and dangerous. Every year someone is killed walking home from a night out in town. Sharp turns, vehicles going too fast, bodies thrown into the ditch of nettles and brambles that runs between the field and the road.

It would've looked like a hit and run.

But this is better. Pinning everything on Sam. I'll be asked questions, of course. He'll deny it. I'll lie. My word against his. It won't be easy, but neither would've been that awful wait, that watchful eye on the local news sites for the discovery of a body, then the jittery panic to see if the dots connected to me.

'Celia.' Jules's voice pulls me back to the road. 'We're going to move you onto the stretcher now. It's going to be a bit uncomfortable but we'll be quick.'

I grab her arm. Her skin is warm compared to the ice of my fingers. 'Where am I going?'

'We're taking you to the emergency department at St James's University Hospital.'

'I'll send someone to follow behind,' the officer says. 'Once you've been treated, Celia, we'll need to talk properly and get more details about what's happened tonight.'

Pain shoots out of my wound, like darts hitting every corner of my body as I'm bundled away. Doors slam and we're rocking and moving. No siren, just the occasional whoop whoop.

I have so many lies to tell. So many ways this could all still fall apart and my life could be over. But it will be all right, just as long as I can keep control of myself, juggle the lies. I should be good at that. I've had enough practice.

Facebook Messenger

You're the only one who knows the truth.
You have to help me.

NINETEEN

SAM

Sam smashes his foot against the metal door again and again and again. He was so close and now it's all gone so wrong. Each twanging crash echoes in his ears, reminding him that he's in a cell, as if the six-by-six space isn't a big enough giveaway. His toe throbs, his foot aches, tears prick his eyes, but he doesn't stop. Can't stop.

If he could just speak to someone. The nurse who checked him over when he got here was nice. But he choked up and couldn't get the words out to explain the madness of the last few hours, and then she got called away and no one has been to see him since.

'I need to talk to someone,' he screams, jamming his finger against the button on the wall that is supposed to call for assistance. *As if.* The effort of shouting makes his face throb. It feels like he's had a fist thrown at him rather than an airbag. He can feel the swelling stretching out from his nose to under his eyes. An ache pulls down his neck and across his shoulders too – the beginnings of whiplash, the nurse warned him.

'You've been lucky,' she said with a kind smile. Lucky? Lucky would've been not getting caught. Lucky would've been not losing his job and then the room in the house share he had. Lucky would've been one of his so-called mates agreeing to lend him the money when he'd called yesterday morning. He didn't blame them. He'd been crashing on sofas, eating their food and taking the piss for weeks now. They'd all had enough of him.

Lucky would've been finding something useful in that house. Something other than a world of more trouble. Or getting to the train station and jumping on a train to London and then to Leeds without the transport police catching him and turfing him out, blocking the station entrances to stop him trying again. Or the taxi driver believing him that he had the money to get to the next station instead of radioing all his mates to tell them not to pick Sam up.

Lucky would've been finding any way to get him to Leeds in time without needing to kidnap someone.

Maybe lucky would've been dying in the crash.

So, no. Sam hasn't been lucky at all. The truth is, he hasn't had a drop of luck his whole goddamn life.

Sam jabs at the buzzer again. It's silent. Probably broken or switched off. He stops. Listens. There's noise all around him. Someone is throwing up in the cell next to him, that deep retching sound that turns his stomach. Someone else is singing from further away, an old Oasis song, the words slurred. There are shouts too. Screaming. Crying. The sounds of the desperate, the dregs, the scum. He is one of them. Always has been. Born bad, a teacher told him once.

'Nothing like your sister, are you?' she'd said then and he'd given her his best couldn't-care-less smirk.

The teacher was right though. He was nothing like Bee. Hard-working, lovely Bee. Sam draws in a breath, but it snags on the emotion blocking his airway.

A door bangs from somewhere, and then the window in the door is opening and the jowly face of an officer appears.

'Please,' Sam says, the words rushing out before the officer can tell him to shut up. 'I need to speak to someone. It's urgent. I need my phone call.' He wants to say more but the words are locked inside him somewhere.

The officer rolls his eyes slightly, but he doesn't laugh. It's pity, not malice, on his face. 'Sir, we are still trying to contact your mother on the numbers you've given us. As soon as we've made contact and informed her of your arrest, I will make sure you have the chance to speak with her, but at the moment we're getting no answer.' The officer's tone is reasonable and calm but does nothing to ease the ticking bomb threatening to explode inside him.

'I know, but—'

'Sir, I understand that this is a distressing situation for you. But shouting isn't going to help you.'

'Can I speak to one of your lot then?' The word 'pig' forms in his mouth, but he shuts it down. His old man's word. It's an automatic reflex, like how he hates Manchester United when he doesn't give a shit about football. 'Like an interview. I need to talk to someone. I have to be somewhere. It's... it's important.' The final word spews out with a sob. He coughs, trying to mask it.

'There won't be any interview happening tonight, so I suggest you get some rest.'

'Tomorrow morning then?' It could be too late by then. The realisation claws at his chest. It has to be OK. There has to be a way. There just has to be.

The officer shakes his head. 'You're down to be moved tomorrow.'

'What? Moved where?'

'You're being held on suspicions of crimes that began in another jurisdiction. You will be transferred to that location tomorrow morning.'

'Jurisdiction? I don't—'

'You're being taken back to Essex, lad.' The hatch closes

with a clang and Sam is alone again. He thinks about kicking the door some more, but the fight has gone out of him. Everything he's done, every stupid thing he's done, and it was all for nothing. They're taking him back to Essex.

It's too late. He's too late.

Sam steps back, his legs suddenly weak, and drops onto the bed. It's not really a bed. More like a raised platform built into the room, barely a foot off the ground. There's a thin blue plastic mat – like the kind they use in schools for PE – that's supposed to be a mattress, and a matching plastic-coated pillow.

He drops his head into his hands and takes a breath, catching the smell of cheap bleach and the stink of his feet, that tang of a day and then some in the same socks and trainers.

He's wearing a pale-grey tracksuit – the same kind they gave out in prison. The first thing they did was take his clothes and his shoes. His jumper was covered in blood from his nosebleed anyway.

Sam peers through his fingers at his feet and briefly considers washing them in the metal sink in the corner, but what's the point? Stinking feet are pretty low down the list of problems.

There are other things above it, way above it. Like just how screwed he is. How many years is he going to get for everything he's done today? He doesn't have a clue about sentencing stuff, but with his police record, it's got to be ten years at least, hasn't it?

Sam did a year once. Twelve months for his second burglary arrest when he was nineteen. He got through it by switching off a part of himself and letting the hours, days, weeks, months tick down. He got his bricklaying qualification and some crappy maths certificate while he was in there. A year is nothing, but ten? Tears blur his vision. If he'd just made it, if he'd just shaken off the daze of the crash that bit quicker, ran that bit faster. He feels it now, that motion of legs pounding the pavement. Cold wind blasting his ears. Shouts behind him. They'd had him cornered, nowhere left to run.

If he'd just made it, ten years wouldn't have mattered. He'd have done it no problem, got some proper exams, learned carpentry or something. But now every second of every day of the years stretching ahead of him will be stained with all the ways he's failed.

Time passes. Sam has no idea how much. There is no clock on the wall, no measure of minutes and hours. He lays on the mat. He stares at the ceiling. He cries. He sleeps – a restless doze, jolting back to consciousness with every holler and bang.

Morning arrives, marked only by the microwave all-day breakfast that is slid into his cell with a cup of tea. Both luke-warm and served in Styrofoam. The breakfast is sausages and potato, swimming in baked beans. He wolfs it down, the food warming his body. It's shit but he's had a lot worse.

Doors crash, cells open and close. The panic returns, hammering inside him. The breakfast turns – a cement mixer – inside him. His thoughts are a stream of swear words and one question he desperately wants to know the answer to but can't bring himself to ask. Is he too late?

He rubs at his head and wishes they'd let him keep his cap on. He hates not wearing his baseball cap. His head aches – a fast pulsing throb. Dehydration and the smack of the airbag in his face, or maybe just his reality being punched into his brains.

Time passes. Too much time. Panic continues to hurtle through him. His breathing is a heaving gasp by the time they come for him, opening the door to his cell and replacing the stale air of his breakfast, his feet and the shit he did a while ago. Two officers in stiff black jackets. A man and a woman, both in their late twenties, both looking like they've drawn the short straw.

'I need to speak to someone.' The words fly out, loud and

desperate. 'Please,' he adds, his legs feeling like they might buckle beneath him.

'Please confirm your name and address,' the female officer says as though he hasn't spoken.

'Sam Grant.' He pauses, thinking of the sofas and floors he's slept on over the last month. Even with everything else going on, the next words still cause a heat to burn in his bruised cheeks. 'I don't have a fixed address. If I could just explain—'

'We're now going to transport you to Hallford police station to answer questions for suspected kidnap, murder and fleeing the scene of a crime. I'm now going to give you a police caution. Sam Grant, you do not have to say anything, but it may harm your defence if you do not mention when questioned something which you may later rely on in court. Anything you do say may be given in evidence. Do you understand?'

Sam understands all right. He knows these bozos aren't going to listen. He knows he's got no choice but to go, to travel all the way back to Essex. His head spins and he clenches his jaw, fighting back frustrated tears threatening to fall. He was so close! Minutes away.

Then he stops. He freezes. Something the officer said has lodged in his mind, like trying to swallow a piece of food without chewing.

'Murder?'

He didn't kill anyone. Did he?

We stand in the shadows. The glow from the streetlights on the road barely stretches to this middle part of the car park where the tarmac is worn and potholed. I don't need to see Lucie's face to know her expression will be set in the same determination I remember so well. An ache cuts through my chest. I want to reach out and touch her, hold her tight for the girl she once was.

'I will go to the police.' Lucie's voice is fierce, shoving any desire to hug her out of me.

If I could just make her understand.

Maybe I step forward because she lurches back. Away. One then two paces.

'I'm going to do it,' she says.

A cold wind whips around the building, bringing with it a spattering of rain that hits my face with the chilling reality of what she's threatening. I shudder inside the fabric of my coat. My hands ball into two tight fists. The moment she leaves this car park, everything I've worked so hard for will be over.

TWENTY

CELIA

There's a patch of brown – a water stain – on one of the polystyrene ceiling tiles. The blotchy shape swims across my vision when I close my eyes to the stark white lights of the emergency room. The medication has dulled the pain in my side, but it's messed up my head too. I can't think straight. I can't hold on to the story I need to tell – puzzle pieces without a picture. Past and present mixed together. Martin's face and then Lucie's. Young and old.

The images are mixed together with flashbacks from the car park. Lucie stepping away from me. *'I'm going to do it.'* The anger burning deep inside me. Then the car flying forward, the thudding blow of Lucie's body hitting the bonnet. Then I'm in Leeds, the airbag smashing into me. The point of the knife at my side. Then Lucie again. That awful thwack as her body hit the tarmac. The sounds – crunching bone, piercing screams – echo in my ears until I feel sick.

I can't stop the flashbacks. The memories. I can't stop shivering either. I'm so cold, but I must get a grip on myself. I am a mother. I have Henry to think of.

The nursing team are sweethearts. One of them phoned Henry for me. They told him I'd been in an accident. They didn't mention where or when or how; they didn't mention Sam or the nightmare of the drive. He must be so worried, imagining the worst, and I long to be able to comfort him, to put my arms around him and pull him close like I did all those nights he dreamed of his father, whispering in his ear that everything would be OK. And it was, eventually. Henry and I have survived so much. We can survive this too, can't we?

The urge to get out of this bed – this hospital, this city – tugs my eyelids open and I stare once more at the stain. How long have I been here? Six hours? Seven? I can't see a window, but it feels like it might be morning now. The voices of the nurses are louder as they bustle in and out, practically tripping over the police officer lingering just outside my bay.

Every few minutes I hear him sharing a joke with a nurse. I'd have sent him to the waiting area, but they are endlessly patient and I know it won't be long before he stops lingering and starts asking the questions I know he will ask.

My head spins. I have to focus. I have to get this right. Or I will go to prison and Henry will be all alone. What kind of mother would I be if I did that?

There's a movement by my bed. I startle, limbs jerking.

'How are you doing, Celia?' The nurse, Jakub, is a small man with black shiny hair and skin that looks pale under the bright white of the hospital lights. It's been a long shift. Jakub has been here longer than I have. He stood beside the doctor who stitched up my side. Patted my hand when I was told no surgery was required, no organs nicked. Just stitches given, rest and painkillers prescribed.

I nod. 'Better, but groggy.'

'Still cold?'

'Yes. I don't think I'll ever feel warm again.'

'It's the shock,' Jakub says, tucking the edge of the blanket tighter around my legs. 'You've been through a lot.'

I give a small nod. He has no idea.

'Celia, my shift is over now. I'm going home. I want to wish you good luck, and also, the police officer wants to talk to you. Is it OK if I send him in?'

I nod again. 'Thank you, Jakub. You've been so kind. You've all been so kind.' I watch him step away, wishing I could call him back, make him stay with me a while longer, but Jakub deserves to go home.

And me – what do I deserve? The question stings.

The police officer steps into my cubicle with an apologetic smile. He is large, like he's been pumped full of jelly from his face and those three chins, all the way down to the thighs that stretch the fabric of his trousers.

I can't imagine this man giving chase to a shoplifter. It makes me despise him and pity him in equal measure. It isn't easy remaining slim. I should know. It requires constant control; constant willpower to turn down those cakes and biscuits in the office kitchen. Birthdays and happy Fridays and all those times a staff member wants an excuse to stuff their face and feels better about themselves if they get others to join in. Then there are those easy, bung-it-in-the-oven dinners. Salty, hot chips. Juicy steaks. Bread. Oh, how I love bread. I've not eaten it in years. Every time I feel tempted, I think of the blue tape measure I wrap around myself on Friday mornings, and the scales I weigh myself on every Tuesday and Saturday.

Martin started me on it, suggesting we both slim down for the wedding. He meant me, of course, but I found I liked the challenge and those weekly measures – the power over my body. There were sacrifices and punishments when we didn't achieve our goals. All those meals skipped. The jingle of those keys that unlocked the padlocks on the food cupboards and fridge. Slipping the keys into a pocket until morning and trying to sleep with hunger rattling around inside us.

Nineteen years later and the weekly weight check-ins are as natural to me as brushing my teeth and applying make-up.

The officer clears his throat. 'Mrs Watson, I'm PC Daniels from Leeds Central police station. If you're feeling up to it now, I need to take a brief statement from you on what happened last night. Before that, though, I should tell you that the case has been handed over to Essex police. I'll be handing over my notes from our conversation today as well as bodycam footage to the detectives assigned to the case.' He taps a finger to a small black camera on his waistcoat.

'Essex?' A flush creeps over my face despite the cold. Already I feel out of my depth and I've not been asked a single question yet. I wish my head would stop spinning. Everything is a mess.

You silly bitch. Martin's voice comes from nowhere. I shut it down, feeling sick. Feeling tired. I thought I could do this, but now I'm here, I'm not so sure.

'It comes down to where the crime took place,' PC Daniels continues. 'And as you were kidnapped in Essex, Essex police will be taking the lead. It will make things much easier for you to make your formal statement, which will need to happen in a police station.' He smiles. It's a wet kind of smile, like he's pleased with himself, like I should be pleased.

'Now,' he says, flipping open his notebook and scratching the folds of his chin, 'could you tell me what happened last night, from the beginning please, Mrs Watson?'

I open my mouth to speak, but nothing comes out. All I see is Lucie's body hitting the front of my car, that thud, that thwack. The deadly still that followed.

A fresh, jittery panic throbs through my body. There is so much that can go wrong, so many lies to tell, and for a moment it feels too much.

I can't do this. I can't.

Facebook Messenger

She watches my every move.

TWENTY-ONE

SAM

Sam's legs jiggle beneath the table of the interview room. He can't stop it. He can't stop the panic from pummelling into his body. His mouth is dry. It's hard to swallow.

He feels the gaze of the duty solicitor on him. Ben Davidson is a skinny man somewhere in that age between not being young but not being old either. He could be late thirties, or early fifties – Sam has no idea.

Davidson has a receding hairline and a cheap suit. He has a brown leather man bag at his feet and a lined notebook on the table beside him. The leathery tang of his aftershave is heavy in the room, scratching at the back of Sam's throat, but it's one up from the body odour wafting from Sam. Davidson sighs, tapping his index finger on the table.

Tap, tap.

Tap, tap.

The movement fast, like Sam's racing pulse.

Sam glances at the clock on the wall, relishing the small freedom of knowing the time. He can't believe it's 4 p.m. already. The journey to Essex, the transfer of custody and waiting for a solicitor, it has eaten up the day. Gone.

He shouldn't have asked for a solicitor. He'd have been straight into an interview room if he hadn't. But maybe a part of him had known it was too late, and Sam is in the kind of trouble that needs help.

He shifts in the chair and a pain shoots out from his neck, down his spine and up to the top of his skull. His head is still aching too – a proper can't-think-straight pain.

He rolls his left shoulder and looks around the interview room. It's the same size as his cell pretty much, without a bog tucked around a corner. Grey walls. Grey table. Grey plastic chairs. The same grey as his police-issue tracksuit and the bleakness he feels inside.

From what he could tell when they brought him in, the police station is a purpose-built cement block that looks like it's from the sixties. The cell they put him in was an exact replica of the one in Leeds, except for the thick blue line across the middle of all the walls. That fecking police blue, as though he might forget where he is. As if he might mistake it for a Premier Inn.

The door opens. Davidson stops tapping as two detectives in suits step into the room. They smile, friendly like, but Sam knows what these women are thinking. The same thing all police think. He's nothing but scum to them.

The atmosphere changes as the detectives sit. Tension twists in his body – screws tightening. Davidson straightens up, clasping his pen in his hand.

Sam already knows the detectives' names. They introduced themselves while he was being processed by the custody officer. They smile at him – DC Sató directly opposite, her dark hair scooped into a high ponytail that swishes with every move of her head. She has black lines drawn around her eyes, making them look bigger, more inquisitive. Her suit is fitted, jacket done up. She looks fresh, put together, ready to pounce.

DC McLachlan sits beside her. Her suit is not as fitted, the dark-blonde hair not as neat. She's wearing big glasses with thick black frames. There's something softer about DC McLachlan, like she might be a laugh down the pub on a Friday night, the kind of woman he'd have tried his luck on if she was a few years younger. If she wasn't police and he wasn't... completely screwed.

Sam wishes it was two different detectives sat opposite him, two men. There is something so competent about these women. He didn't exactly have a lot of hope that he was walking out of this police station, but there was a whisper of it, a minute speck, but it disappears as he looks between the detectives. They have the look of two people with something to prove.

DC Sató looks to Davidson, then McLachlan. They nod. McLachlan starts the recording. Finally, it's time to talk. The thought makes Sam's head spin, his pulse race faster, harder. How can he make them see that he had no choice? That he didn't mean for anyone to get hurt. They'd have done the same in his shoes.

Sató gives the opening lines of the interview. The date, the time, the place. The usual bollocks about rights he's heard before. Sam gives his name and date of birth and there's a pause, a moment of silence, where nobody moves and all he can hear is the pounding of his pulse in his ears.

From beside him, Davidson clears his throat, another mark of impatience. Sam wonders what he's so keen to get back to, and what it means for him that the one person who's meant to help him would rather be somewhere else.

DC Sató flicks a glance at the solicitor, a quick 'piss off' flashing in her eyes that Sam would've smirked at if it wasn't for the gushing panic rushing through him. She leans her arms on the table, her focus now on Sam. 'As you know, Sam, you were arrested yesterday evening by West Yorkshire Police. You were cautioned at the scene, but I will caution you again now.'

Sam barely listens as Sató reads out the police caution,

going into detail about what it means, as if it makes any differ-ence to Sam now whether he understands or not.

'You were arrested and are being held under caution for the following offences – murder by reckless driving, kidnap, inflicting grievous bodily harm with an offensive weapon and fleeing the scene of a crime, all taking place on Tuesday seventh of November.

'The purpose of the interview today is to find out what happened between the hours of six p.m. and nine-thirty p.m. last night. Do you understand?' Sató's face is unreadable, hard. Her eyes don't leave his.

Sam nods. The murder charge makes his stomach flip. He can't wrap his mind around Celia being dead. The knife barely pushed against her before he was pulling it back. He didn't even mean to stab her. She just sort of fell into him.

'For the purpose of the recording, the defendant is nodding,' Sató says.

Another pause. Sató checks something in the folder in front of her before looking back at Sam. 'I saw your baseball cap in evidence. The logo is Memphis Tigers, isn't it? What's the story there? Are you a basketball fan?'

Sam shakes his head before glancing at the black recording device at the edge of the table and adding a 'No'. He takes a breath, his stomach unknotting a fraction. He knows this is a softening-up thing, an attempt to engage him with pally-pally chit-chat but, despite himself, it's working. 'I just like tigers and I like wearing baseball caps.' He rubs at his shaved head with both hands, feeling the stubble growing back.

'Would you feel more comfortable with your cap on now, Sam?'

He thinks. Then nods. 'Yeah. Yes please.'

'We can get that for you. It's just being processed for evidence, but I'll make sure there's a rush on it and if there's no evidence we need from it, then I'll get it back to you as soon as I can.'

'Thanks,' he mumbles.

'So,' Sató says, pressing her hands together as she leans forward on the table in an I'm-listening gesture, 'what happened yesterday, Sam? Can you take me through it?'

He bites at the stubby nail on his little finger, his face growing hot in a way that makes his nose throb. How much do they know? Where do they expect him to start? They know about the car, of course. But what about before that, the morning when he thought there was no one watching?

Something flashes in her eyes – fear? Uncertainty? I can no longer read her as I once did. That lost little girl who needed me.

She turns. The wisps of her long hair lift up, flying around her in the wind. I wonder a hundred things about her in that movement. I wonder about all the small things in her life. Does she have a boyfriend? Who does she talk to when she's sad? Happy? What does she think when she looks back at the time she spent in my house? Does she wonder, like I do, what her life would be like right now if she'd just trusted me?

Lucie starts to move – long hurried strides towards the red barriers of the exit.

'Lucie, wait! Let's talk some more.'

She glances back, a furtive look, before shaking her head. 'There's nothing more to talk about.'

I see it then – the expression in her eyes. She thinks I'm a monster.

As I watch her go, a rage starts to build. A scream rattles deep inside me, catching in my throat. For a split second I see myself lurching forward, pulling Lucie back, snatching at that long hair, pleading with her again.

TWENTY-TWO

CELIA

'Mrs Watson?' PC Daniels raises his eyebrows. He's waiting for my story.

Saliva fills my mouth. Panic grips. I swallow and press my hand to my chest. The shock is no longer bubble wrap, but a heavy blanket smothering me and I can't shake it off.

I can't make a mistake, and yet I can barely make sense of my own thoughts. 'A man came up to my car,' I say, a gasping start. 'I was... I was getting in my car to drive home. He jumped in and held a knife to my side. He forced me to drive him to Leeds.' The words feel wooden, clunky in my mouth. It's the truth at least.

'And' – PC Daniels looks down at his notes, his face arranging into a look of sympathy – 'the body in the boot. You said at the scene that the victim's name was Lucie Gilbert. What can you tell me about that?'

'Lucie.' I whisper her name. 'She's an old family friend. Was,' I correct myself, tears falling from my eyes. 'She saw him – that man. He called himself Sam. She saw him get in my car and she... she tried to stop him, but we were already driving and he grabbed the wheel from me and we... we hit her.' I stumble over the lies and the truth, a tangled mesh. 'My car hit her. I tried to brake but I couldn't stop in time.'

'And this happened where?'

I pause, thoughts disjointed, the answer out of reach. Then it comes. 'In the car park behind the building where I work. It's on a road called Brook Street.' I reel off the address.

'Does the car park have CCTV?'

'No, I don't think so. It's just a bit of tarmac behind the building for staff to use.'

'OK. You never know though. I'll make a note.'

Panic swoops through me. I mentally scan the walls of the office building, trying to remember if there are cameras. There aren't. I'm almost certain. Almost but not completely.

'What happened next?' PC Daniels asks.

'He made me stop the car and then he made me... He made me put her body in the boot.' Sweat pricks at my skin. 'I begged him to let me go. I told him I had a son, and he said... he said he'd kill me if I didn't do what I was told.'

The bright white lights of the hospital are like spotlights on me, pointing, jeering. *She's lying.* I close my eyes, remembering the weight of Lucie in my arms, the struggle to hoist her body into the boot, how warm her skin felt in my hands.

The ward spins around me. The nausea returns and I reach slowly for the cardboard bowl Jakub left by my bed earlier, hugging it to my body.

Even if what I'm saying isn't true, the emotion – the crushing sadness, the guilt – it's as real as I am.

'And when you arrived in Leeds?' PC Daniels prompts me to continue.

I stare at him, unblinking, and just like that we've moved on from what happened to Lucie. Could it be that easy? I take a breath. 'Leeds?'

'Yes. What happened when you escaped?'

'I... knew he was going to kill me. I could tell we were

getting close and I didn't know what to do, but then I saw the police car and I just reacted. I crashed the car and he... he tried to stop me by stabbing me.'

'Thank you, Mrs Watson. You've been very brave,' he says with a sympathetic smile, and for a moment I think he might reach out and pat my hand.

'Is that it?' I ask, failing to mask the hope in my voice.

'For now, yes.' He gives me another reassuring smile that makes his cheeks bunch like a hamster. 'I'll pass this all on to the investigating officers and they'll be in touch. I believe you're being discharged soon. Do you have someone who can come to collect you?'

I shake my head.

He thinks for a moment, tapping his pen against his bottom lip. 'Would you like me to arrange transport? Considering the circumstances, I feel we should make sure you get home safely.'

'No.' My reply comes out too fast. 'I mean, thank you, but I'll get myself home. I don't feel ready to sit in a car for a long journey again just yet,' I say, tacking on an extra lie. It's not the car; it's the company. I can't sit side by side with PC Daniels or another of his colleagues for hours. Not with my thoughts so jumbled. The questions they might ask. The answers I might let slip.

PC Daniels leaves, wishing me good luck, and then I'm mercifully alone.

An hour later, I'm discharged with a little paper bag of pain medication, and I hobble outside and into a bright grey day.

The cold hits my skin and I pull my cardigan around myself. The green fabric is torn now and stained with the rusty brown of my blood. I long for my coat, but I left it in the boot with Lucie's body after I'd shoved Sam's jacket in beneath her cold limbs, making it look like the jacket was there before the body.

It's why I asked for it at the roadside, and one of the reasons

I opened the boot. If I'd had time to reach the car jack, a weapon against Sam, I'd have done that too, but there were other things I needed to do when I opened the boot to stare at Lucie's frozen features.

———

Facebook Messenger

There is no one else I can turn to!
You see that, right?
You started this!

TWENTY-THREE

SAM

'I was walking up near Springfield Road, yeah,' Sam says, starting with the middle, with what they know. Sató's eyes watch him as he talks, focused, alert. It's unnerving, the intensity of her gaze. 'And I had my thumb out for a lift 'cause I was trying to get back to Leeds, like. And then this woman pulled over and we got chatting and she said she'd take me.'

There's another sigh from Davidson. Sam knows it's stupid to lie, but he does it anyway. He hears his old man's voice in his head. *'It's up to the pigs to prove the shit they're accusing you of, lad. Keep your mouth shut or lie through your teeth. Got it?'*

It worked once before. He'd been arrested in Bradford for robbing a designer clothes shop with Deano and Paul, all three of them wearing the stolen merch. But Sam just kept telling them that he bought the clothes from a bloke in the pub and eventually they let him go. He doubts it will work this time, but what has he got to lose?

'So Celia Watson just offered you a lift all the way to Leeds? Just like that?' Sató asks.

'Yeah. She said she liked to help people,' he adds, remembering she'd told him that.

'Right. And why were you going to Leeds last night?'

He pauses. Swallows. The emotion threatening to escape feels red raw, like the time he came off the back of Deano's motorbike in shorts and took the skin off his left calf. Like that but on the inside.

'I had to get there,' he mumbles. 'There was an emergency.' He sniffs, wiping his nose on the back of his hand, sending a shot of pain across his bruised face and making him wince.

'What kind of emergency?'

'My sister.' He forces the words out, but they are barely a whisper.

'I'm sorry, Sam,' Sató says. 'I can see this is upsetting for you, but could you speak up for the recording please? Take your time.'

He nods, tries to breathe. 'My sister – Bee. She needed me.'

'And what happened when you got to Leeds?'

'Nothing. We were almost there when she – Celia, I mean – started acting crazy and crashed the car.'

DC Sató nods like she believes him, and then she sits back in her chair.

'I'm going to show you a photograph now, Sam,' DC McLachlan says in her Scottish accent. It's the same accent as a guy from Aberdeen he met inside. Sam wonders if that's where she's from and how she ended up working for Essex police.

She reels off a spiel for the recording before sliding a photograph towards him.

Sam recognises it straight away. It's the knife he stole off the old boy in the house yesterday. He shakes his head a fraction. How was it only yesterday? It feels like months ago. Another lifetime. Another version of himself, when he still thought everything would work out.

Then he blinks and the realisation of everything he's done comes flooding back through him. He can't believe he took that knife. His heart starts to beat sickeningly fast as images of the house flash across his mind. He thought it was empty.

It wasn't.

'Can you tell me what this is?' McLachlan says as Sató folds her arms, that steely gaze still on him.

'A knife,' he says, fighting to talk over the tightness in his airway as he waits for them to mention the attempted burglary.

'Do you recognise it?'

'Looks like any old kitchen knife.'

'It was found in Celia's car in the passenger footwell.'

'It's not mine.' The words come out too fast.

'It's currently being tested for fingerprints. Whose prints do you think we're going to find on it?'

'Not mine,' he repeats, sounding like, feeling like, a toddler. Why the hell didn't he think to wear gloves? The answer is simple. He didn't think. From the second he got that first text from his mum yesterday, it's like his brain shut down. He closes his eyes for a second; his head is still pounding. It all feels too much.

'If you try anything, I'll kill you.'

His voice. His words. His threat.

It just came out. He didn't mean it. Didn't mean to hurt her. And he definitely didn't mean to kill her. He was going to tell her to pull over round the corner from the house and jump out, run for it. He knew she'd go to the police. But it would've taken time and that's all he'd needed. A little time.

'This knife was used to stab Celia in the abdomen as she tried to escape. She says that you stabbed her.'

'What do you mean?' His eyes flick from McLachlan to Sató and back to McLachlan. 'You said Celia was dead. You said I'm being charged with murder.'

'Celia Watson isn't dead, Sam,' McLachlan says, her head tilting to one side, and Sam catches a flash of confusion in her expression. 'She's very much alive and telling a different version of last night's events.'

'If she isn't dead, then why are you charging me for murder?' he asks, turning to look at his solicitor. Surely this is the point to jump in and get that charge dropped. He didn't kill Celia. The relief surges through him and he tries not to think about the old man in the PJs, just hours before Celia.

McLachlan tucks the photo of the knife back in the folder and then it's Sató's turn again.

'Let's rewind a moment,' she says, ignoring his question. 'And talk about when you got into Celia's car. At what point did you see Lucie Gilbert?'

'Who?' Sam rubs at his head. He doesn't understand the question. Celia mentioned someone called Lucie in the car too. 'I don't know no Lucie.' He bites at a hangnail on his index finger. It comes free, causing a sharp pain. He doesn't like this, this not knowing what they're talking about.

'Perhaps you'll recognise her photo,' Sató says as McLachlan flips through her folder again. There's another shift in the room, like they're all holding their breath, like they all know something he doesn't. Three pairs of eyes watch his face as McLachlan talks to the recording once more and slides a second photograph across the table.

Sam looks down, gasping, pushing back. 'What is this?' His words are loud, almost a shout. He doesn't understand.

The photo is an open car boot – a silver car – and inside is the body of a girl with grey-blonde hair covering part of her face. But not all of it. Not the pale blue of her eyes, which stare up at him and at nothing at all. Dead eyes.

I made her. Me. I saw something in her. I nurtured and encouraged and loved her. No one else believed in Lucie, least of all herself. It was my belief, my patience and time, that built up her confidence. And this is how she repays me? Blackmail and threats.

The anger blisters beneath my skin.

She has no idea of the truth. No idea what she's about to do to me and Henry.

'Lucie?' I call out to her, taking a step forward, almost stumbling on the uneven tarmac.

She doesn't respond, and I realise the time for talking is over.

TWENTY-FOUR

CELIA

There's a single taxi waiting in the rank and I walk slowly towards it, one hand on my side, the other clutching the box of medicine.

I have no phone. I can't call Henry and check he's getting himself up for college like he does every Wednesday. A whole night alone. I hope he's eaten something, looked after himself. I hope he's OK.

I have no purse either. Just a single bank card one of the officers retrieved from my bag, the one I threw in the boot in my struggle with Lucie's body. She really was a dead weight. I tried her legs first and then her torso, but each time she dropped back to the ground in a heap. In the end I picked her up like a sleeping child – one arm under her legs, the other under her back. It wasn't easy and she was a slight little thing, really. God knows what I'd have done if she'd been any heavier.

My body shivers – the cold, the thought of Lucie's body in my arms, of what I did. My mouth is so dry, my throat scratchy. I push thoughts of her to one side and focus on putting one foot in front of the other.

It's an hour before I'm on the 8 a.m. train to London. I ease myself slowly into my seat, a hand pressing gently to my wound. I close my eyes and wonder how the hell I'll survive the lies I'm tangling myself in. One slip, one thoughtless comment, and it will all be over for me.

And that's before I consider the forensic evidence that could trip me up. I've tried to be careful – putting Sam's jacket in the boot so his DNA was on Lucie's body, and then later making sure he had to grab the wheel, leaving his fingerprints behind. And the final move – throwing myself on Sam's knife. I had to make the police see how dangerous he was, that there could be no doubt that he was the kind of person who would kill a young woman who got in his way, stab another who tried to escape him.

The train pulls away and we jostle through brown empty fields and towns with dark-red brick houses sloping on hillsides, then new estates built with gardens right up to the railway line. I sip at a scalding-hot green tea and go through the story I told to PC Daniels in my head.

Talking to Lucie in the deserted office car park. True. Her walking away. True. Sam coming out of the darkness, jumping into my car as I start the engine. Lie. Lucie turning and seeing my car approach. True. Lucie trying to stop the kidnap. Lie. Sam grabbing the wheel, forcing the car to change direction at the last minute. Lie. My car slamming into Lucie's body. True. Lucie dying on impact. True. Lifting her body into the boot of my car and driving away. True.

I replay it over and over but the lies and truth knit together in a tangled mess that makes my breath stick in my throat. I try to grab at my thoughts, drifting fuzzy and distant across my mind. I must not underestimate the police. They are not all going to be bumbling overweight PCs. There will be something I've not thought of. Something that supports the story Sam will tell.

It could be Lucie's phone. The police have that now.

I threw her bag in the boot straight after her body, planning to drop her phone in the river just as soon as I'd found a safe ditch to hide her in.

Another shiver. It's not Lucie this time that makes my blood run cold; it's Sam. That moment on the roadside when I stuffed his jacket beneath Lucie's legs then fumbled in her bag for her phone, desperate to lob it into the central reservation and destroy whatever evidence was on there.

I couldn't find it. Couldn't reach it. Then Sam was coming towards me and there was barely time to slam the boot shut before he could see what was inside.

Questions, images, thoughts rush through my mind at the same speed as the empty dark fields rushing by my window. My heart is hammering in my chest and it feels for a moment like I might pass out.

Slow breaths, I tell myself, focusing on a buzzard drifting across the murky grey sky, waiting for a mouse or a rabbit to appear. I close my eyes and say a silent prayer that Lucie's phone was in the pocket of her coat, that it shattered as easily as her body did, but then I remember the ringtone coming from the boot as we drove. Was that Lucie's phone or mine? There's so much I don't know.

Facebook Messenger

Do you believe me?

TWENTY-FIVE

SAM

Bile rises to the back of his throat. Acrid and burning. Those eyes continue to stare back at him. He can't look anymore. Nothing is making sense.

'I don't understand,' he says.

'I'm sorry to have upset you, Sam,' Sató replies, her tone still so even. 'This is the body of Lucie Gilbert. She was found in the boot of Celia's car. Can you tell me about how she got there?'

Sam's eyes find Sató's. He shakes his head, a furtive back and forth.

She says nothing. She waits.

He fights to find the words over the pounding in his head. 'I didn't do this.' His voice is loud in the silent room. Tears threaten at his eyes again. He's messed everything up. 'You have to believe me. I didn't kill that girl.' He lifts a hand to his forehead. He's shaking. There's a buzzing in his ears.

He looks to his solicitor, then at the detectives, pleading with them to see the truth. They don't. He can tell. 'I wanna break. I wanna speak to him,' he says, looking at Davidson.

His words are like magic. Suddenly it's all over. For now.

Sató nods to DC McLachlan. The recording is paused and the detectives leave.

The moment the door closes, Sam slumps against the table, face buried in his arms. His head hurts so much. All he wants is to go back to his cell and sleep. The girl in the boot flashes in his thoughts. How did she get there? How did she die? They said murder by reckless driving, but that doesn't make sense. He wasn't driving, Celia was, and they didn't hit anyone.

'Sam.' Davidson touches his arm. 'Let's talk.'

He forces his body upright and turns to Davidson. There are pointy black strands of hair poking out of the solicitor's nose. Sam tries not to stare but his eyes keep going back to them.

'These are very serious charges, Sam,' Davidson says in a stern kind of way, like a parent talking to a child. 'And there is strong evidence against you, not to mention a credible witness.'

'I didn't kill anyone,' Sam says in a voice he doesn't recognise as his own. He thinks of yesterday morning – Tuesday – before the car journey, before Celia and the mess he's now in. The lurch of fear at being found out. The panic shooting through him. He made a mistake then too, but he didn't kill anyone. He's sure of it.

'How do you expect them to believe that when you're lying to them?'

His old man's words come back to him again. *'Don't give 'em nothing.'* His dad. He hates that word – dad. It belongs in a cosy Netflix film about a man who steps up to care for his kids. It doesn't describe his old man, who only used the house as a place to sleep and to store whatever crap he stole. Who would get in their faces and scream at them for everything, for nothing. Who took Sam with him to the multi-storey car park in Leeds city centre and made him keep watch while he stole catalytic converters out of parked cars. Sam had been eight years old at the time and so terrified that he'd wet himself. His old man had laughed the whole way home. The same old man that kicked his sister Bee out the house at fifteen because she had a boyfriend. The same man who ignored his wife's drinking, because it suited him that she was never really there.

Sam wonders briefly where his old man is right now. He left their mum a few years back and Sam hasn't seen him since. At least his mum pulled herself together after he left. Enough to be there for Bee anyway. Maybe Sam will bump into his old man inside. The thought makes him wish he was dead. Gone. Sam can't kill himself, but he'd give anything to not be here anymore, in this world of trouble. Then he thinks of Bee and it's like his whole insides get tangled in heavy stones, filling him with a pain that he doesn't think will ever stop.

'My advice' – Davidson's voice jolts Sam's thoughts back to the interview room – 'if you want to take it, is to start telling the truth. Regardless of what you say in these interviews, I believe there is enough evidence that the Criminal Prosecution Service will bring charges against you. You were arrested fleeing the scene of the crime and there's a witness who can no doubt identify you. And that's just the start. They're gathering more evidence as we speak. Will they find your DNA in the car and on the knife?' Davidson continues without waiting for an answer. 'And even if they don't, there will be traffic cameras along the route you drove that will show you in that car, Sam. Your best hope right now is to cooperate and hope it goes in your favour further down the line at sentencing. If, like you say, you didn't kill this girl—'

'I didn't. I don't even know her,' Sam cries out, willing himself to calm down, but he can't. He has to make them see.

'Then we have to explain your side of the story.' Davidson reaches into his man bag and pulls out a Twix, pushing it towards Sam. 'Have this,' he says. 'The sugar will help. Then let's go through what really happened before you have to tell it all to the detectives.'

. . .

Half an hour later, Davidson calls Sató and McLachlan back in and they take their seats. The recording is started with another run-through of the date and time and all that crap.

Sató places an unopened can of Coke in front of Sam. It's cold in his hands as he pulls at the ring. The can hisses that sweet sound of release, reminding him of being a kid; hot summers hanging out at the park. 'Thanks,' he says, taking a long sip. The fizzing sugar coats his teeth and zips through his body.

'I was able to get your cap for you too,' Sató says, placing his black baseball cap on the table.

Sam fingers the fabric embroidery of the tiger on the front. It feels strange in his hands, like it isn't his cap anymore, but he pulls it onto his head and feels better, like a part of him has been given back.

Sató leans forward, her hands on the table, her eyes fixing on him. 'So, Sam, you've had a chance to talk to your solicitor. How are you feeling now? Are you ready to carry on talking?'

Sam nods, pressing his lips together, trapping in the jittery nerves rising up inside of him. Then he remembers he has to speak and whispers a 'Yes'.

Davidson clears his throat. 'My client would like to revise his initial account of the events of yesterday evening.'

Sam scrunches his eyes shut for a moment, wondering if now is the time to tell them everything. How long before they connect him to the burglary and the old boy with the walking stick?

The engine of my car strains – a choking whine. For a moment I think it will be too much, that the engine will flood or give up altogether. Then what?

I grit my teeth, desperate to shout and scream and cry, but my anger is a red haze over my thoughts and all I manage is a hissed whisper only I hear. 'Lucie.'

The engine holds, the speed picks up. Too fast. Too fast. I can't stop it. I can't think clearly.

The exit for the car park approaches – the red barriers and the empty road beyond. What would happen if another car was to appear now? Or a person, a lone shopper taking a shortcut home?

But it's too late to stop now. No one can save her.

Lucie turns. Her mouth gapes, a perfect O. She throws up her arms as though they alone will save her.

TWENTY-SIX

CELIA

Somehow I make it home; trembling and weak as I climb out of the taxi – a shadow of the woman I was yesterday. The air is cold but not as biting as last night in Leeds, and as I step onto the pavement it feels as though the dead-end road with its thirteen houses is holding its breath, watching me, waiting to see what I'll do.

I wonder which neighbours are standing out of sight behind net curtains. We don't talk. I know their names but nothing else, going out of my way to avoid those titbit exchanges about the garden or the weather that so easily lead to more. It's safer. The less anyone knows about our lives, the better.

My house is the odd one out. It sits at the very end of the road, facing out to the neat rows of six identical homes on each side. Behind it is a wasteland. A wooded no man's land between us and the industrial estate that's not big enough for dog walkers to enjoy.

There is nothing remarkable about my house. It's the kind of three-bed, one-bathroom style that sprung up in housing estates on the edge of towns all over the country back in the seventies. It isn't beautiful, but it isn't ugly either. It's just a house with a garage stuck on one side with a red metal door that needs a fresh coat of paint.

There's a thick laurel bush in the front garden that blocks the view of the front door and part of the living-room window. Like the fir trees in the back, the laurel gives an extra layer of protection. We're not overlooked on either side, but it never hurts to be vigilant. Martin's words, but I tend to agree.

I shuffle towards the house and imagine my neighbours staring. Can they tell so much has changed since I walked out of there yesterday? That in twenty-four hours my life has shifted irrevocably?

Twenty-two hours ago, Lucie was alive.

Twenty hours ago, I was held at knifepoint.

Seventeen hours ago, I was lying on cold, wet tarmac.

Nine hours ago, I was in hospital.

None of it feels real.

The taxi shuffles back and forth, a three-point turn that takes five goes, before driving away. I wait until it's disappeared out of the road before turning towards the house.

My eyes linger on the garage and I feel the jolt of my heart starting to pound again. I think of the white door in the kitchen that leads into that dank space. I locked it Monday evening. I'm sure of it. I always lock it. I always check. But it feels like I've been away for days, weeks, and I don't know what awaits me in that dark windowless space. My life may be unrecognisable from the one I was living yesterday, but there are still things Henry can't know, things about his father that could – would – destroy him.

I bend cautiously, retrieving the spare key that's hidden beneath the third plant pot to the left of the front door, and let myself in. I'm greeted by the scent of white jasmine from the diffuser on the window ledge. Its familiarity wraps itself around me like a hug. But beneath it lingers another smell. Metal and dirt and body odour all mixed up. I stagger back, knocking into the door frame, yelping from the pain shooting out of my side.

Every part of me wants to turn away. To run. To never look back, but this is our home – mine and Henry's – and I must go in.

'Henry?' I step forward and listen.

Silence.

Fear clutches at my chest.

'Henry?' My voice is shrill and I reach for my handbag that isn't there, and the phone that's in an evidence bag in a police station somewhere.

Reality dawns.

I've never been the type to be on my phone all hours like my line manager, Deborah, who is forever scrolling, swiping and tapping. But I'm no technophobe either, and so when three weeks before Henry's fifteenth birthday, he began nagging and begging for his own phone, like he'd done every Christmas and birthday since he was twelve, I finally relented. And despite my reservations about the world away from me it would open, I found I liked Henry having a phone. It was suddenly so easy to open the tracking app and see that little square on the map.

And then I realise exactly where Henry is. It's Wednesday afternoon. He's at sixth form like he is every weekday.

The fluttering relief is brief. Henry may be where he's supposed to be, but I am not and the thought tips me off-kilter, as though I'm about to capsize. I look down at my clothes. They are dirty and bloodstained and creased, but worse than that, they are Tuesday's clothes and it's not Tuesday anymore.

My thoughts spiral into a twisted darkness. Images of yesterday pummel my mind, then further back to all the terrible things I have done. I make it, staggering to the living room, and sit down to call the office from the black landline phone on the side table.

I haven't missed a day at work in years. Not since Henry had an abscess on his tooth when he was fourteen. I wonder if they've been calling. I wonder what they're thinking. Nothing good. They never do when it comes to me.

It takes longer than it should to reach the back office. The direct number is in my phone and without it I have to go through the call centre. I'm put on hold and pinged around the office until finally Deborah's voice comes on the line.

'Hello, this Deborah.'

'Deborah, it's Celia.'

'Celia, hello.' There's annoyance to her voice, poorly hidden in a mock amusement where she drags out 'hello', raising her tone high for the *hell* and lowering it for the *o*. What there isn't in her tone is concern and it bothers me that she doesn't know me well enough to consider that if I'm not in the office and I haven't called in, then I have a good reason. I'm not like Jo on the desk next to me, who takes a day off anytime she gets a tummy ache. I'm reliable.

A flash of anger – lightning just before the storm. Deborah really is a stupid woman. I could do her job ten times better than she does. She runs the office like it's a school staff room, a place for gossip and chat rather than helping people.

'Are you all right?' Deborah asks.

'Yes, well, no, actually. I was... kidnapped last night in my car.' The words don't sound real, even to me. 'I... I've been stabbed.'

'Oh my God, you're joking?'

'No. I was getting into my car to drive home.'

'It happened here?' Deborah's voice squeaks in my ear, making me wince.

'Yes,' I reply, sticking with the lie.

'Oh my God, you poor woman. Is there anything we can do?'

'No, thank you. I will need a few days at home. I'm sorry to let you down.'

'Of course, of course. You'll need more than a few days. Take a week and give me a call back next Wednesday. I don't want you rushing back before you're ready,' she says, sounding almost gleeful at the prospect.

'One week will be quite enough.' My tone is suddenly snippy and leaves a silence in its wake. One week will be too much.

'Whatever you need,' Deborah says after a pause. 'I must get on. Take care, Celia.' And she's gone, leaving me with the anger hot on my face. I shouldn't have snapped.

I'm not well liked at Citizens Advice, but then, I don't like any of my co-workers either. They are nosy, needy flappers who stuff their saggy faces with chocolate biscuits while moaning about their weight. They don't understand me. They don't like that I keep my private life to myself; they don't like that when new protocols are emailed in from above, I accept the change and adapt, while they coo and protest and grumble. They don't like that I am there because of a genuine desire to help people, something I'm barely allowed to do anymore. Not after Kathryn Deakin's husband complained.

Oh, Kathryn. You silly woman. I thought you were stronger. I thought you were more like me.

She was my age – Kathryn – but looked closer to sixty with her greying hair and frumpy clothes. She wanted to know how to set up her own bank account. 'Will there be letters? I don't want my husband to find out.' I knew the moment she walked in what was happening to her. There's a way to spot the victims. The way they carry themselves. An air about them I recognised so very well.

Of course, there is red tape on what we can advise and what we can't. If they don't ask, we don't offer, but I wanted her to know about the women's refuge houses, the places she would be safe. I gave her practical advice, ways she could start hiding a bit of money here or there. Little things. Shopping in the reduced section at 6 p.m. and peeling off the stickers before going home to show the full price. Little by little, I explained, until she had enough.

Her husband came in the next day, red-faced with fury, a vein bulging in his forehead. He screamed at me. An actual battle cry of a noise. I sat still, calm. I didn't show my fear. Deborah stepped in and he was ushered to a back office, placated.

'You can't overstep like that,' Deborah said to me later, going so far as to tsk me.

'She needed help,' I said, standing my ground. I was not going to apologise for trying to save someone's life.

'That may be, but it wasn't your place to give it. This isn't the first time you've overstepped, Celia. You're a valued member of the team and we don't want to lose you, but I think for now it would be better if you stuck to answering the phones and supporting the back office.'

I remember the heat that crawled over my skin, the fury. How dare they move me? I did more than any of them would dream of doing. I wasn't just a friendly ear to listen. I was actually helping people.

The same anger catches in my throat, and I rest my head against the sofa cushions and try to let it go.

Exhaustion overwhelms me. My eyes flutter then close for the briefest of moments. Then bam, the glint of silver slashes across my thoughts – the knife at my side. I give an involuntary flinch, causing a pain to shoot across my abdomen.

My breath comes in short raspy gasps. I stare around me, taking in the familiarity of the living room. It hasn't changed much over the years. A new TV and stand, a new cream leather sofa. The walls are still the yellowy cream of magnolia that I love. I really cannot stand the concept walls I see everywhere I go – big bold blues or slate grey on one wall. It looks messy to me. Disorderly.

I'm desperate for a cup of tea or a glass of water, but I'm too tired, too weak to move. My thoughts jumble again. It must be the shock. I rub my eyes and it's then that I smell it again: that earthy unwashed scent. I don't have to look up to know Martin has stepped out of his hiding place and is in the living room.

I freeze and try not to show it. Every muscle in my body tenses. He shouldn't be here. It's not part of our rules.

Martin. My husband. The man Lucie accused me of murdering – the man no one except me has seen for thirteen years – stands before me.

'Henry will be back soon,' I hiss.

'I'll only be a minute,' he says, always pushing his luck. 'I had to find out what happened last night.'

I keep my eyes shut tight. I can't bear to look at him, but I tell him about Sam and the car ride, unburdening the truth this one and only time.

'You should never have got involved with her back then,' Martin says.

He means Lucie, of course, and I can't help the sarcasm from dripping into my reply. 'How useful to point that out. I was trying to help. Someone had to.'

'Well, you didn't help. You killed her. This mess we're in is all your fault.'

'Shut up, shut up, shut up.' I shout the words and bury my head in my hands. I will not look at the pale sagging face of the man I hate. Nausea burns the back of my throat.

This isn't me. I don't shrink and hide, but nothing feels right today.

'Get back now.' Anger carries and my voice is a growl and for now at least Martin listens. I keep my eyes closed, silent tears falling down my face. And then there's another sound.

Not Martin this time but Henry. A key scratching in the front door. My boy is home.

My eyes fly open. He must not see his father.

Facebook Messenger

I'm a prisoner in this house.

TWENTY-SEVEN

SAM

'All right, then,' Sató says with a small smile, 'let's begin. Sam, tell me what happened yesterday evening at approximately six-fifteen p.m.'

'I was walking near Springfield Road like I said. I was heading to the A12 to hitch-hike. I had to get to Leeds. It was an emergency and I'd tried everything. Like, everything. I'd called everyone in my contacts. You can check my phone. And asked them to lend me the money for the train fare, but... no one would. Then I tried begging on the streets but only made a few quid and I didn't have time. So I...' Sam pauses. He swallows. The gruff shouts of the old boy fill his thoughts. *'Oi, you. Get out. Get out.'*

Sam shakes the memory away. 'So I went to bunk the train, but the guard saw me and called the transport police, and they kicked me off. I was going to hitch-hike but no one would stop and then I panicked and there was this car that just stopped at these traffic lights and I could see it was a woman in the driving seat and... I dunno. I didn't think. I just opened the passenger door and told her to drive me to Leeds.'

'Did you use a weapon?'

He nods, hating himself. The worst kind of scum. 'Yeah. That knife you showed me. I took it from... a friend's kitchen 'cause I didn't have anywhere to stay that night and I wanted protection. I wasn't going to use it or anything. I just wanted her to drive me to Leeds.' Sam fiddles with the Coke can and takes another sip. The caffeine and sugar have made him antsy but he feels better too, more in control of himself.

'And what happened on the journey?'

'Nothing,' he says. 'I knew she was scared, like, but so was I and I just had to get back, see? But there was no girl. I swear I've never seen that Lucie person before until you showed me that photo.'

It doesn't take long to tell them the rest – the journey, then Leeds, the police car, the crash, running. When he's done, Sam slumps against the chair and lifts his hat up, repositioning it back onto his head. Then Sató makes him tell it all again, teasing out every detail Sam can remember.

'Why did you run from the scene, Sam?' she asks on their third run-through.

'I... I had to be in Leeds. It was an emergency.'

'You keep saying that, and I want to believe you, but I need more information.'

'My sister,' he says, his voice cracking. 'She...' He sniffs, wiping the snot as it falls from his nose. 'She got cancer. Really bad. I didn't know how bad or I would've gone back sooner. But I got a call from my mum. She said Bee got an infection and was dying. They didn't think she'd last the night and she was asking for me. It was her dying wish.' His chin trembles; a thickness forms in his throat. He can't stop it now – the grief he's kept trapped inside him since that phone call from his mum. It's a battering wave that washes through him, releasing in a loud heaving sob. Then another and another. 'I had to go... I had to.'

'I'm so sorry, Sam,' Sató says and she sounds like she means it.

He can't stop crying; he'll never stop crying, it feels like. 'I don't even know if she died last night or if she's still alive.'

'Why don't we give you a minute to compose yourself and I'll see if I can find out about your sister.'

He nods and gives them Bee's address and phone number, as well as his mum's, and then they pause the interview. Through tear-blurred vision, Sam watches the detectives and Davidson stand. Sató moves towards the door first and he thinks she limps slightly on her left leg. There's a grimace on her face too.

They leave and he's alone. Sam wipes his face again, leaving streaks of tears on the pale-grey cuffs. He bites another fingernail as a numbness presses down on him, and instead of thinking about Bee or the body of that girl and the world of trouble he is in, he finds himself thinking about DS Sató's limp.

It takes him a moment to realise why it's stuck in his thoughts and why it makes him feel better – the limp makes her human. Before the limp, Sam saw DS Sató as police. As someone with boxes to tick, arrests to make, scum to lock up. She is still all those things, but now he sees her as human too. And humans make mistakes. They mess up. Humans listen. They have their own opinions, and maybe DS Sató with her nice suit and eyeliner will listen to him. Maybe, if he keeps telling the truth from now on, she'll believe him. The thought gives Sam the first whisper of hope he's felt in a long time.

He sees it then – the utter stupidity of what he's done. The panic, the grief, it was blinding. He sees now that he should've made his mum put Bee on the phone, said his goodbyes that way.

Bee will still be alive. She has to be. Sam repeats the words, a chant in his thoughts, blocking everything else out as the door to the interview room opens and Davidson, Sató and McLachlan step back inside.

Sam closes his eyes, powerless to stop the weight of it all pressing down on him – a wall of bricks he alone can't hold up. It's Bee and it's him, what he's done – Celia, the old man and that girl in the boot they think he killed.

Time seems to stop.

The car is still moving, speeding at its target, and yet Lucie and I are away from it, alone in the space between one second and the next.

We stare at each other, and finally I see the Lucie I remember. The lost little girl who needed me then.

And now?

Yes, now too. Only I can save her.

The second ticks by and Lucie's face contorts – twisting in horror as realisation dawns.

It's too late. I won't help her.

In the final cowardly moment, I close my eyes, blocking out the sight but not the sounds. There's a thud first – the car hitting her body. If she tries to scream, I don't hear it over my own.

TWENTY-EIGHT

CELIA

I lurch forward, trying to stand, to rush to my darling boy, to waft away the stink of my husband that lingers in my nose. The pain makes me gasp then freeze. There's a white burning in my side, stretching up and up to the corners of my brain.

'Henry,' I call out, collapsing onto the cushions, my breathing ragged, sweat glowing on my face.

He appears in the doorway and I drink him in like a tonic – the best medicine. He's in a blazer and tie just as he was yesterday morning. His hair is a little rumpled now, the waves finally fighting back. It makes him look younger.

'Mummy,' he says, relief and worry knitting across his features. He strides towards me so fast I find myself flinching back, clutching at my side. He falters, slows, staring from my face to my stomach, before moving more cautiously. He sits down beside me and takes my hand in his. It's warm, his skin soft.

'Is someone else here?' he asks with a frown, looking back to the doorway. 'I thought I heard voices.'

I shake my head. 'Just the TV,' I say. It's off and the remote is out of reach on the coffee table but he doesn't notice.

Questions rise to the surface. I want to know everything about his day. Every little thing, minute by minute. The urge is visceral. 'Tell me—'

'What happened?' Henry's question cuts over mine. 'Are you all right?'

'I'm fine.' I move my lips into a smile, fighting back the threatening tears. Lucie's face flashes before my eyes. That long grey-blonde hair that is still so popular. It suited her. She looked beautiful. Beautiful and lost.

Did I really have no choice? The question is unnerving.

I wait for the image to pass but it doesn't. It freezes like a lost connection on a Zoom call.

'Mum?'

'Huh?'

'What happened?'

'I... er... a car accident,' I say at last. 'I was injured. Nothing serious. Everything is fine.'

He opens his mouth to say more, but it's me that gets there first this time. 'Were you OK last night, darling? Did you eat something? I'm sorry I wasn't here.'

'I'm nearly eighteen, Mum. I was fine. I had some toast. I was worried about you. I tried to call but you didn't answer. I thought about calling the police. I was just about to when the hospital phoned me and told me you'd had an accident.' Our eyes meet and I think he'll carry on with his questions, but something drags his attention away from me and down to the phone now gripped in his hand. I try not to bristle as he loses himself to the screen. The worry deepens in the contours of his face.

'Who's that?' The question jumps out of my mouth before I can stop it.

'No one.' He pulls his hand away, leaning back.

'Don't lie to me,' I snap.

He shakes his head and when he lifts his eyes and looks at me, it's as though I'm a caged animal – wild and unpredictable – ready to pounce, instead of his mother, the woman who has been there for him every single day of his life; the one person who will love him no matter what.

'I'm not,' he says, showing me the screen. 'It's a Fantasy Football league alert, see?'

'Football? You don't like football.'

'The lads at school talk about it a lot. I've got into it a bit.' He shrugs and I feel instantly bad.

'I'm sorry, I didn't mean to snap.'

'It's OK.' He retreats to the doorway. There is something so Martin in his posture – the slouch against the door frame, the slump of his shoulders. It's a fight not to bark at him, to tell him to straighten up, but I hold it in. I remind myself that this is my sweet boy, not my husband.

'Go change out of your uniform please.'

Henry hesitates. I can almost see the questions forming on his lips, before he moves on. 'I was worried last night,' he says eventually. 'I thought something really bad had happened. The nurse said you'd been in an accident but didn't say any more. Just that you were OK.'

I bite the inside of my lip and smile again. 'I'm sorry. I'm home now. Everything will be all right,' I say, reassuring myself as much as him.

His eyes find mine and he holds my gaze as though waiting for more. When it doesn't come, he says, 'I'll change then make us a cup of tea.'

'Thank you, darling. And then let's go over your revision. It's chemistry tonight.'

He nods before disappearing up the stairs. A few minutes later he's down again and in the kitchen. I rest my head on the cushion and close my eyes as the kettle hums into life.

I thought seeing Henry would be a comfort, a reminder that he is safe, I am safe. But all it has done is remind me of the stakes. There is so much to lose. The police will come now. After all the years I've waited for the knock at the door, now it's coming – and I'm in no state to answer it.

TWENTY-NINE

SAM

Sam should've stayed in Leeds. None of this would've happened if he hadn't left. He's never felt at home in Essex. The people here look down on him like he's bird shit on their shoe. Sam sees it in their faces. On the street. In the shops. Everywhere. Like there's something in his DNA that makes him less human than them.

But staying in Leeds after he got out of prison meant staying in his old life with his old friends. He'd have slipped back into it as easily as he'd slipped into the clothes waiting for him in his old bedroom. It wouldn't have been long before Deano would've mentioned a house he liked the look of, or a mate of a mate that needed a hand. Easy money. And he'd made a promise.

Sam had done a lot of thinking inside. Not much else to do. He'd started to think for the first time about wanting more for himself, about having a choice. Bee's weekly visits had helped. Her relentless optimism. 'Sam, you can be anything you want to be; you can be so much more than this.' She'd taken his hand over the table and the rest of the room had fallen away. He hadn't seen the guards in the corner or the other lads with their families; it had just been him and Bee and her words, her belief in him, and for a little while he'd tried to believe in himself too.

He'd moved home when he'd got out, living back with his mum, feeling crapper by the day, and then Kev from inside had called and said he was out too. He'd told Sam about his cousin working on a building site in Essex. 'There's work for anyone with a bricklayer qualification. Even us.'

Sam had told Bee about it and she'd said to go. So he'd packed a bag, hugged her goodbye and left.

It had been good at first. He'd rented a room in a house with Kev and some of the other workers who'd come down from Leeds. Kev's cousin had been right. There was plenty of work. There were new housing sites going up everywhere. For the first time in Sam's life, he had a proper job, money in his pocket, mates to drink down the pub with who wanted to talk girls and films and sports, and not which house they'd like to score.

Then they'd had the break-in at the site. Tools taken. Thousands of pounds of equipment. Some materials too. The police thought it was someone who worked on the site. One of the lads had pointed the finger at Sam.

For anyone else, there might have been the benefit of the doubt, but not for a criminal, a thief. He'd been fired on the spot and within weeks he was crashing on his mates' floors, trying to find more work, failing, running out of money as fast as he was running out of friends. He'd wanted to go home, but he couldn't let Bee see he'd failed.

And now it's too late. He can see it on Satő's face as they file back into the room – Davidson first, holding two bottles of water, then McLachlan, then Satő. She sits down opposite him again, her face a mask of sympathy that squeezes his throat shut tight.

'No.' He croaks the word as tears blur the room and fall in two streams down his face.

'I'm very sorry, Sam,' Sató says. 'I've just spoken with your mother. Your sister, Bee, died at ten-thirty last night.'

He shakes his head from side to side. His chest feels like it's been cracked open, the hurt a physical pain. Where was he the moment she took her last breath? He pictures himself running through the streets, feet hitting the wet pavements, the shouts of the police giving chase. Another minute and he'd have been away, he'd have made it.

'Your mum said that she was happy in the end, Sam,' Sató continues. 'She told your mum to tell you that she loves you and she'll always be proud of you.'

A chasm rips open inside of him. He's falling into a dark, dark pit and there is no escape.

A firm hand clasps his arm. Davidson. 'Might I suggest we take a break? It's now eight p.m. We've been in this room for four hours. My client has told you everything he knows and is visibly upset from the death of a loved one. I suggest we reconvene tomorrow morning.'

There is back and forth between Sató and Davidson. Formalities being agreed. The conversation drifts over Sam's head, distant and inconsequential. Nothing matters anymore. Can't they see that?

After a while, he's led to a holding cell and given a tray of food he doesn't touch. He lies on the plastic mat, pulling himself into the tightest ball he can manage and cries himself to sleep. It's all over. The one person who loved him, who truly saw him, is gone. He is alone in the world. He is lost.

I don't want to look. Not yet, not now, but I'm powerless to stop my eyes from flying open as the car jolts to a stop.

I'm panting. Emotions rush at me, just like the car at little Lucie. It's disbelief, it's shock, it's sorrow. I cry out again. An anguished scream, not me, not human.

Lucie's body is flying through the air, hurtling up, up, up.

The hot rage inside me leaves me in a whoosh of horror as she slams against the side of the building. The noise is a sickening thud I know will haunt me forever.

A sob catches in my throat as Lucie's body falls into the shadows.

THIRTY

CELIA

The knock at the door comes as I'm cleaning up the breakfast dishes. I'm bone-achingly tired. Like those early days with Henry when he was a baby, crying for milk and love every few hours. Except it wasn't the screams of a baby keeping me awake at night, it was Lucie. The sound of her body hitting my car, shaking me awake anytime I drifted close to sleep. Sounds that made my breath come in a rush and my chest ache with the speed of my pounding heart.

I was hot, feverish, my thoughts just as muddled. One minute it was Lucie's scream, the next it was Martin's, and then he was there – in my room, standing over my bed in the bleak hours of the night. He sat on the edge of the bed and watched me pretend to sleep. It's like he senses the weakness in me, the control slipping through my fingers.

My eyes move to the door that leads to the garage. I shuffle over, pull at the handle. Nothing happens.

It's locked.

I'll open it tomorrow, get back to my routine, however much I hate it some days.

I check the time as I move slowly towards the front door. It's gone eight. I should be dressed, shoes on, packing my lunch. Today is Thursday. Black trousers and the blue blouse with the pearl buttons. Four Ryvita crackers. A Red Lady apple. One low-fat Rich Tea. The thought of the routine soothes me until I look down at the beige dressing gown I've had since before Henry was born and feel cast adrift.

The knock comes again. It is not the hesitant tapping of a neighbour sorry to disturb or the one tap of the Amazon delivery driver letting me know there's a parcel on my doorstep. This knock is loud – three confident taps that leave me in no doubt who will be on my doorstep.

It's the exact knock I've waited thirteen years to hear. The thought causes a panic to grab at me. Suddenly the years fall away and I'm being dragged back to that day in the kitchen.

'You're a self-righteous bitch, Celia. You know what? I've had enough. I'm leaving and I'm taking Henry with me. You'll never see that boy again.'

The fury inside me was a deep well that rose up so fast I was half blind with it. Years of being married to this loser of a man. I gripped the frying pan in my hand and I told him, 'No. You're not taking Henry away from me. I won't let you.'

He laughed, of course. That grating chuckle. He always laughed when I got mad, but this time it died on his lips when he turned and saw me coming at him.

It's the tremor taking hold of my body that brings me back to the present. I take a shaking breath and try to steady myself. Thirteen years of waiting. I should be ready for this, except they are not here to ask about a husband who dropped off the face of the planet thirteen years ago. They are here because a girl died last night. A girl was murdered, and I am to blame.

My legs feel rubbery with each step closer. Then Henry appears at the top of the stairs. He's wearing his white school shirt and a curious expression on his face.

'It's the police,' I tell him.

His eyes widen in alarm.

'Nothing to worry about,' I say. 'They just want to check how I'm doing after the accident,' I add, my voice softer now. I wish I could believe my own words.

He hesitates a moment longer as though torn between offering to stay with me and wanting to escape.

'Get your bag sorted for school. You need to leave soon,' I say, making the decision for him. Henry nods and disappears upstairs.

'Hello,' I say, opening the door to the two women on my doorstep. They are standing side by side, both in suits. Beyond them I catch sight of a silver hatchback. There are no markings on the car, but everything about these women screams police.

'Celia Watson?' the first woman asks. She's tall. Six foot something. Long legs. A slim frame that looks like it knows the inside of a gym. Her hair is silky black and deadly straight, hanging in a neat ponytail down her back. Her make-up is flawless, the eyeliner curving the shape of her eyes. She looks nothing like the washed-out, over-worked TV detectives I half expected. Instead, this woman seems to command a respect that makes me instantly alert. The desire to flee, to turn on my heel and rush through the house, out into the garden, away away, thrums through me. But I stay rooted, unable to run even if I could.

I nod and take her outstretched hand. A firm grip to my feeble one. 'I'm DC Sara Sató. This is my colleague, DC Amanda McLachlan. Sorry it's early. We're getting a jump on things today. May we come in please?'

'Of course.' I move back, my hands fluttering around the neck of my dressing gown as they step into the hall. 'I'm... er... sorry I'm not dressed yet. It's most unusual for me but it's been a very upsetting couple of days. I'm still quite shaken by it.'

'We completely understand, Mrs Watson,' DC McLachlan

says, surprising me with a Scottish accent. In contrast to DC
Sató, DC McLachlan looks scruffy. There's a coffee stain on her
shirt and wisps of blonde hair sticking out from behind her ears,
but her smile is warm and puts me at ease.

'Call me Celia please.'

My hands remain on my dressing gown. I'm still shaking
and I'm glad DC Sató sees.

'Would you mind' – I gesture to the living room – 'if we sit
down? I'm still in a lot of pain.'

DC Sató nods and follows me into the room as I ease myself
carefully onto the sofa.

I am the victim, I remind myself. This is about me and Sam
– a madman who kidnapped me, who deserves to go to prison
for the rest of his pathetic life. What does it matter if murder is
tacked onto the list of his other charges?

'Why don't I make us some tea?' DC McLachlan asks.

My refusal lodges in my mouth. 'Don't,' I want to say. 'Don't
you dare go in my kitchen. Don't open my cupboards or touch
my things with your greasy fingerprints. Don't you snoop.' I
keep it in and grit my teeth, forcing a nod. 'Thank you,' I say.

I try not to wince at the sound of clattering and watch DC
Sató move towards the armchair by the window.

'May I sit down?' she asks.

'Please do.'

She perches right on the edge, back straight, one leg
stretched out with her hand on the knee, rubbing it slightly as
though it's sore. A netball injury, I decide. She looks like the
type for aggressive team games.

From above us there's the whoosh of a tap running. 'My
son,' I say to fill the silence. 'Henry. He's seventeen and doing
his A levels. He wants to study medicine.'

DC Sató lifts an eyebrow to show she's heard, but nothing
in her face suggests she's impressed in that way most people are
when I tell them about Henry.

I lower my voice before I continue. 'He doesn't know what happened. He thinks it was a car accident and I... I'd like to keep it that way.' The words come out in a whispered rush and DC Sató nods this time.

'What about your husband, Celia?' she asks. 'Is he home this morning?'

The question blindsides me and even though I do my best to mask it, I'm sure the surprise flashes on my face. His voice echoes so loud in my head it's like he's in the room with us. *It's your fault she's dead.*

I recover quickly, clutching at my side as though it's the pain that's caused me to falter. 'Sorry,' I say. 'What was the question?'

'I asked if your husband was here this morning?'

'Oh.' I shake my head. 'No. Martin left us years ago.'

'I see.'

What do you see? I want to ask. What do you know? But I can't get the words out. My thoughts are frozen. All I see is Martin in the doorway of the living room yesterday. How quickly my control has slipped.

THIRTY-ONE

SAM

It's hours before he wakes. The light is still on in the cell, harsh and unwelcoming. He has no idea what time it is. There is shouting from somewhere, banging too, but no doors are opening and closing, no movement of prisoners, so he guesses it's the middle of the night or the early hours. His eyes are puffy to the point of barely opening – swollen from the bruises and the crying. His head still throbs.

There's a queasiness to his stomach and his mouth feels furry with the remnants of the Coke he drank earlier. He empties his bladder and drinks the bottle of water in one go before filling it up at the sink and drinking that too. He eats the tomato pasta dish. It's cold, the sauce congealing at the edges, but it's not the worst food he's eaten in his life.

Bee might've been good at a lot of things, she might have been the most organised person he knew, the kindest too, but she was a terrible cook. No matter what it was – cheese on toast, pasta, rice – it was either burned or raw, never anywhere in the middle. Sam always jokes to Bee that he's putting his life in his hands eating her food.

Joked.

Cooked.

Bee won't be burning anything anymore.

He waits for the emotion to hit him again but it's numbness he finds.

He can't believe she's gone. If he could swap places with her, he would.

When Bee was kicked out of the house three months before her GCSEs for having a boyfriend, she could've given up, thought sod it, like Sam did. What was the point of exams anyway? But she didn't. She worked harder, living in a group home social services found for her, miles away from school.

She went to college and studied events management, and found a job in one of the big hotels helping organise weddings. A proper nine-to-five job with a good salary. She got her own place – a studio apartment in the city centre. And all the time, she still went back every Sunday to visit their mum and get yelled at by their dad. Their father had twisted the story as soon as she'd got a wage, making out that she thought she was too good for her family, ditching them after all they'd done. She never shouted back, never disagreed. She took it and then she went back to her life.

When Sam got out of prison, Bee was the only one who believed he could turn his life around. She was wrong.

His heart starts to sprint suddenly like a racehorse, hooves pounding the course. He thinks of the old boy in the tartan pyjamas. Where is he now? Why haven't the police asked him about that morning?

He's glad Bee isn't here to see him break his promise. Not break... Smash. Obliterate. He wonders if she really said those things about him at the end, about being proud, or if Sató just said it to make him feel better. He knows it's not the kind of thing his mum would make up. He was always her disappointment.

The enormity of his situation is glaring at him from all four walls, but he can't process it. Snippets of Sató's final words to him echo through his mind. An offer of condolences, the offer of a break, but a warning too. 'We will be talking again tomorrow. Another woman is dead. Her name is Lucie Gilbert. And we need to find out what happened to her.'

Except Sam doesn't know what happened to her. He doesn't know who she was, how she died or how she got into the boot of Celia's car. But he knows one thing – he didn't put her there; he didn't have anything to do with it. If there was a body in Celia's boot, then it was there when he climbed into the car.

The car journey seems otherworldly now. His mum had been messaging him, begging him to hurry, telling him he was letting Bee down, as if he didn't already know that. Sam had been frantic; a right state.

What had Celia said to him?

Think.

Something about Lucie and money. Yeah, that was it.

'If it's about Lucie and the money.'

Something else occurs to him – Celia opened the boot. He remembers now: when they stopped by the roadside, Celia insisting she needed a piss, and his own bladder telling him he had to go. The moment his back was turned, she was up and moving around to the back of the car.

She opened the boot, but she didn't scream or cry or shout. Lucie's body had to have been in there because they didn't stop again until the crash, which means Celia knew it was there. She knew when Sam got into that car that she had a dead body in the boot.

I move. Unsteady. Stumbling forward.

Sounds come back into focus. Beyond the ragged catch of my breath in my throat I catch a car door banging and the rumble of buses on the main high street, reminding me of life beyond this car park, a world still turning.

I think of Henry, my darling boy, and the mess I've brought to our lives. I really did just want to help.

The exhaust fumes scratch at the back of my throat as I carry on moving. Another gust of wind hits my damp cheeks and I realise as I inch around the front of the car that I'm crying.

I see her leg first. Bent out at the strangest angle. My body reacts, jerking back, my hip hitting the edge of the car. The stinging pain is a welcome distraction as I fight back the growing need to vomit.

There is no blistering rage now, just fear. Fear and guilt.

What have I done?

THIRTY-TWO

CELIA

DC McLachlan returns with a tray carrying three mugs of tea. There's a little bowl of sugar too, and I wonder where she found it. I try not to think of the scattering of granules sticky on my countertops.

She steps towards me and lowers the tray. The mugs are too full, too milky, and droplets of tea land on my dressing gown as I lift a mug towards me. 'Thank you,' I say, wondering how someone so incompetent at making a cup of tea has risen to a detective in the police force.

McLachlan places the tray on the coffee table, but neither she nor Sató reach for the remaining mugs.

'So,' Sató begins before pausing. Quiet footsteps sound on the stairs. Henry may be a teenager now, but the need to move softly, precisely, is ingrained in him, etched through his DNA. He will make a brilliant surgeon one day.

Henry appears in the doorway. I don't breathe for a moment, taking him in like I always do. I try to see what the detectives must see – this almost man. Handsome features – a nice nose, a strong jaw. That thick brown hair and the dusting of freckles now faded, almost lost. They'll reappear in the summer when the sun blazes down. He looks so smart in his uniform. He really is perfect as he stands before us.

Of course they don't see the boy who still has nightmares that shake him awake some nights, who still sucks his thumb in his sleep. Who licks all the flavouring off a crisp before eating it. The boy who spent hours and hours building a matchstick Buckingham Palace during those endless days of lockdown just for something to do. These things are for my eyes only.

'Henry, darling,' I say. 'This is DC Sató and DC McLachlan. They just want to talk to me about my car accident. Nothing to worry about.' Again, I wish it was true.

He freezes. It's just a second. A flinch really, before he gives his Head Boy, straight-A smile. 'Hi, I'm Henry.' He steps into the room, leaning down to kiss my cheek.

'Won't you be late?' I ask.

'It's Thursday,' he says and I catch the subtle smell of his deodorant – woody with that manufactured masculine smell. 'I have a free period first, remember?'

I nod. Of course. How could I forget?

'I'm going to the school library to finish my homework though,' he adds.

'Have a good day.'

Another moment of hesitation as though he's expecting me to say something, for the detectives to ask a question maybe, and then he lifts his hand in a wave and leaves. A beat passes before the front door opens and closes with a soft clatter.

DC Sató allows a silence to draw out as though she's turning a page, beginning a new chapter. 'Celia,' she begins, 'I hope we'll not take up too much of your time. We have a brief statement that you made in the hospital yesterday to PC Daniels from West Yorkshire Police. What we need from you today is for you to tell us what happened. From the beginning please.'

I nod. I swallow. I knew this was coming. 'It's still all a bit fuzzy. I think it's the shock. I can't seem to shake it.' I shiver for emphasis and draw my hands tighter around my mug of tea.

'We understand,' she says. 'But it is necessary for us to hear in person what happened. A man is being held in custody at Hallford police station and it's imperative we build a complete picture for our case against him.'

I give what I hope is a wobbly smile before taking a breath and telling the story of Lucie calling me. Our meeting in the car park after work. Her walking away, me getting into my car. Sam coming out of the darkness. My words are hurried and stuttering, but the story is easier this time than it was with PC Daniels. I've replayed it so many times in my mind that it feels real, and I'm rather pleased with my performance.

'And what did Lucie want when she arranged to meet you?' DC Satō's tone is soft, her face open. There is no hint of suspicion and yet I can't help but wonder if it's there.

'Help,' I say. 'She was in trouble. She didn't tell me what. Just that she needed some money.' Easy tears fill my eyes as I talk about Lucie. My sadness for her, my grief, it is real despite the lies I'm weaving. 'I... er... don't know what the money was for, but she looked very worried.'

'Did you give her money?'

'Not then. I didn't have any on me and certainly not the amount she asked for, which was sixty thousand pounds. I hadn't seen Lucie for thirteen years, but she's always been a rather troubled girl.' I paint a picture of Lucie growing up in the council flats. Our meeting in school and my desire to help her. I skip over the part about Lucie wanting to be a doctor. I mention Lucie's mother's neglect and a difficult child who has grown into a lost woman.

'I told her I'd do my best to help her and we arranged to meet in a few days' time. That's when she went to leave. I wasn't really going to lend her that kind of money. I don't have it, but I thought if she'd meet me for a warm drink in the daytime then maybe we could talk a bit more and I could find another way to help her.' I sniff and wipe away the tears lying damp on my cheeks.

I expect more questions, holes poked in my story, but DC Sató stands and brushes down her trousers. 'Thank you, Celia. We'll leave you to rest now. Here are my details,' she says, placing a plain white card on the coffee table. 'My contact information is on there if you think of anything else. I've written your crime number on the back as well. We'll need you to come to the station to give a formal statement in the next day or two please.'

My body feels light, floaty, as I go to stand. It's the same feeling I had in the hospital after speaking to PC Daniels. Can it really be this simple?

'Don't get up,' DC Sató says, motioning for me to stay seated. I give a feeble nod.

'Thank you, detectives.'

'DC McLachlan will keep you updated with the investigation,' Sató says and there's a nod from her colleague as they move to the doorway. 'We have an officer at the station scouring the traffic cameras for Tuesday evening alongside any CCTV footage of the buildings surrounding the car park.'

'Footage?' The question is out before I can stop it. A rush of heat floods my face.

Sató pauses, turning slowly to look at me. Our eyes meet and I force myself not to look away. 'Yes,' she confirms. 'We may get lucky and have everything we need on camera.'

She continues to stare – questioning and curious. I force myself to nod. 'Of course. That would be good.' Inside, a scream wails through my mind.

The second the front door is closed, I shut my eyes, my breath coming short and gasping. The question drums in my mind in time with my hammering heart – what will they find on the footage?

Facebook Messenger

I'm scared of what she's capable of!

THIRTY-THREE

SAM

The truth smacks Sam square between the eyes with the same force as the airbag. He had nothing to do with Lucie's death, but Celia did. He can't believe it's taken him this long to twig. Celia had everything to do with it, and now she's trying to pin it all on him.

He slumps back onto the mat and stares at the ceiling. He thinks of Bee and the last time he saw her. She'd had her hair cut again – a pixie cut, she'd called it – that shaped her face, making her smile seem even wider. 'You've got this,' she'd said to him as Kev's van pulled up on the street. She'd pushed a carrier bag into his hands. 'Sandwiches for the journey. Don't worry, they're shop-bought. I didn't make them.' She'd laughed. 'Love you, little brother.'

'Love you, big sis,' he'd replied.

It was an hour into the journey before he'd opened the carrier bag and found the envelope. Five twenty-pound notes and a Post-it with three words written on it: *Proud of you xx*

Tears sting at the edges of Sam's eyes. He isn't sure he believes in heaven and all that, but he imagines Bee looking down on him. She wouldn't be proud right now. She'd be horrified. Regret and loathing slink over him like a slow and lazy snake, coiling and squeezing until he's trapped, until he can't breathe.

'I'm so sorry, Bee,' he says, his voice a hoarse whisper. 'I was just trying to get home. I didn't kill that girl.'

It suddenly seems important to him – this one truth. He did not kill Lucie Gilbert. There has to be some evidence, some way to prove he's innocent.

Sam sits up, rubbing his hands over his face. He stands, pacing the room, stretching out his body. At the end of the last interview, a darkness had swallowed him up. He'd just been told his sister had died less than an hour after he'd made it to Leeds. He'd been minutes away from her and she'd died.

He hadn't thought it mattered what they charged him with, what happened to him. It wasn't going to change anything. It wasn't going to bring Bee back. But sitting in this cell, he thinks it does matter. He has to prove he didn't kill that girl. For Bee and for himself.

There's a ringing in my ears, drowning out my gasping breath, my pounding heartbeat. I inch forward again, ignoring the pain in my hip from where I knocked it on the car. Her leg comes into view once more and this time I keep moving.

Is she dead? The question tears at something inside me. Do I want her to be?

'Lucie?' Her name comes out in a croaking sob.

She was going to destroy everything. She was going to ruin my life, ruin Henry's life too. He won't cope without me.

I wanted to stop her but I didn't want her to die. Really, truly, I didn't.

THIRTY-FOUR

CELIA

The day passes.

I gaze at nothing, my thoughts racing and sticking and racing again. At some point I sleep, drifting off on the sofa and losing all sense of time, waking to darkness, my wound throbbing. My mouth is bone dry and I long for water and some painkillers.

'Henry?' I call into the darkness, gritting my teeth to the pain as I stand.

'In here.'

He means the kitchen. He's at the table, his maths books spread around him. He's wearing a red polo shirt and the dark-blue chinos I bought him last Christmas that are already looking a little short in the leg. There is something not quite right about the outfit but I can't think what it is. My mind is jumbled. Incoherent.

The bright kitchen light makes me squint. I glance at the clock. It's only 6 p.m. It feels like midnight. I'm still in my dressing gown, cold now, my skin grimy with however many hours, days, it's been since I washed.

'How was school?' My voice is hoarse. I get myself a glass of water, gulping it back then filling it again and easing myself into a chair at the table.

'Fine,' he says, but there's a sheepish look to him.

'What?'

'It was in the news.' His eyes draw to his phone.

'What was?' I ask.

'A man kidnapped a woman in her car.'

A stillness takes over the room. The unasked question hangs between us.

'It was in the news?' I ask, repeating his words as though they haven't sunk in.

He taps at his phone screen and turns it towards me. It's the headline of a local news site – *Man arrested for kidnapping local woman.* I scan the article. The only details are the time and date. A woman in her forties, a man in his twenties. No mention of Lucie or the charge for murder. I'm relieved and then I'm not. Why would they leave out the juicy detail of a dead body? Are the police holding it back? Do they know Sam is innocent?

'Mum?' Henry bites his lip, uncertain, scared. He looks suddenly so young, closer to a boy than a man. 'It was you, wasn't it?'

'I... I didn't want to worry you, that's all. I'm fine,' I reply, placing his phone between us on the table. Instantly, he's reaching for it.

'Is that why the police came this morning?'

I nod. 'They just want to make sure they have all the facts before they charge this man.' There's a pause, a moment where I should mention Lucie, but I don't. How can I tell my precious boy what I've done?

'What are you not telling me?' He frowns, and when I shake my head, something in his expression hardens. A flash of Martin. There are so many things I'm not telling him, I wouldn't know where to begin.

'Darling,' I say, 'I promise you, everything is going to be fine. All you need to do is concentrate on your revision.'

Still, Henry's gaze remains on me.

He's getting harder to lie to.

Sometimes I catch him looking at me – a fleeting distrust.

He's no longer my little boy, but I'll carry on these lies, doing all I can to protect him. He may not remember the first five years of his life, but they have shaped him more than the twelve that have followed.

He glances at the screen of his phone before tucking it in his pocket and standing, packing up his books.

'What are you doing?' I ask.

'Packing up.'

'It's not six-thirty.' I don't mean for my tone to sound hard, but it lands anyway.

He glances at the clock. 'It will be in five minutes.'

I bite my tongue, keeping in my reply. He's right, of course. It is only five minutes and he works so hard. Stopping early just this once won't matter, I tell myself as my insides knot. It's another change to the routine I'm not sure I can handle.

Henry catches my eye and stops. 'What?'

'Nothing.'

'Mum, what?'

'I was just thinking that you've worked so hard for so long, and at this point five minutes could be the difference between an A and an A star, you know that. Details matter, Henry, especially with places to study medicine so competitive. But I wasn't going to say anything because I know it's been a difficult week for you and I'm sorry about that.'

He sighs, then nods. 'You're right.' He drops back into the chair and flips open his notebook. I stay where I am, silent, patient. When the five minutes are up, Henry looks at me again and I nod this time.

'Are we still having casserole for dinner?'

'Oh.' I rub a hand to my forehead. It's Thursday. Chicken casserole night. Except I usually prep in the morning and pop the slow cooker on. 'I've not put it on.'

Sudden tears build in my eyes. I'm hot all over.

'Why don't we eat the pasta tonight? The sauce is still in the fridge.' His words are soft as though he knows it's madness to suggest a change in routine. A few years ago, when he was fourteen or fifteen, he suggested fish and chips on Saturday night when he knew it was fajita night. I lost my temper. Crashing around in the kitchen, banging pots too hard on the surfaces. We ate our fajitas in a stormy silence that night and he never suggested a change again. Until now. But this is different.

And that's when I realise what's wrong with his clothes. The red polo shirt. It's part of his Friday outfit. Today is supposed to be a blue Gap hoody and chinos. Surprise morphs into a gushing anger. It's the final straw on top of a day where I didn't dress in my own Thursday outfit. I didn't go to work. I didn't put the casserole on. Nothing has been right.

'Henry' – my voice is too loud for the kitchen – 'why are you wearing the wrong clothes?'

He stares at me, eyes wide, a furtive glance down to his top and then back to me. 'What does it matter?' If he was aiming for defiance, he has fallen short, but he continues anyway. 'What does it matter if I wear red on Thursday or we eat fish on Tuesday? What does any of it matter?'

I gasp. It's so unlike Henry to talk back like this. I thought he understood how important routines are, but here he is, so much like his father, asking pointless questions. 'I've told you,' I reply, 'routines keep us on track. We know where we are and what we're doing. I thought you understood.' Tears form in my eyes and I watch Henry's face fall just like I knew it would.

'I'm sorry,' he blurts out. 'Don't cry, Mummy.' He's up and out of his chair in a flash, leaning over to hug me. 'I'll go change.'

I nod. 'You're right about the pasta. We can eat that tonight. You can't eat cereal and toast for a third night in a row.'

'I can cook,' he says, straightening up.

'No, no,' I say too quickly. 'You pack your things away.' His expression changes again. Worry to resignation. I try to imagine him boiling water, stirring sauce on the stove. The thought releases an uncomfortable queasiness in my belly. The water will boil over; the sauce will splat on my walls.

I know it doesn't matter, shouldn't matter. How will he learn how to cook if I don't let him try? And yet I can't do it. Everything in my life feels broken, disrupted. I need to do this. For the routine, for Henry. What kind of mother will I be if I don't cook my darling boy dinner?

'Mum,' Henry says, hovering in the doorway now, a habit I'm starting to hate, 'are you really OK?'

I pause, allowing the silence to draw out. How do I tell him what I've done, what kind of monster I am? 'I'm sorry, darling. I don't think I can talk about it tonight.'

'All right,' he says with a shrug.

I must get control of myself. I've done so much to keep Henry safe and by my side. It will all be for nothing if I push him away and lose control now.

My eyes drag to the garage door, a chill moving through my body. Martin will be enjoying this – Henry's sudden resistance, my feeble state. Already I feel my control has slipped; already he's breaking the rules we agreed on all those years ago. I briefly wonder about another bolt on the garage door. This one on the kitchen side only. Something like the ones on the bedrooms when Henry was little.

It wasn't a lie what I told Lucie. Martin did sleepwalk and he did almost knock a toddling one-year-old Henry down the stairs once, but the locks had other uses. Like when I needed a little break, mostly from Martin's whining.

Of course, I wish I'd locked Henry in his room that night Martin threatened to leave.

I move slowly across the kitchen to the fridge and pull out the tub of pasta sauce to heat up, and while I make dinner, I allow myself to think of an alternative reality where Henry didn't see Martin on the kitchen floor and Lucie didn't jump to conclusions and instead she kept coming for dinner – a sister to Henry, a daughter to me. I would've been the best kind of mother to both of them.

But I did hit Martin, knocking him out cold. And Henry saw him on the floor.

Martin didn't die from the blow; Lucie was wrong about that. It would have been easier if he had. I panicked and dragged him into the garage, tied him up, and when he came to, he begged for his life.

He promised to change. He painted a picture of a different life, away from the arguments and the bullying. And like a fool, I listened.

Facebook Messenger

This is the only way!
I can't live like this anymore.

THIRTY-FIVE

SAM

It's a different interview room today. The same but flipped around. The recording device is on the right instead of the left.

Davidson pulls out the chair beside Sam. He's wearing a grey suit with a baby pink shirt and matching tie. It reminds Sam of the red Adidas T-shirt he had once, when he was nine or ten. It was his favourite T-shirt, his lucky T-shirt he used to think. Something about the fit, the way it sat on him, it made him feel more than he was. He washed it every three days and hung it on a radiator to dry overnight. The colour faded, but Sam didn't care. Until his dad walked into the living room and whacked him over the back of the head. A hard stinging slap. 'Whatcha doing wearing a girly T-shirt? Take it off.'

Sam pulled the T-shirt over his stinging head and watched as his dad threw it in the bin, pushing it right down onto the scrapings of the burned dinner Bee had tried to cook them because their mum was in bed. He remembers thinking it couldn't have been a lucky T-shirt, after all. Luck was something other people enjoyed, not Sam. He hasn't worn anything red or pink since.

He stares at the clock on the wall. It's 1.55 p.m. Like the

strange expanse between Christmas and New Year, it takes Sam a moment to place the day – Thursday. He's been waiting for the interview all morning. Pacing up and down in his cell, standing by the door every time he heard footsteps.

He thought they'd drag him back in first thing, but Sam has eaten two extra meals after the cold pasta – another breakfast microwave meal slightly better than the first. Better beans, he thinks. And at lunch they brought him a cheese sandwich. He's drunk two cups of tea and plenty of water. He's brushed his teeth and rubbed a damp soap under his armpits. The best he could do.

DC Sató and DC McLachlan sit in the same positions as before, Sató opposite. She's wearing a navy suit today and a white shirt with a large pointy collar. DC McLachlan is wearing a shirt too – pale blue with iron creases down the sides and a black cardigan. There's a gap between the buttons of her shirt where her breasts push against the fabric. Sam catches a glimpse of white lace and quickly looks away.

DC McLachlan starts the recording, sending a burst of nerves darting through his body. Sató reels off the date and time, then location. He's asked to give his name again and he does.

'Sam, how are you? Is there anything you need?' Sató asks. Another warm-up.

He shakes his head and pulls his cap lower. 'No, thanks.'

'That's good. The reason we're interviewing you today is to go over some of the details you gave us yesterday and talk through some of the evidence we now have. Does that sound OK?'

He nods. 'Yeah, fine.' It wasn't really a question.

He spends half an hour answering the same stuff as yesterday. Then Sató opens her folder and Sam gets a feeling the real interview is just beginning.

'I'm going to show you a photograph of a jacket,' she says. 'Can you tell me if you recognise it please, Sam?'

The jacket is puffy and black with a badge on the arm to make it look like a fancy brand, but it's not. It's from one of the stalls on Hallford Market. Sam knows this because it's his jacket. He nicked it last month when the weather turned and he found himself not only flat broke, homeless and jobless, but cold too. 'It's mine,' Sam says before the photo is halfway across the table.

'We found this jacket in Celia's car.' She places another photo in front of him. It's the body again – that girl with the dead eyes, but it's not the same photo as before. This one is zoomed in on her legs. 'Can you see this here?' Sató says, tapping the photo and not waiting for a reply. 'It's your jacket and it's underneath Lucie's body. Celia has told us that you took it off in a moment of anger after Lucie was hit by the car and lying dead on the road. You threw your jacket into the boot before you forced Celia to put Lucie's body in on top of it.'

'What? That's not true,' he cries out, desperate to be believed. He has to make them see.

'Then how do you explain your jacket being found beneath a body that you claim not to have seen until our interview yesterday?'

'She put it there – Celia, I mean.' The words fly out. 'I told you how she went to the boot of the car...' He trails off, a red heat flushing his face. He'd forgotten to tell them about Celia's movements when they'd stopped by the side of the road. Stupid!

'When was this, Sam? You haven't mentioned this to us.' Sató looks to McLachlan, who shakes her head. 'I'm happy to review yesterday's recordings and we can go back through what you've said.'

'I forgot,' he stammers. 'I know it sounds bad, but it's the truth.'

'What exactly did you forget to tell us?' There's a note of exasperation in Sató's voice.

He takes a breath, willing himself to calm down as he explains Celia's sudden rush to the boot. 'She put my jacket in there.'

'Underneath a body?' Sató asks, raising an eyebrow.

'Yeah. She must've.'

'I see. So you didn't see Lucie running back towards the car which you had just forced Celia to drive away in. You didn't grab the wheel from Celia and cause her to hit Lucie, then force Celia to put Lucie's body in the boot of the car?'

'NO.' His voice is loud, making his head hurt. 'That isn't what happened.'

'OK, Sam.' McLachlan leans forward and Sató tucks the photo back into the folder, and he's suddenly reminded of the wrestling shows he used to watch and the deadly tag teams. He can see them now facing up against Team Hell No.

'We are currently processing the evidence from Celia's car,' McLachlan continues. 'We don't have the DNA results back yet, but we do have fingerprint analysis. Your fingerprints have been found on the steering wheel, which supports Celia's claim that you grabbed the wheel, forcing the car to hit Lucie.'

'No.' He shakes his head. He can't believe this. 'It's not true.'

'In that case, can you explain how your fingerprints came to be on the steering wheel?'

He tells them about Celia being upset and him having to grab the wheel. It sounds too convenient. An explanation for everything. Frustrated tears threaten behind his eyes.

They go through the whole story again. Start to finish. Sam stumbles over his words. He's told it so many times that it's taken on a film-like image in his head, an unreal quality. The truth doesn't feel true anymore. He's given another can of Coke and a ham sandwich and a break. Davidson tells him he's doing well. It doesn't feel that way to him, and it's a relief when Sató calls time on the interview.

'A judge has granted us an additional seventy-two hours, Sam,' she explains. 'Ninety-six hours in total from when you were brought here yesterday. We'll continue with our interview tomorrow morning, if that's OK.'

Sam nods, exhausted. What choice does he have?

Only later, in his cell, does he wonder why they've asked for extra time. They have the evidence, they have a credible witness and they have a criminal in custody. What more are they hoping to find?

'Lucie?' I say her name again, my voice a husky whisper.

No reply. No groan of pain. No plea for help. A shiver races through me.

My hands shake as I dig in my bag and pull out my phone. I need to call an ambulance. I need to do something. But my eyes drag back to her body and I falter, cry out. 'Lucie.' It's not a question this time and I drop my phone back into my bag.

Her body is an unnatural heap – a rag doll thrown to the floor. There is a trickle of something dark by her ear – blood, I think. Her legs are tangled and one of her arms is splayed out on the wet tarmac. The other is twisted under her body. But it's her eyes I keep drawing back to. Wide and vacant.

'Oh, Lucie.' I'm sorry. I'm so sorry.

THIRTY-SIX

CELIA

The detectives return after we've eaten the pasta. That same confident knock-knock-knock at the front door that has my thoughts spinning off in every direction. I glance furtively around the kitchen and to the weather-beaten summer house at the back of the garden, and then to the door that leads to the garage.

Thirteen years of truth is lurking just out of sight. How hard would they have to scratch the surface to see it?

'Mum?' Henry raises his eyebrows. 'Are you going to answer it?'

I nod. 'Go upstairs and pack your school bag and recheck your maths answers.'

He snatches up his phone and his books and moves silently upstairs. I listen for the sound of his bedroom door closing but hear nothing. Is he hiding just out of sight, listening? There's a fluttering in my stomach as I reach one hand for the front door, the other rubbing at the base of my neck.

DC Sató and DC McLachlan are full of apologies for disturbing me in the evening. I lead them into the living room, catching the stale smell of my own body odour in the room lingering beneath the white jasmine. I pat at my hair, smoothing down the bumps and tucking wisps behind my ears. It shouldn't matter what I look like, and really, isn't this what a victim of a traumatic kidnapping should look like? And yet, I feel uncomfortable, fidgety, wishing I was wearing my blue blouse and black trousers instead of the same tatty dressing gown as this morning.

This is why I can't concentrate. Why my thoughts skitter and jump, questions racing. It isn't just the shock and the pain, the knowledge of what I've done. It's the disruption to my routine. It's what I told Henry – routines keep us on track. I don't know who I am without them.

DC McLachlan makes tea again, placing another overly full mug in my hands that I won't drink. I barely touched my dinner. Pasta on a Thursday. It didn't feel right.

'Is everything all right?' I ask when DC Sató has perched on the sofa and I can't bear the silence anymore. 'It's just I'm rather tired.'

'We have a few inconsistencies to clarify, if you don't mind, Celia. We'll try not to keep you any longer than we need.'

Inconsistencies? My face grows hot at the word, but I nod. What more can I do?

'So, we're in a bit of a tricky situation and we hope you can help clear something up for us,' DC Sató continues, her tone friendly, still that apologetic air, and yet there's something else there – a curiosity. No. It's suspicion. They know I'm lying. My pulse quickens.

'You said that Sam got into your car on Brook Street where you park when you're working at Citizens Advice. Is that correct?'

I nod again. Unease creeps over me.

'Would you mind showing me where in the car park it happened? I've got an aerial photograph right here.'

DC McLachlan pulls out an A4 sheet and places it on the

coffee table between us. It's a Google Earth image, a bird's-eye view. The paper has been folded in two, the line snaking unevenly across the page. Laziness. How difficult is it to fold a piece of paper correctly?

I pretend to stare at the photograph, questions racing through my head. What do they know? What do I say?

'Just a rough idea would really help,' DC Sató pushes.

'I... I'm not sure,' I say at last. 'It all happened so fast. I feel a bit confused by it all.' My pulse thunders in my ears. My chest is tight with the effort of trying to breathe slowly. I pray my face gives nothing away.

There's a pause. DC Sató leans forward another fraction, clutching at her knee again. Any moment now I expect her to fall off the chair. 'The thing is, Celia, Sam has admitted to us that he did get in your car and force you to drive him to Leeds, but he's saying that it happened on Springfield Road at a set of traffic lights.'

'That boy is a criminal,' I hiss. 'Of course he's going to lie.'

'That may be, but we have found one image so far from a traffic camera that appears to corroborate Sam's story.'

No. The word screams in my head. A coldness rushes through me.

DC McLachlan steps forward and places a glossy photo on top of the car-park printout. There is no fold in this one, nothing to obscure the image. It's grainy but in colour and surprisingly clear. I can even see the pinched expression on my face, the hunch of my shoulders as I lean over the wheel. And an empty passenger seat beside me.

'This was from a camera on Nelson Avenue. As you can see from the date and time stamp in the corner, it shows you driving away from the Brook Street car park alone.'

DC Sató stops then. She doesn't ask a question. She doesn't have to. Her statement hangs in the air, a noose above my head.

'I... I'm sorry.' My voice falters and shakes. 'I was in shock and confused in the hospital. When PC Daniels asked me what happened, I got muddled and I couldn't remember. And then when it came back to me afterwards, I thought it would look bad if I changed my statement. And so I lied to you. I'm sorry.' I lift my head and force my eyes to connect with DC Satō's piercing gaze.

'Right,' she says, with a nod. 'It would be better now if you tell us the whole truth. Starting with where you met Lucie and how she fits in to this.'

'Everything I told you about Lucie was the truth.' Tears form easily in my eyes. There's a creak of a floorboard and I know the one – the top step of the stairs. Henry. My eyes dart to the detectives. If they heard the noise they don't show it. 'But after we talked, I offered to give her a lift.' My mind blanks for a moment. I can see the question forming in the detectives' minds. If I met Lucie at Brook Street car park and drove her somewhere then why isn't she in the photo? And then the obvious conclusion – unless she was already in the boot.

A second ticks by and I'm aware of the silence. I frown, touching my hand to my side, buying myself time.

'Sorry, the pain comes and goes. So... er... Lucie refused at first, shaking her head and looking over her shoulder. It seemed like she was scared of someone.' I force myself to maintain eye contact, to ignore the pull to look down. 'When she finally agreed, she got in the back and sort of crouched down in the seat.'

'Where did she want to go?'

Another pause. I cough. The movement sends a shot of pain down my side, but I cough again. I can't think. Thoughts rush too fast through my mind, like the car journey with Sam, the road flying by.

'Would you like me to get you a glass of water, Celia?' DC McLachlan asks me.

'Yes please.'

The detective disappears, returning with a glass of water that I gulp back.

'I am sorry,' I say again, dabbing at my mouth. 'I didn't want you to think that I was an unreliable witness, and I... I didn't want to stop that man being charged for what he did.'

'I see.'

She doesn't.

'Lucie wanted me to drop her near Springfield Road. She had a friend near there that she was staying with. We pulled up to a set of traffic lights and she got out. She told me she'd call me the next day. She was walking away when Sam jumped in the car.'

DC Sató makes me tell the story all over again. Lucie in the car park, in the back of the car. Then getting out. Sam forcing me to drive. Grabbing the wheel and mowing Lucie down. Lies on top of lies until I feel they might drown me. But what choice do I have now but to keep going and hope there's no CCTV footage on Springfield Road?

'His fingerprints will be on the wheel, right? Evidence I'm telling the truth.'

'Your car has been transferred to Essex police and is currently being processed by our forensics team,' DC Sató replies. 'If there's anything else you've failed to tell us, Celia, then now is the time.' Her eyes burn into me.

I shake my head, feeling scolded.

'Good then. We'll leave you to rest now, Celia. We're continuing our investigation and we'll be speaking to people who knew Lucie to build a better picture of her movements and her life before she came to see you on Tuesday. We'll also be appealing for witnesses who might have seen what happened. Especially if your memory could still be a little murky.'

Is that a threat? A warning of more questions to come? A sickness roils in my stomach. What have I done?

'And Sam,' I say to fill the silence. 'What is he saying?'

DC Sató pauses, her head tilting slightly to the side as though she's assessing me. I wish I could take the question back. The pinch of a frown appears on her brow. 'I'm afraid I can't tell you that.'

'But he's guilty. He was arrested at the scene. Surely that's enough?'

'We wouldn't be doing our jobs if we didn't investigate properly,' DC McLachlan says, a boilerplate answer.

They stand and just as I'm about to ask when I'll hear from them again, DC Sató takes a step forward, but her left leg gives way and she stumbles, her face a mask of pain. She rights herself quickly, straightening her jacket.

'Are you all right?' I ask, looking from her to DC McLachlan. The detective doesn't react. It's as though she hasn't seen it.

'We'll be in touch, Mrs Watson,' DC Sató says by way of reply.

I startle at the use of my surname. I'm not sure if it's a reaction to her stumble or because of something I've said. Either way, I don't like the formality, or how the air feels thick with guilt and the stink of lies that I'm sure they sense.

They leave and Henry appears at the top of the stairs. I can see from his face that he's been lurking, listening. He'll know about Lucie now. His expression is pinched – confusion and worry. A fear starts to unravel inside me. It's nothing like the urgent panic I felt on Tuesday with Sam and the knife at my side. This fear is darker – talons stretching around my heart. Squeezing. Scratching. What will happen to me now? To us?

Facebook Messenger

I don't know how this will end for me!

THIRTY-SEVEN

SAM

Sam leans against the cell wall, sliding his body to the floor. He drops his head into his hands. They don't believe him. They never will believe him.

He bangs his head against the wall, one, two, three times, and imagines standing in the stuffy heat of a courtroom in a cheap suit and an itchy shirt that he'll have begged his mum to buy for him.

He imagines a jury – lots of nice, middle-class citizens doing their duty, looking first to him and then to Celia as she takes a seat in the witness box. She'll be wearing pearls, he thinks. She looks the type. Pearls and one of those silky shirts, and her hair in that bun she had the other day. She'll look like a kindly school teacher, the kind of woman people trust to walk their dog or water their plants while they're on holiday. She'll look innocent. And he'll look guilty.

They'll lap up every word she says. They'll look at Sam like he's a liar. And why wouldn't they? He's a thug, isn't he? A criminal with a record. The only person who ever saw him as something else, something more, was Bee, and she's gone.

A door bangs from somewhere on the block, shaking Sam from his thoughts. He listens to two sets of footsteps and his heart pounds in his chest. The footsteps stop outside his door. Someone shouts a barrage of abuse Sam barely hears.

This is it.

Sató and McLachlan are going to open his cell and tell him he's being charged with kidnap and murder and being shipped off to prison while he waits for the trial.

He's totally screwed. He can't catch his breath.

But it's not Sató who opens the door. It's one of the custody officers and beside him is his solicitor, Davidson, looking pale-faced and exhausted.

'Just five minutes or you'll have to wait for an interview room to become free,' the custody officer says with a hard glance to both Sam and then Davidson.

'Thank you, Frank,' Davidson says, stepping into the cell.

It's too small for both of them. The smell of Davidson's aftershave clogs the air; his presence feels claustrophobic.

Davidson smiles and leans against the opposite wall. If Sam stretched out his leg, he'd be able to touch Davidson's shiny brown shoes. 'Hey, Sam, how you doing?'

'Pretty shit.' Sam rests his head in his hands, rubbing them over his cap.

Davidson nods. 'Look, I've been speaking to the detectives. I assume you know that they presented the evidence against you to the CPS, and it's the CPS who decide whether to bring charges?'

'Yeah.' Sam's mouth is suddenly dry. Is Davidson about to mention the old boy in the tartan pyjamas?

'OK, good. So the CPS are prepared to drop the murder charge—'

'What?' Sam leaps up. 'They believe me?' Relief swoops through him so fast he feels dizzy with it.

'Hang on, Sam. They're prepared to drop the murder charge if you plead guilty to both kidnap and manslaughter.'

The relief disappears as quickly as it arrived. Sam sinks back to the floor, feeling empty.

'Manslaughter? For Lucie?' The question seems so dumb that Sam bangs his head against the wall. The impact makes the bruises around his nose ache.

Davidson nods. 'You've already admitted to kidnap. If you plead guilty to manslaughter too, it would mean no lengthy trial. I'm guessing you don't have the funds to pay for a barrister?'

'The ones in wigs?' he asks, thinking of the last barrister he met. The guy didn't even look at Sam as he was led into court for the burglary charge. The hearing was over so fast, he was sentenced and back in the transport van without more than a few words.

'Yes. You would of course be appointed a barrister by the court, but if you plead guilty, there is no trial. A judge will decide your sentence, which will be reduced by one third for a guilty plea. It also looks good for the parole board down the line. You could be out in' – Davidson thinks for a moment – 'ten years with good behaviour. You'll only be in your early thirties. Still the chance to live your life and make some good decisions for yourself. There is something good inside you, Sam. You've made some bad choices. My advice now is to make a good one.'

There's something so Bee about Davidson's comment that it stings right in the centre of his heart. That's all Bee wanted for him – to turn things around, to live his best life – a life that has been so cruelly snatched away from her.

'But I didn't kill Lucie.'

There's a pause. Davidson looks up. 'I believe you, Sam. But you're a bright boy and I'm sure you know how this is likely to go in a courtroom. It's not about the truth and what I believe; it's what can be proved. It's the story the barristers paint to a jury.'

Sam knows Davidson is right. He'd been thinking the same thing earlier, but it needles him. Surely a courtroom is the one place where the truth really does matter.

'And if I plead not guilty?'

'The CPS will charge you with murder. If you're found guilty, it'll be life in prison. Twenty-five years.'

Sam lifts his head and stares at the ceiling, letting the stark white light blur his vision. 'So in a trial, it will be my word against Celia's?'

'Yes. Alongside the evidence, which is pretty damning. Your jacket was found underneath the body, Sam. Your DNA will be on Lucie's body from the jacket. Celia is saying you grabbed the wheel and forced the car to hit Lucie. There is evidence to support everything she's saying.'

Sam closes his eyes and nods slowly, remembering Celia's outburst, those sobs. He'd felt sorry for her. He'd hated himself for causing her so much anguish. Had it all been part of her plan to get his fingerprints on the wheel?

'A judge has granted additional time to put a case together, which is why you're still here. The detectives are taking today to build the case, Sam. Dotting the Is and crossing the Ts. You've got a few hours until you're called back in.' Davidson pauses and Sam opens his eyes and looks up. Only then does Davidson continue, his expression half sympathy, half pleading. 'Think about what I've said.'

The custody officer returns and Davidson stands, giving Sam a pat on the shoulder as he leaves.

Alone again, Sam thinks.

He's going to prison. He deserves to go to prison. And not just for what he did to Celia. It feels like he's been holding his breath from the moment he was arrested, waiting for someone to mention the house on Moorcroft Road.

It was a stupid thing to do. Reckless and yet so familiar. Sam couldn't even blame it on his desperation to get home at that point because it was before his mum's text. But Kev had finally got sick of him crashing on his sofa; he'd run out of friends and money and places to sleep and was facing a night on the street.

The house had appeared before him like a beacon. A neglected Victorian-style detached in deep-red brick, set back from the road. It had the look of a place that might have a wodge of cash under a mattress. A place that was empty.

Sam's pulse drummed in his ears as he knocked and waited. No answer. He walked round the block and tried again. Same result. In and out in five minutes just like all the other times back home, before he'd got caught anyway. Five minutes. That's all it would take, he told himself as he turned a blind eye to the promise he'd made his sister and jimmied up the kitchen window at the back.

The house was everything he'd expected. Grand on the outside, run-down on the inside. It was dated and dirty, neglected. The kitchen had beige swirl-patterned tiles on the walls and dark wood cupboards, installed in a decade long before Sam was born.

Sam was sure the rest of the house would be the same, just as he was sure that he'd find hidden cash somewhere. Under the mattress or in a biscuit tin behind the coffee mugs? Sam wondered, allowing himself a small smile as he stepped across the room.

The man appeared in the doorway before Sam could open a single cupboard. He was old. Like ninety or something. Tall, big once, but hunched over now and wearing red tartan pyjamas with a collar and buttons down the middle. He had a white beard, thinning grey hair and a brown walking stick.

'Oi,' he said. 'Oi, you. Get out. Get out.' His voice was raspy and loud and sent a jolt of panic straight into Sam's chest. He didn't mean to pick up the knife, but it was there on the draining board and then it was in Sam's hand and he was waving it about, telling the old boy to stay back.

The man's face drained of colour and he fell back against the worktop like he was fainting or something, and Sam took his chance and shoved by him, running straight out the front door.

It was aggravated burglary. And there's no way DC Sató wouldn't have connected the dots. The man would've described Sam's appearance. He'd have mentioned the knife too. So either the man didn't report it, which seemed unlikely, or he couldn't report it because he never got up after Sam rushed him.

Tears spill onto his cheeks. His chest tightens, every breath a short gasp.

He didn't kill Lucie, but he deserves to go to prison.

If he does what Davidson suggests and pleads guilty, maybe he will only get ten years. But if he pleads not guilty and they start to build a case, then maybe they'll connect him to the old boy in the PJs who Sam hadn't known was there. He wonders why they haven't asked him about it yet. Could the old bloke not have reported it? Or maybe his eyesight was rubbish.

It'll be twenty-five years at least if they do find out. Aggravated burglary and kidnap. The offer is a no-brainer, even Sam can see that.

But he didn't kill Lucie. And that feels important.

His despair hangs in the air. He can taste it in his mouth like the dust of the building sites. It doesn't matter what he decides to do now, his life is over. He broke his promise to Bee – the only person who loved him – and now she's dead.

Sam thinks his mum might have loved him once when he was little, maybe, but if she feels anything now, it's nothing more than a distant obligation. It was Bee who stood up for him. Bee stood up for everyone, for what she believed in. She never gave up on him or anything else.

He wishes she was here now so he could ask her what to do. Would she tell him to plead guilty and serve his time, go on to be something more for the rest of his life? Or would she tell him to stand up for himself for the first time in his life?

A door crashes shut somewhere along the row of cells. Someone cries out. A wailing kind of noise. Sam rests his head in his hands again, smelling the tang of the industrial soap on his skin and wishes Bee was here. As the time ticks on slowly, Sam thinks of the old boy and wishes a lot of things.

Tears flow hot and silent down my cold cheeks. I shiver again as much from the chill in the air as the ice running through my veins.

Lucie is dead.

The thought doesn't feel real and yet I can't stop repeating it in my mind.

I don't know how long I stand over her body. Seconds? Minutes? Time feels distorted.

If it wasn't for the sound of the traffic from the high street, the beeping of a delivery van reversing, bus doors opening with a whoosh, I would think it was the dead of night. How can it be only early evening? How can I have just been leaving work? My breath catches in my throat, a sharp gasp. The car park is empty of other cars, but that doesn't mean someone won't come out from one of the buildings, a shortcut on their way home.

I need to do something. I can't be seen like this.

Another sound slices through the darkness. Closer. I freeze as the engine of my car cuts out.

THIRTY-EIGHT

CELIA

In bed that night, my mind continues to race like the fairground ride Martin dragged me on once when we were dating. Fast and spinning, blurring the night, and sending a queasiness through me. There is too much going on, too many plates I'm trying to keep from crashing to the floor. Is it plates or balls? Or bowls? I can't think straight.

'They know,' Martin says from the other side of the bed.

I keep my back to him, ignoring the undisguised glee in his voice. I hate the fact that he's here, sitting so close, just a wall away from Henry.

It didn't used to be like this. For years and years, I had everything under control. Martin knew his place and he followed the rules, coming into the house only when I gave permission, only when Henry was out. It's another reason why the routines are so important. A schedule. A plan. It wasn't perfect and no way to live for either of us, but there was a point of no return long ago in the darkness of the garage, and this is all we have now.

But my ability to keep Martin in check has slipped away this week along with everything else – my routine, my ability to sleep, my moral compass. My sanity feels not far behind and I'm powerless to stop Martin.

'They might suspect, but they don't know,' I whisper. 'They can't know everything.'

I rub at my eyes but nothing can dispel the image of Lucie's body collapsed on the ground, that glassy stare; the tang of exhaust fumes clogging my senses. A cold chill floods through my veins, prickling at the skin of my forearms and then down my body, like I'm outside in a swimsuit in winter.

They can't know everything yet, I tell myself again. But how much digging would it take to discover that Martin disappeared thirteen years ago? Disappeared, not died. There had to be a distinction. Death meant questions asked. Disappeared meant no longer at this address. It meant I could tell people he'd run off with someone else.

But there's a trail somewhere leading back to me if someone felt inclined to look hard enough. Martin still has an accountancy business as a sole trader, after all. We wouldn't survive on my salary alone, especially with the money I've tucked away year after year after year for Henry's medical degree.

The business has a PO box address paid for out of an umbrella company account, but keep peeling back those layers and it will eventually lead back to Martin, to here. It only takes the police to ask for the company accounts to know that the money is all transferred to my personal account.

'What are you going to do?' Martin asks.

The exhaustion is a thick cloud over my thoughts, but there is a fear pulsing through me – tiny particles of panic rushing through my body, making sleep impossible.

'I can't leave.' I whisper the words to myself but Martin hears. He always does.

'No,' he agrees, 'there's no escape for you.'

'So I carry on. I keep lying.'

He grunts at that before falling quiet.

I must drift off at some point because I wake with a jolt – a knife to my side, a scream in my throat. With a shaking hand, I turn on the lamp. The room is empty.

From the bathroom, I catch the gush of water, indications that Henry is awake and getting ready for sixth form. I must drag myself up too. My head is full of voices. Martin's and DC Sató's, and Lucie's. Sam's too. I don't know how much longer I can do this.

Fridays are not a day I work at Citizens Advice. Fridays are for unlocking the garage. Fridays are for opening the laptop I keep hidden in there and answering emails from the handful of Martin's clients who've stuck by him.

It was surprisingly easy for Martin to disappear. His colleagues were more than happy to believe he'd run away. Reading between the lines, I did them a favour. He'd always been a bit handsy with the office women.

I created a new email address and contacted his clients, painting a picture of a move to the remote island of Anglesey, off the north-west coast of Wales. He proposed a method of remote working long before it was the done thing like it is now. He offered far lower rates if they stuck by him. The same accountancy job of managing their books and accounts he'd been doing for years, but cheaper.

Five clients said no, but three said yes and since then a few recommendations have come in and three is now ten. Ten clients that I manage on Fridays while Henry is out and thinks I'm cleaning and doing the washing.

And so it feels normal to be sitting at the kitchen table dressed in my usual Friday outfit – a floral green-and-pink top with loose grey trousers, a long grey cardigan. The waistband of my trousers rubs a little against my wound, but it's worth it to feel a small sense of normality.

I've showered today too. My hair is pinned back in its bun. My face is still pale, but a little mascara and some concealer hides the worst of it.

Henry is sitting opposite me, spooning Cheerios into his mouth, and staring at his phone. He knows I hate phones at the table, but perhaps, like Martin, he senses that I'm too weak to argue. When Henry is done, he stands and kisses me goodbye. I catch the scent of his deodorant and the sweet milky smell of the cereal.

'Have a good day,' I say, following him to the front door, where he hoists his school bag onto his back.

'You too. What will you do?' he asks, eying my outfit.

'The usual,' I reply. 'Just cleaning and changing the bedding. As best I can anyway,' I add with a hand to my side.

He nods, reaching for the door handle when he turns back to me. 'I think we should talk about what happened.' It's not a question and I find myself shrinking away a little at the directness of the statement. 'I heard what the detectives said.'

I shake my head. 'Something terrible happened and a man has been arrested and will be going to prison for a long time. There is nothing else to say.'

Henry fixes me with a look that is too adult on his features. It's the kind of look that tells me he knows better, but he opens the front door to leave and there on my doorstep for the third time in twenty-four hours are Detectives Sató and McLachlan.

They step aside and Henry gives them a winning smile, kisses my cheek again before striding away. I wish I could go with him. I wish I could slam the door shut and pretend I'm not in, but it's too late for that now.

DC Sató is wearing another power suit – charcoal grey with a blue striped shirt and silver cufflinks. It's the kind of outfit that would look good with high heels but she's wearing sensible flats, perfect for chasing down criminals, I imagine, although I notice the way she's favouring her right leg and pretending not to.

In contrast, DC McLachlan is wearing one of those jumpers with shirt collars and tails sewn in. Shumpers, Deborah calls them at work, always grinning as she says it as though she made up the word herself. DC McLachlan's face is make-up free again but there's something sparking in her eyes – anticipation, I think. Whatever it is, I don't like it.

'Hello again, detectives,' I say with all the smile I can muster. 'How can I help you today?' I open the door wide, gesturing for them to come in; readying myself for McLachlan and her awful tea, but neither detective moves.

'Some more... inconsistencies.' DC Sató pauses before the word inconsistencies, like she's thinking over her choices, like there might be another word that fits better and we all know what it is – lies. 'In relation to the picture we're building of Lucie's life in the run-up to her death.'

Fear flutters in my chest. What do they know? That question again, screaming in my head, crashing at the sides, desperate to be asked, shouted.

'What kind of inconsistencies?' I frown. 'I've already told you that before Tuesday night, I hadn't spoken to or seen Lucie for thirteen years. I'm not sure I can help.'

'And that is one of a few things you've said to us, Celia, that we'd like to continue talking about.'

'Come in then,' I say, but again they don't move.

'Actually, we'd like to continue our discussion at the station please, if you don't mind.'

'Not at all.' My tone is a notch higher than the breezy reply I was aiming for. 'When would you like me to come in?'

'Now. We can drive you.'

'Right.' My nod is too vigorous. 'Let me get my keys and my jacket.' I turn around, lost suddenly, overwhelmed. The last thing I need right now on top of a mind I can't keep straight and exhaustion and shock is to be wrong-footed, and I'm sure that's what they are aiming for – catching me off-guard.

What can they know?

Something. It has to be something. They wouldn't drag me to the police station at a moment's notice for nothing.

On the driveway, DC Sató opens the passenger door and motions for me to get in, and then we're driving out of the close, them in the front, me in the back, like a suspect. A criminal. I close my eyes, drifting unmoored, keeling.

I glance back at the house and for a moment I think I see Martin stood at the living-room window. I gasp and DC Sató follows my gaze, but we are already on the main road and there is nothing to see.

The car has that sickly pine freshener smell to it that claws at the back of my throat just like the exhaust fumes of my car that night. Images flash through my mind. Lucie standing in the damp darkness. My car ploughing towards her too fast. Her body hurtling to the ground.

A single tear traces down my cheek.

A door opens. Footsteps approaching.

'She's dead,' I whisper.

'Good.' The voice is harsh and scratchy. Goosebumps rage across my body. I look up and I'm hit with a thousand memories of a past I've tried so hard to forget.

I thought we were free. I thought we were safe. We'll never be either. I drop to my knees and weep for Lucie and for myself.

PART III

Facebook Messenger, 11 days before

Henry Watson

Are you the Lucie who used
to come to my house for tea
about thirteen years ago?

THIRTY-NINE

LUCIE

11 days before

Lucie blinks in the bright grey London daylight and stifles a yawn as the warmth of the lecture theatre is replaced by a welcome chill. It's the kind of cold that would normally make her want to shove her hands in her coat pockets, tuck her head down and hurry home to a steaming mug of tea in front of *Pointless* or curl up in bed with the latest Lisa Jewell novel. But she keeps her coat unzipped a while longer, glad for the goosebumps tickling her skin and the feeling of being shaken awake.

'That was—' she begins, raising her eyebrows as she turns to Jo.

'The most boring lecture in history,' Jo replies in her North London accent, making a face somewhere between exasperated and zombie-dead.

Lucie laughs. 'I was going to say intense, but your description works just as well.'

'At least it's the weekend now. And we're in the hospital observing on Monday,' Jo continues as they stroll across the square courtyard in the direction of the main road. 'Who are you working under?'

'Doctor Sheldon.'

'Lucky. I've got Doctor White,' Jo says with a groan.

'He's not that bad.'

'Correction,' Jo says. 'He's not that bad to you, because you're his star pupil.' Jo grins as she waves her hands in the air. 'Everyone, copy Lucie right now. She is right and you are all wrong.'

'Oi!' Lucie smirks at Jo's teasing and her friend's throaty cackle of a laugh before giving her a nudge with her elbow. 'He does not say that. You just have to read the suggested reading as well as the set pieces before his class.'

'I know, I know. And you know I love you, really.'

From across the quadrangle, a group of twenty or so students pile out of a lecture hall.

'First years,' Jo mumbles and Lucie nods. The group hurry by, on their way to their next lecture or more likely the Student Union bar. A boy straggles a few paces behind the group. As he passes by, he turns, flashing Lucie a wide smile that causes a blush to creep up her face.

'Someone has an admirer,' Jo says, her voice low in Lucie's ear.

'He was looking at you,' Lucie replies, glancing at her friend.

Jo is a head taller than Lucie and beautiful in that effortless kind of way with black Afro curls currently hidden beneath a mustard-yellow bobble hat. She's wearing a bright-red scarf around her neck, which should clash with her hat but just looks chic on Jo. She has flawless skin and eyes that always seem to be dancing with laughter or mischief.

She's muscular, too, from years on the River Thames with the women's rowing team, when she's not sat beside Lucie in the library or vegging with her on the sofa.

'He was not,' Jo says.

'Well, he's way too young for me.'

'You always say that.'

'Because it's true.' And it is. Lucie deferred her place at university for two years after her A levels so she could save enough money for the psychology degree and then the clinical doctorate at the prestigious King's College in the south of the city. She's always felt older than everyone else. Turning up on the first day of freshers week with that same sense of standing out, of being different, that she's felt her whole life.

Except for Jo, who is kind and silly – scrawling little biro cartoons of dogs on any scrap of paper she finds and leaving them around the house for Lucie and Natalie, their other house-mate. Dogs sleeping. Dogs eating, dancing in ball gowns, studying at the library, lying on a therapist's couch. Lucie has a whole drawer of them and they always make her smile.

'The age thing is just an excuse,' Jo says in a sing-song voice.

'An excuse for what?' Lucie rolls her eyes, knowing she won't like the answer.

'For the fact that you still see yourself as a flat-chested carrot-top goofy teen instead of the smoking-hot woman you are.'

Lucie laughs, her cheeks flushing as she wonders if Jo is right. She knows she's grown into her gangly limbs, which are now an athletic frame. Her freckles are still just as bright orange but the foundation she wears is thick and hides them well. And then there's her hair – her one luxury. Every six weeks, she goes to the salon on Brixton High Street and has her roots bleached and grey-blonde highlights added.

'Were we ever that young and stupid?' Lucie asks, changing the subject and nodding to the students now giving each other piggybacks across the grass, one of them knocking into the branch of an oak tree and toppling off in a fit of giggles.

'Yes.' Jo grins. 'But we were more refined.'

Lucie misses it. That buzz of finally starting out. The possibilities, the hunger, the drive she had. It's still there. She still wants to be a clinical psychologist more than anything in the world, but with only seven months until they qualify, that excitement is muffled by the weight of responsibility on her shoulders to help those patients she treats.

Lucie glances up at her friend and wonders if, beneath her playful teasing and easy-to-laugh manner, Jo feels that same pressure. She doesn't know how she'd have got through the last five years without Jo by her side.

Jo, who suggested they live together in their second year, finding a house for them a bus ride or walk away from campus and the library. Their friend Natalie joined them too and still lives in the house, despite dropping out in her third year. She trained as a chef instead and eventually landed a job at a Mayfair restaurant where she got both Lucie and Jo jobs as waiting staff.

Sometimes, Lucie lies awake at night, fizzing with an energy she can't explain, wondering where they'll be living next year, and the one after that. Whatever happens, she knows they'll always be friends.

A gust of wind buffets against them as they leave the shelter of the buildings and turn onto the main road. There's a long line of red buses in stationary traffic, the smell of diesel heavy in the air.

'Looks like we're walking home,' Jo says.

'After that bloke tried to chat us up on the bus yesterday, I'm more than happy to walk,' Lucie says, pulling her phone out of her pocket to check the time.

Jo gives a dramatic shiver. 'True. He was a creep. But we'd better get a wriggle on. We're working at seven and I need to iron my uniform and I've got to rewrite something for Doctor White.'

Jo launches into a rant about her report on a patient with

generalised anxiety disorder, but Lucie is only half listening. Her feet slow, then stop altogether. Someone shouts a 'Watch out' from behind her and an electric scooter zips by, but Lucie's focus is only on her phone and the Facebook Messenger app, the message on the screen from someone called Henry Watson.

> Are you the Lucie who used to come to my house for tea
> about thirteen years ago?

'Luce? You all right?' Jo asks from beside her.

'Yeah, sorry. Go ahead without me. I just need a minute.' Lucie's voice feels far away as thoughts of little Henry fill her head. She imagines five-year-old fingers tapping out the message and then almost laughs at herself. He'll be older now. Sixteen or seventeen, she guesses. Lucie taps on the profile picture at the top of the message and Facebook opens. The picture is a badge of a football team she's never heard of and the account is private.

'I'll wait for you,' Jo says, guiding Lucie out of the flow of people and e-scooters. 'What's up?'

'It's... I got a message from someone I used to know. It's just thrown me a bit.'

'A boy?' Jo asked with a waggle of her eyebrows.

'It's nothing like that. It's complicated. I don't know where to begin.'

They start to walk again and Lucie wants to explain about Celia and Henry and the summer when she was thirteen that she spent with them. And Martin too. Memories fly out of somewhere, draining the colour from her face, the energy from her legs.

They normally tell each other everything. Jo is the only person Lucie has told about her tendency to obsess over people and occasionally things, crying on her shoulder in the second year after Lucie followed a boy she'd been dating home one night, to check if he was cheating on her. He caught her and dumped her on the spot.

Lucie has worked hard since then to keep a check on the obsessive side of her personality. She knows it comes from insecurity, rearing up during exams. After another date in her third year ended with Lucie spending four hours trawling through his social media accounts, learning everything she could about him, she decided to swear off dating and focus only on her studies, despite Jo's encouragements.

And yet, Lucie can't find the words to tell Jo about Celia and Henry and Martin. Like a barrier is stopping her. It's guilt, maybe, Lucie thinks. She left Celia's house that day and never looked back.

They walk the rest of the way home in silence, Lucie lost in thought, Jo not pushing her to talk.

'Come on,' Jo says, nudging her as they reach the front door of their terraced house on the end of a long road of matching houses that back onto the overground railway line, two roads back from Brixton Road. 'I forgot my keys again. You'll have to let us in.'

Lucie opens the front door and catches the smell of cooked chicken. A second later, Natalie sticks her head out from the kitchen, waving a wooden spoon. 'Perfect timing,' she says. 'Thought you'd both need to eat before your shift. And before you ask, no, I haven't done the washing-up yet, but I will. There didn't seem any point when I was cooking anyway.'

The afternoon turns into evening. The streetlights flicker on outside, the grey sky now black. Lucie perches on the sofa between Jo and Natalie, scooping forkfuls of buttery new potatoes and chicken into her mouth while the others shout wrong answers at an ITV quiz show that Lucie is only half watching. She swaps her jeans and jumper for sheer tights and a black dress and jumps on the Tube with Jo as they head against the rush-hour traffic towards Central London.

She's going through the motions, barely there. Her mind is lost to Henry. How did he find her? Why has he messaged her? Now, after all this time. How is he? How is Celia? Question after question after question.

A nervous energy swarms inside her. She doesn't know any of the answers, but she wants to find out. Where's the harm in that?

She fires off a reply to Henry's message before stashing her bag into one of the lockers in the staff area. Then she takes a deep breath and finds her best 'I-deserve-a-big-tip' smile before heading to table nine to take their drinks order, but all the while her thoughts remain on Henry and what happened in that house all those years ago.

FORTY

CELIA

The silence in the police car is an oppressive beast – thickening and bruising with every passing minute. It's a struggle to breathe normally. My lungs feel as though they are screaming for more air.

I keep my head down, smoothing over the soft material of my green top with the pink flower print. My Friday top. Today is Friday. Later, Henry will sit at the table and revise biology. I will cook gammon and mash – Henry's favourite.

I cling to these thoughts like a security blanket, worn and paper-thin, but still Lucie pushes through.

It's true I didn't want her to leave the car park. I didn't want her to go to the police, but I didn't want her to die either. It's my fault she's dead. It was me who put her body in the boot of my car to take somewhere safe, hidden. I've done terrible things, but I didn't kill Lucie.

The silence continues. The only noise is the hum of the engine and the pounding of my pulse in my ears. I'm desperate to say something but then the concrete block of Hallford police station comes into view and I lose my nerve.

I've passed the station a thousand and more times in my life, but I've never paid much attention to the blue railings, the ramp, the glass doors. We pause outside and I see a woman sitting on the steps hunched over her phone. There are tears streaming down her face and I feel a pang of sympathy for whatever mess she's in. I want to call out, offer to help, but I'm hardly in a position to do so.

DC McLachlan flicks the indicator and we turn a corner, around to the back of the building and a car park filled with police cars and vans, and rows of unmarked cars.

We walk together across the car park, three in a line with DC Sató on my left and McLachlan on my right. The smell of cigarettes hangs in the air as we approach a thick silver door with a keypad on the side. My feet feel heavy and unmovable.

I didn't kill Lucie, but neither did Sam. The thought flashes in my mind and the guilt hits me hard – a roiling fire in the pit of my belly. Guilt for Lucie. Her blood is on my hands. Guilt for Henry and the mess I've dragged him into. And Martin too. Even after all this time, there is a pang for him. It keeps coming in that way that I think only women can understand.

My mouth fills with saliva and I swallow and swallow again, pushing it back with the words of my confession threatening to escape.

The moment we're inside, DC Sató guides me along a corridor, her hand firmly placed on my upper arm as though she thinks I'm a flight risk. I walk slowly, bending over a little, a hand clutched to my side, taking my sweet time. Gathering my strength for what is to come.

We turn down a long corridor with freshly painted walls and white ceilings, bright lights. There are doors on both sides of the corridor. Some with names. We pass a victim suite, and interview rooms eight, seven, six and five. We turn into an older part of the building with peeling blue paint and scuffed floors. Sató's grip on my arm tightens a fraction – a brief squeeze where it seems like she's leaning against me rather than guiding me. Then we're stopping and McLachlan is opening the door to interview room four, motioning for me to step inside.

'If you could wait in here, we'll be with you shortly,' McLachlan says, nodding to one of the chairs in the corner. The door shuts with a firm click and I wonder briefly if it's locked and what would happen if I tried to open it.

At least it's not a cell, I think, taking in the four grimy grey walls and a battered-looking table that takes up most of the room. I do as I'm told and sit on one of the plastic chairs facing the door. And I wait.

There's a clock on the wall – a black square with red numbers and a flashing colon. I stare at it until the minute changes from three to four and dab the edge of my finger on the perspiration forming on my upper lip. Where have they gone – DC Sató and her sidekick? It's a tactic – like bringing me here when we could have talked at the house; like the silence in the car and now this. It's all designed to unnerve me as though I'm not already unnerved, broken.

My thoughts begin to unravel like the black ribbon of an old cassette tape, pulled out, chewed up. I think of the lie I told PC Daniels in Leeds about Sam jumping in my car in the car park. A stupid error. It's made them distrust me. I should've thought of traffic cameras. I should've stayed closer to the truth.

Sam dominates my thoughts. Is he sitting in a cell somewhere nearby, or maybe another interview room? I wonder what we'd say to each other if we were sat together now.

He's bad, I remind myself. Evil. The kind of man who holds a knife to people's sides and forces them to do things. He might not have killed Lucie, but that doesn't mean he hasn't killed someone else.

The clock continues to flash. Blinking at me. I dab at my lip a second time and try to slow my breathing, slow the thumping beat of my heart. I have the sudden desire to pace up and down in the tiny space beside the table, but the black dome of a camera on the ceiling keeps me in my seat.

Minutes pass. Five then ten then twenty. Finally, the door opens and DC Sató steps into the room, DC McLachlan walking just behind. There is no cup of tea or water, no sympathetic smile this time. Another game. They don't want me comfortable, that much is certain. Fear prickles at my skin. It's not the same gasping panic of the car journey to Leeds, more a slow inescapable burn. I consider asking for a solicitor, but would that suggest I'm guilty of something?

The detectives settle in their seats, their movements slow and deliberate. They are telling me that they have all the time in the world. My pulse quickens again, a pummelling beat vibrating through me. I place my hands in my lap, sit back in my chair, feigning calm. Control. It's not about what I've done or what they suspect I've done. It's about what they can prove.

'I'm sorry to have kept you,' DC Sató begins with a tight smile.

'No problem.' I return her smile, resisting the urge to dab at the sweat on my upper lip again.

'The purpose of this interview is to record a formal statement of the events of Tuesday seventh of November. I'd like to start at the beginning with the phone call from Lucie Gilbert. We know from your phone records that this call took place at one minute past five.'

'You want me to go through it all again?' I ask. Relief is a cool ointment flooding through my veins. Is that it? Is that why I'm here? A formal statement.

'It's important to document the events formally now and I think you'll agree that there have been several inconsistencies in your story, Celia. I'm sure you can appreciate the importance of getting to the truth. A woman with a promising life ahead of her is dead, and a young man is under arrest on suspicion of her murder.'

'Good.' The word slips out and I regret it instantly. 'I mean, I'm glad he's been arrested. What happened to Lucie is awful,' I say, and the emotion choking my voice is real.

'Indeed,' Sató says. 'Would you mind if we record your statement, Celia? It's the best way to keep an accurate record.'

'Of course,' I say, my eyes flicking to a black recording device on the table.

And then we begin. I take them through every step of the evening, my fictional tale that feels so real. Except at night, when the truth seeps out and I hear that deafening thud of my car hitting Lucie's body, and Martin's mocking words: *This is your fault.*

Martin is right in some ways, but not completely. And if either of us should be feeling guilty for Lucie's death, it's him.

'Thank you,' Sató says when I'm done. She sits back in her seat and I think we're finished, but then DC McLachlan leans forward, pulling a piece of paper out of the folder in front of her.

My mouth turns bone dry; my vision blurs as I feel the lies wobbling like a Jenga tower, swaying from side to side, waiting to see if it will steady itself or tumble down.

'Last night I spoke to Lucie's housemate and best friend. She was very upset to hear of Lucie's death. And she has painted a very different picture of Lucie. Did you know for instance that Lucie was in her final year of studying for a doctorate in psychology at a university in London?'

I shake my head. Easy tears fill my eyes. A doctorate. So she was following her dreams after all. Psychology, not medicine. I wonder if I had a hand in that. Either way, I was wrong about Lucie. I thought she was trouble. That she'd done nothing with her life and now she was after money. I saw what I wanted to see that night.

The urge to drop my face into my hands and cry is almost overwhelming, but I clench my muscles and fight it, push it back, tuck it down. However much I cared for Lucie, she is gone. I can't bring her back. I must think of myself now, and Henry.

'Lucie's friend was very surprised when we asked her if she knew of any trouble Lucie was in. She was adamant that Lucie was top of the class. She had a good job working at a restaurant in Mayfair and was careful with her money. There was only one thing this friend could think of that would have caused her a problem. And that was you.' DC McLachlan's words are delivered matter of fact as though this is any other update, a sharing of information, but her face is set in a hard mask that sends another bolt of fear through my body.

'Me?'

A nod from DC McLachlan.

'I can't think why. Perhaps this friend misunderstood.'

'Lucie's phone was broken beyond repair.' DC McLachlan continues as though I've not spoken and I feel another whoosh of relief. 'We're waiting for access to her cloud to see her messages, but in the meantime Lucie's friend's phone was absolutely fine. She showed us a message Lucie sent her. Would you like me to read it out?'

'By all means,' I say. Inside I scream a 'No'.

DC Sató shuffles through the papers in the file in front of her and takes out a single piece of paper. She looks at it for a moment and then lifts her gaze to me as she reads out the message. '"If anything happens to me, it was Celia!"' She pauses for a beat, lets the words settle around us. 'Can you think of any reason why Lucie would have sent that message to her friend?'

The silence that follows is charged – electric. The eyes of the detectives burn my face. I feel myself flailing – the Jenga tower finally tumbling.

Facebook Messenger, 11 days before

Lucie Gilbert

Hi, Henry, yes it's me!
Good to hear from you.
Hope all is well :-)

Henry Watson

I'm OK thanks.
I'm looking for my dad.
Do you know where he is?

FORTY-ONE

LUCIE

10 days before

I'm looking for my dad.

The message arrived shortly after Lucie had pressed send but it wasn't until her break – five minutes to nip to the toilet and glug back some water – that she saw it and now those five words circle her thoughts as she smiles at the Lush clientele in their designer clothes and glittering jewellery, taking orders of beetroot-infused noodles and tuna tartare, and the chef's special for the evening – braised beef ragu.

Do you know where he is?

The question is a constant prod in her mind as she tops up glasses and walks back and forth to the kitchen a hundred times and more. It sticks in her thoughts as she, Jo and Natalie pile into an Uber at 1 a.m., too drained to talk beyond moaning about their sore feet and comparing their tips for the night. At home, Lucie strips off her clothes, pulls on her PJs and falls into bed without bothering to wash away the thick layer of make-up she always wears to work, as much a part of the uniform as the black dress and sheer tights.

She closes her eyes and the message flitters into the oblivion of exhaustion and sleep, returning – a pestering alarm in her head – to shake her awake at 6 a.m.

I'm looking for my dad. Do you know where he is?

Lucie turns over in bed and stares into the dark gloom of her room. There's enough light from the street outside to make out the wall of built-in wardrobes and the desk in the corner, piled high with the psychology textbooks that used to sit on the shelf above her bed, until the weight of them broke the brackets and the whole thing collapsed.

There's a wintry chill to the room, almost damp-like, that makes her pull her duvet up to her chin. It's another hour before the heating clicks on – a thirty-minute burst that barely takes the edge off the biting cold, but it's all they can afford on top of the rent.

Lucie hates the winter months in this house. Sometimes, first thing, when she's awake but her eyes are still closed, she thinks she's back in the single bed of her mum's old flat and feels an inexplicable need to get up, get out, study harder, longer.

With a long sigh, she throws off the covers. She doesn't want to be awake yet, but she is, and there's nothing she can do to stop Henry's question from playing over in her mind and the answer from forming.

Yes. I think I do.

Lucie hasn't thought about Celia much over the years. The day after she ran out of their house, she threw herself into her coursework and revision, finishing school with all A grades. It was only during a counselling module in her second year at university that Lucie began to think about that summer. 'You can't be a clinical psychologist and unpick the complexities of other people's lives without first unpicking what makes you

you,' her tutor said – a woman with floaty skirts and thick horn-rimmed glasses that always made Lucie think of the wolf in *Little Red Riding Hood. All the better to see you with.*

And so Lucie dutifully looked back at her childhood and the neglect she felt but hadn't understood when she was young. The physical – the lack of nutrition, of basic care needs – and the emotional too.

She knows that neglect now manifests itself in certain aspects of her personality, like her ability to obsess over stupid things – Walnut Whips, fitness trackers, the effect of climate change... each month something always seems to grab her.

She can be clingy and jealous too, which is why she's been single since the guy who dumped her for following him.

Her mother was the root of her neglect, but then along came Celia like a fairy godmother, giving Lucie everything she was missing – stability, nutrition, love, support. Lucie thrived on it. Positively basked in it. In those months, she shed the self-doubt and insecurities, as though Celia's belief in her solidified into something real. Even after she ran away from Celia's house that day, she'd kept hold of that belief, the determination to succeed, dogged tunnel vision.

But Lucie hasn't thought about Henry at all until yesterday. That sweet little boy with brown hair and the whispered make-believe games. He almost felt like a little brother, until she turned her back on him, left him in Celia's controlling grasp.

It was self-preservation, Lucie thinks now with a pang of guilt that hits her gut.

She shivers beneath the duvet, remembering the absolute certainty she felt standing in Celia's kitchen. She had been so sure that Celia had killed Martin and buried him in the garden. And what had she done with that information? She'd run home, thrown herself into bed and the next morning, when she'd woken up, none of it had seemed real.

She convinced herself that no one would believe her, convinced herself she'd been wrong, and so she pushed Henry and Martin into a cupboard in the back of her mind and she shut the door.

Looking back, it's hard to know what really happened to Martin. Henry wasn't the only child with an active imagination. Lucie was only thirteen. She'd spent most of her childhood lost in books, re-reading *Matilda* until she knew entire chapters word for word. Moving on to John Grisham, Stephen King and Dean Koontz. How had reading about dead bodies, buried secrets and horror affected her reasoning? Isn't it possible she completely misread the situation?

More importantly, what does she do now? Henry's question has flung open the door in her mind to that part of her life, and although there's a part of her that wants to kick it shut again, she won't. She's not a teenager anymore. If there's even the slightest possibility that those long-forgotten suspicions are real, then she needs to do something.

She showers and pulls on a pair of jeans and a burgundy hoody two sizes too big, with sleeves that fall over her hands and a soft fleece layer inside. She snuggles into it before padding silently downstairs, picking up her bag, slipping on her parka and stepping out into the dark street.

Despite the early hour on a Saturday, there is still traffic on the main road. She can hear the hum of it as she walks down the residential street towards the high street.

She walks on auto-pilot to the twenty-four-hour café on Denmark Hill that serves huge cafetières of coffee and doesn't mind Lucie studying at a table in the corner until the library opens. And yet the moment she catches the scent of bacon and eggs in the air, she knows she won't go in today.

A bus pulls up at the stop beside her and without any thought to her plans, Lucie hops on. She makes her way across

London to Liverpool Street station. She buys a train ticket at the machine inside the huge glass-domed building and within an hour is making her way back to Hallford, to Henry, and all the while one question gnaws at her thoughts – did Celia kill Martin?

FORTY-TWO

CELIA

There's a ringing in my ears. A dread in the pit of my belly. The detectives stare, waiting for me to speak, to explain why Lucie – a young woman who wasn't troubled at all but had her life together, everything to live for – would text her best friend a warning about me.

My mind is empty. A blank space. A void. I have nothing. No answer to give. No lie to tell.

Tears swim in my vision. I really did think Lucie's life must have been a mess. Why else had she come to me for money? I try to swallow but the rock of emotion is lodged deep in my throat.

'You are the horrible one. You are evil.' Her voice was angry, desperate. I couldn't understand why she'd think that unless... unless she was in some kind of trouble and looking for help.

Oh, Lucie. You poor girl. Why did you come to see me?

I clear my throat, then cough. The effort tugs at my abdominal muscles, sending a shot of pain out from my wound that makes me wince.

'I'm sorry,' I say. 'Could I have a glass of water please?'

Sató nods. 'Of course.' If she knows I'm trying to delay my answer, she doesn't show it. A moment later she stands and leaves the room, returning in under a minute with a bottle of water and a plastic cup.

'Thank you.' My hand shakes as I pour the water into the cup. Droplets drip onto the table – tiny puddles betraying my nerves. I take a sip, holding the water in my mouth a moment too long as I fight to swallow down the emotion still blocking my throat.

'So, Celia,' McLachlan says, 'the text Lucie sent – "If anything happens to me, it was Celia!" – why do you think she would send that, if, as you say, she came to you for help?'

I shake my head. 'I... er... don't know. I'm sorry, but I'm completely baffled. Before Tuesday, I... I hadn't spoken to Lucie for thirteen years.' The truth for once. 'You've got my phone – you can check. There's no passcode on my phone.'

'We have,' Sató says, looking down at her notes.

'Did Lucie tell her friend anything else?' I ask, panic flittering through my veins. 'I wish I could help you,' I say when it's clear neither of the detectives is going to answer my question, 'but I'm really tired. As you can imagine, I'm having trouble sleeping after my kidnap. If there's nothing else, perhaps we could talk again tomorrow?'

McLachlan looks as though she's about to nod but Sató speaks first. 'We understand and we don't want to cause you any undue distress, but I do have a few more questions.'

I bite back a scream. Beneath the table my hands close into two fists. The air in the room is suddenly stifling. I wonder if the air-con has been turned off. Another game. 'I really can't help you when it comes to Lucie. What possible reason could I have for hurting her?'

'That's a question we'd very much like to know the answer to,' Sató says, leaning forward, pen flicking between her fingers.

'I've told you, I've no idea what Lucie was doing that night or why she was scared, why she asked for money or why she wanted me to take her to Springfield Road.' Sweat is collecting beneath my breasts, dampening my bra, and I fight the urge to pull down the wires digging into my skin.

'I wonder, Mrs Watson,' Sató says, 'can you tell us where we might be able to find your husband – Martin Watson?'

The sudden change of direction prods at my side as sharp as Sam's knife. 'Martin? You want to speak to Martin?'

'Yes,' Sató says. 'You said when we spoke yesterday that you haven't seen or heard from your husband for years. Do you know where he is?'

A flush pours into my face. 'No,' I lie. Martin's presence in my room last night flits into my thoughts. I shove it away, block it off as though the detectives might be able to see the image playing in my eyes. 'He... he wasn't a nice man,' I say, filling the silence and catching a sympathetic look from DC McLachlan.

'When did you last have contact with him?'

'Gosh,' I exhale as though trying to remember. 'It was a long time ago. He left when Henry was five, I think. He'd had enough of family life. He called a few times after he left but then nothing. I always assumed he'd got himself a new life somewhere.' The lies continue to burn on my face.

'It's quite unusual to disappear, though, don't you think?' Sató pushes.

'I'm... er... not sure what you mean.'

'To leave his wife and young son and his job. Here one day, gone the next. It's actually not that easy to do, you know. I had a quick look for him and it really is very peculiar. I spoke to Timpson and Gough, the accountancy firm I believe he last worked at. They said they hadn't seen or heard from Martin Watson since 2010. Thirteen years ago.'

She knows. The realisation sucks the air from my lungs.

'I think,' I say, doing everything I can to keep my voice

steady, 'that is the point of doing a runner though, isn't it? For someone not to be found.'

'Yes, I guess you're right. It's interesting that Martin did a runner, as you say, exactly the same number of years ago that you last saw Lucie. Quite a coincidence, don't you think?'

Tears fight to break free. Anger and hurt and guilt – a gale, a torrent. The emotions I've kept bottled up, screwed down tight all this time.

'That's all it is. A coincidence. The summer ended, Lucie grew up a bit and stopped coming for tea. My husband left me. Of course, if you do manage to track him down, please let me know. I'm very interested to discuss backdating child support payments.' It's a step too far. I see it the moment the words are out of my mouth. I see the business account. The payments to my personal account. I'm digging myself a hole. A grave.

'What does Martin have to do with any of this?' I ask, trying to push on from the words I can't take back. 'I thought you wanted to talk about Tuesday, which I've done. I really am very tired and would like to go home now.'

'Of course.' Sató nods, collecting the file on the table.

The movement sends a shaky relief through me. It's over.

'We're just trying to build a full picture of Lucie's life. I'm sure you can understand that we don't want to miss anything.'

I nod and the detectives stand.

DC McLachlan leads me through a warren of corridors and I find myself pushing through a door into the main entrance of the station. 'Are you sure you don't want a lift home?' she asks.

I shake my head and smile. 'Thank you but I'm sure you have a lot more important things to do. I'm happy to get a taxi.'

She nods and leaves me to step through the automatic doors. A blustery wind hits me from the side, threatening to sweep me right off my feet. That toppling Jenga tower again, except it's not my lies that threaten to tumble now, it's me.

Facebook Messenger, 10 days before

Henry Watson

Sorry if my last message was weird!
I should've explained that I haven't
seen my dad since I was five.
I barely remember him to be honest.
But I recently found your name written
down in the back of an old book
and it made me think that maybe
you might remember something.
Sorry!!
My mum doesn't like to talk about it
so I don't have anyone I can ask.
I'm rambling now so I'll go. I'm
sure you don't have a clue what
I'm talking about which is completely fine!
Sorry for disturbing you.

FORTY-THREE

LUCIE

10 days before

Celia's house looks the same as Lucie remembers, right down to the green of the laurel bush in the front garden and the red front door beyond. She can just catch a glimpse of that red from her position on the corner of the road by the street sign. A green dog bin has been added to the grass verge since Lucie was last here. There's a bag sticking out the lid. She keeps her distance, glad for the wintry chill keeping the smell at bay.

She stares at the house and feels a strange sense of stepping back in time. It's mixed in with something else – nostalgia – a longing for something she no longer has, a kind of innocence, but there is something uncomfortable about the feeling too. And yet she can't help think that there's something sinister about the house now. The way it sits facing out onto the road. Alone. No one to peek in, to see what might be going on inside. The thought makes her shiver.

Should she be here? The message replays in her mind.

I'm looking for my father. Do you know where he is?

It would be so easy to say no. To wish Henry luck in his

search and carry on with her life. But then the other message came through, all garbled and apologetic and Lucie knows she won't do that. She has grown up never knowing her father. And while she knows she's OK, she can't pretend there hasn't been a missing piece to her life. Even if her dad is the deadbeat loser her mother always told her he was, it would still be nice to have a name, a photo, something to connect to the fifty per cent of her DNA that she shares with him.

She could have a whole extended family out there that she doesn't know about. Grandparents and uncles and aunts. Cousins and half siblings even. It's a wishful daydream Lucie works hard to keep in check.

A few summers ago, she tried to track down the fair that came to town all those years ago. She badgered her mum for a name and a description, getting nothing more than a sighed eye roll and a 'Don't waste your time, Luce.' But she had anyway. Emailing Hallford Council and then the library and the local paper, and spending hours scrolling websites. Late nights. Early mornings. It became one of her obsessions.

She found nothing. Travelling fairs from the nineties don't exactly have a big online footprint. In the end, Jo had given Lucie the talking-to she needed, reminding her that the present and the future mattered more than the past, and Lucie had thrown herself back into her studies.

So Lucie knows all too well the grating sense of not knowing. But what she doesn't know is how it would feel if someone told her that her father was dead. Would it stifle the daydream once and for all or would it just open a whole abyss of questions?

And how can she tell Henry she thinks his dad is dead without telling him how she knows? It's the first thing he'll ask, and that's on top of the fact that Lucie isn't even sure of how much she remembers.

Whatever she does next, one thing is certain – she can't just blurt out her suspicions on Messenger. She needs to talk to Henry. She needs to see how he's doing.

Lucie starts to walk, following the pavement down towards the house. Her heart starts to race as she draws nearer. What is she going to say? What does she think is going to happen? The question makes her falter. Reassess. She can't knock on Celia's front door on a Saturday morning to tell a teenage boy she hasn't seen for over a decade that his dad is buried in the garden. And what if Celia answers – what then?

Lucie spins around, one foot almost tripping over the other as she hurries back to the street.

She's almost at the road sign when there's a noise behind her. The bang of a door closing. Lucie throws a glance over her shoulder and watches a boy step out from behind the laurel bush and onto Celia's driveway.

He's tall and slender, wearing a white Aran knitted jumper and a navy coat. It has to be Henry, Lucie thinks, making her way to the edge of the close before crossing the main road, uncertain where she's going or what to do next. She's come all this way, given up a day of study. What harm is there in saying hello?

In seconds, Henry is out of the road too and striding along in the direction of town. He doesn't look to have seen her. Lucie follows, her heart jittering a little.

Henry walks fast, head down, holding the straps of his backpack as though its contents is heavy. They approach the edge of town and she jogs a little to keep up, worrying she'll lose him in the shopping crowds.

The high street has changed since she was last here. The large department store sits empty, the windows cloudy white. The paving stones have been replaced with cobbled stones with two long strips of flat pavement where mobility scooters and pushchairs weave around each other. Lucie spots a Hotel

Chocolat and makes a mental note to buy something for Jo and Natalie before she leaves.

They reach the end of the high street and Henry ducks up a narrow walkway of boutique shops – a jewellers and an art gallery, and then it's the bus station with the stink of petrol in the air and people looking cold, waiting in silent queues. And suddenly Lucie knows exactly what's in Henry's backpack – books. He's going to the library.

It's the same glass structure she remembers, right down to the lime-green doors and the display of Must Reads just beyond the checkout desk. Her feet slow. She takes in the familiar smell of books and the soft murmur of voices and it feels a little like coming home. She thinks of all the books she's borrowed from this place and the worlds it opened up to her in the four walls of her bedroom. And even though she reads on her Kindle now, she still has the urge to check out a dozen books and lug them home like a magpie with its shiny treasure.

Lucie smiles to herself, but when she pulls her eyes away from the books, Henry is gone. She hurries forward, looking down the aisles and at the lime-green armchairs and then the children's corner with its bright Snakes and Ladders rug, but he's nowhere. She turns around again, wondering if he could've left already. The jittery feeling returns and she doesn't know why.

Then she spots the staircase and the sign pointing up – Computers, Reference Books, Study Area. Her feet tap the stairs in rhythm with her heart and when she throws open the glass door she finds more book shelves holding thick red and green volumes of encyclopaedias now old and outdated; no match for Google.

Straight ahead of her is a bank of computers. Each one is busy. Two elderly women bunch around one. Another has a student type, another a young mum, rocking a pushchair with her foot as she types.

Beyond the computers are groups of tables and chairs – empty apart from one. She's found him.

Henry's head is bent, forehead resting on the palm of one hand, while the other writes slowly in a notebook. Every minute or so he looks at the textbook in front of him before putting pen to paper again.

Lucie hesitates for a second and then moves to a bookshelf, pretending to browse as she watches Henry work. Her gaze fixed, unable to look away.

His message plays again in her thoughts.

She thinks again of the five-year-old boy she cared for. A minute passes and then she finds herself moving forward. He looks up as she approaches, his eyes staring straight into hers, and Lucie knows there is no going back.

FORTY-FOUR

CELIA

The lies echo in my head. So many lies.

I should never have told DS Sató that Martin called me after he left.

'They might be able to access phone records from back then,' Martin says, reading my thoughts.

He's been sitting on the edge of the bed for hours now. I've given up trying to get him to leave as the thick sludge of exhaustion seeps into every corner of my mind.

'Maybe,' I whisper. I keep my body turned away, but I can smell him – that metallic smell mixed with his body odour. I wish he wasn't here. I wish I'd run away when I had the chance; thrown some clothes into a bag for me and Henry and gone all those years ago when he was unconscious on the kitchen floor.

I thought it was impossible, but nothing could've been harder than this. And there's nothing I can do to make him leave. We are both trapped in our lies.

I think of Henry, and my chest squeezes in on itself, crushing. He was sullen tonight. I saw suspicion in his eyes when he looked at me.

'This is all your fault,' I say. 'You created this mess we're in. You killed her.'

'How much does the boy know?' Martin asks, ignoring my accusation.

'More than I'd like, but I can't exactly ask him, can I?'

'You said he didn't remember Lucie.' Martin's tone is accusing. Beneath the covers, my hands form two fists.

'I might have been wrong.'

'You've been wrong about a lot of things, it seems.' His comment hits where it hurts, where he intended. 'You know nothing.'

I was wrong about Lucie. She was following her dreams. She was going to be a doctor. She looked so wild that night, hair blowing in the wind, clothes wrinkled and damp-looking. But I should've known she'd make it without my help, although I like to think I still had a hand in it.

That night in the car park twists and coils in my thoughts. The real version and then the lies I've spun to the police, over and over until it's something else entirely – a grotesque nightmare I'm desperate to wake from. Except, I'm not asleep.

My heart beats so hard against my ribs, it feels like my chest will crack open.

What have I done?

My mind unravels as I think of the choices I made that brought me here. Which turn was a dead end? Should I never have picked up the phone to Lucie that night? No. She'd have found me anyway – the trouble would've come.

I didn't want her to die.

The guilt is a razor blade slicing my insides. It's in my blood too – splinters of glass. But Lucie's death had to happen. I see that now. It was the only way to save us – to protect Henry and the life I've built for him. Maybe it was always going to happen – Lucie coming back into my life and then her death. Events were set in motion long before I picked up the phone and agreed to meet her.

And it wasn't putting her in the boot of my car either that led me to this corner of hell, because I had to get her away from the office car park and any connection to me.

So was it Sam? Should I have rolled the dice and hoped he'd let me live when we reached our destination? Could I have driven away from that nightmare journey, dumped Lucie's body somewhere in Leeds and gone home again? But the terror. I still feel it now, clutching at me. That absolute certainty that I was going to die, and Henry would be all alone in the world.

Tears spill from my eyes, sliding down my face and onto my pillow. I try to ignore Martin; I try to sleep. Everything will be clearer if I could just sleep.

The small hours of the night wrap themselves around me, tight and uncomfortable. There is no sleep. No rest. As dawn approaches, I cry again, pathetic, half-hearted sobs.

I can blame Martin all I want, but I played my part. Lucie is dead because of me too. A beautiful life ended too soon.

The guilt becomes all-consuming, eating me alive from the inside out. I can't go on like this.

An idea starts to worm its way into my mind. A realisation. It's the guilt that is keeping me in this hell. The lies too. So many lies for so many years. But there is a way out – I could confess. I gasp as the thought takes hold.

I see myself walking to the police station, sitting in that grimy little room and allowing the guilt to spill out of me. 'I am the reason Lucie is dead. It wasn't Sam. It was me.'

Yes. That's it. That's the answer.

I thought I was saving us – Henry and me – when I dragged Lucie's body to the boot of the car and hefted her in. She was already dead, I reasoned. What good would going to prison do when Henry needed me?

But Henry is not a little boy anymore. He's eighteen next

month. I need to face the truth – I've done all I can to protect him and keep him safe. It won't be easy for him, and the thought of not seeing him every day, of not knowing where he is or what he's doing, fills me with unspeakable dread, but I will live with it. It will be easier than this guilt, this hell. All these secrets I've been holding on to so tight.

A dizzying lightness takes hold in my head. How have I stayed quiet all these years? A sob escapes and then another and another. My body shakes with the tears and the relief pouring out of me. I will go to the police station as soon as it's light. I will tell them everything. Almost everything, I correct.

The thought is soothing and I fall into a listless sleep, jolting awake to find Henry in the doorway, holding a cup of tea. He smiles at me and moves around the bed with no sign of the sullenness that clouded him yesterday. I wonder if he was lying awake last night too, thinking and planning for himself.

'I thought you might like a cup of tea in bed,' he says.

'Thank you, darling,' I reply, my voice croaky.

'How are you feeling?'

'Tired. I didn't sleep well again.'

'I thought I heard you talking to someone,' he says, and my body tenses. I try not to react. 'I worried the police had called you.' His eyes fix on me then flick to the landline receiver by the bed.

I swallow and push myself up on my pillows. 'I was just muttering to myself.'

'Right.' He gaze remains on me. 'What are you doing today?'

'The usual,' I reply. 'Some shopping and then cooking this afternoon. I'll get a taxi to the supermarket.'

He shakes his head. 'I'll do the shopping, Mum. You need to rest.'

I stare at my darling boy. His face is earnest but determined.

I want to protest. Saturdays are for food shopping and batch cooking. It's all I have. I'm falling apart without my routines.

'Mum' – Henry raises his eyebrows like he knows what I'm thinking – 'I'm doing the shopping. I've got your bank card right here.' He taps the back pocket of his jeans. 'Oh, and here.' He places a white box on the bed. 'I got you a new phone. It's all set up with the same number and everything.'

'What?' I stare at the box and then Henry. 'How?'

'I called the phone company. You've got insurance for loss and theft. I told them it was theft and gave them the crime number that detective wrote on the card that's in the living room. They didn't want to speak to me as I'm not the account holder but the woman in the call centre had a son my age and she felt sorry for us. This just got delivered. I'm going to take care of you now, Mum,' Henry continues. 'You've taken care of me all these years and now it's my turn.'

I find myself nodding and Henry seems happy and turns to leave. He's grown so much over the last few months, filled out from a gangly teenager to something more manly. I stare at the profile of his back and catch my breath. He really does look so much like Martin.

Fear is an ugly beast that looms just above my head, ready to swoop down, and I remember the plan I made last night and what I must do this morning. It's the only way to really be free – from my secrets and lies, from Martin. I see that now.

FORTY-FIVE

LUCIE

10 days before

Something sparks on Henry's face – a questioning recognition where his lips part and one eyebrow raises, and Lucie thinks of her Facebook profile picture that surely he would've looked at, the same way she tried to look at his.

The hush of the library feels suddenly too intense, like the shelves of books are holding their breath, waiting to see what will happen next. The air is stuffy and warm, just like the lecture theatres. It makes her want to spin around and rush out into the cold fresh air.

For a fleeting moment, she regrets stepping forward. It didn't feel real up to now, the following, the watching – a game. He could've been any teenage boy. Now up close, his eyes on her and his expression lifting, he is little Henry. A grown-up version, but that boy with the warm chubby hands and the endless games of Lego is still there; she can see him.

'Lucie?' he asks as he moves, chair scraping against the wood flooring. And then he's standing up, towering over her, still the question on his face, but there's a nervousness to him too.

She nods and closes the gap between them, moving to stand by the chairs on the opposite side of the table. 'Hi.' She smiles, wanting to tell him how much he's grown, changed, but she keeps it in.

There's a moment between them where they both pause, awkward and uncertain how to move forward. Lucie makes the first move, pulling out the chair and sitting down. Henry sits too, leaning his body towards her. There's a biro in one hand and he chews the end for a second before pressing it to his chin instead.

'Hi,' he says again, making her smile with the nervous energy radiating from him. She's about to say hello again too when he continues. 'I didn't... I mean, I just messaged you and now you're here.' He tilts his head to one side, a silent question of how and why. It's the same inquisitive glance she remembers from little Henry. 'How did you know I'd be here?'

She hesitates a moment. 'I went to your house—'

'You saw my mum?' His voice is a hissed whisper, urgent, scared maybe, Lucie thinks, and she gives a quick shake of her head.

'I didn't really have a plan,' she says. 'I went to the house just out of curiosity, I think, and then I saw you and sort of followed you here.'

He gives a relieved nod like it's the most reasonable thing in the world to stalk someone through town. 'I can't believe it's you.' He scrunches up his face. 'I sort of remember you, but it's a bit vague in my head. I thought you had red hair.' He gives an awkward smile.

Lucie reaches to touch the bleached ends of her ponytail. 'I did. But I got sick of being called carrot top,' she says, and he huffs a laugh.

They fall silent. It's awkward again. Lucie wonders how

they go from this to talking about his dead father buried in his garden. It's too hard, too much. She can't tell him. She was a fool for ever thinking she could. There's another pang inside her – this one a longing to be back in London, sharing a bag of Quavers with Jo, watching reruns of *Frasier*. She should get back. She's working at Lush tonight.

'You wanted to know—' she starts to say at the same moment as Henry speaks.

'Where do you—' he says.

They laugh. And she motions for him to go first.

'Do you still live around here?'

'No. I'm in London now. I'm studying clinical psychology. I haven't been back here for years. My mum married a bloke from Southend and lives there now.'

'Oh, wow. Which university? I'm going to apply to a few London ones.'

'King's College.'

'No way. That's my first choice.'

'Really? What do you want to study?'

'Medicine.'

Lucie makes a noise, a soft 'huh'. 'Your mum must be pleased.'

'Yeah. She is.' Something in Henry's face changes at the mention of Celia. His eyes flick to the door as though he's expecting her to burst through it. It's the same spark of some-thing she saw a moment ago when he'd asked if she'd spoken to Celia. It's the same look she remembers from thirteen years ago when Henry would get excited and giggle or shout and then clamp his hands over his mouth, eyes always darting to the doorway.

A sinking sensation drags Lucie down. She remembers Celia's backhanded compliments about how she should wear her hair, how she should talk or chew her food. The prying way she wanted to know every minute detail of Lucie's day and how happy Lucie had been to share it, thinking it was interest. Kindness.

But there was a part of Lucie that has always wondered, right up until a few moments ago, if she'd misunderstood, got it all wrong. If she'd misremembered. If the memories had warped in her mind, if she could trust what she felt.

Seeing Henry's face, she knows she wasn't wrong. Celia is still that same controlling woman she remembers. Then another thought strikes her. If those memories were right, then what does it mean for the ones about Martin?

'Why did you stop coming for dinner?' he asks, shaking Lucie from her thoughts. His words come out in a rush as though he's been wanting to ask them for thirteen years.

It would be easy to lie. To make an excuse about studying and her own mum wanting her home, but there's something so hollow and desperate in Henry's expression that Lucie doesn't want to lie. She's never been any good at it anyway.

'There were a few reasons,' Lucie says. 'At first I was really grateful to your mum for inviting me for tea and paying me attention, but then I started to feel like...' Her voice trails off.

'It got a bit much?' Henry prompts.

'Yes. She wanted me to wear my hair a certain way and do things her way. Stupid stuff, I guess, but I don't know, I wasn't her daughter, so I just stopped coming.' There's more she needs to say. So much more, but it's a start.

Henry nods, chewing on his lower lip. 'She has always liked her routines.'

'I remember that. Certain clothes on certain days.'

Henry huffs a laugh. 'She still does that.' He looks down at his own jumper, the smile dying on his lips. 'These are my Saturday clothes.'

'She was quite controlling,' Lucie says, voice gentle, probing.

He looks up at her then, eyes wide, and slowly he nods. 'Yeah. She still is.'

Another silence. Lucie watches an elderly man shuffle down the aisles, stopping at the philosophy section and running his hands along the books. He doesn't take one, just stands there, as though absorbing wisdom through proximity.

'What were the other reasons you stopped coming?' Henry asks.

'Huh?'

'You said there were a few reasons.'

Her gaze returns to Henry. He is looking at her with such expectancy, such hope that the truth feels like a crushing weight pinning her to the ground. 'You wanted to know about your dad,' she says, her voice low.

'Yeah.' His face brightens.

'Why did you think I'd know anything?' she asks.

Henry's face flushes. 'I don't really know. I was just this little kid when he left.'

'Five years old.'

'Yeah, exactly. I know my memories are probably all muddled up, but I remember everything being normal. Mum and Dad together. I remember you coming for dinner a lot, and then in my head, it's like everything stopped at the same time. It's hard to explain. It's more like a feeling. I know that sounds weird.'

Lucie shakes her head. 'It's not weird at all. It's exactly what happened. I only met your dad once in all the times I was there. It felt to me – and bear in mind that I was only thirteen myself – but it felt like Celia was keeping me away from him. Then once, when I was babysitting, he came home early.' She pauses. Swallows. She's breathless and doesn't know why. 'You used to love playing Lego,' she says, aware she's swerving into a different conversation, but she's not ready to talk about Martin yet.

To her relief, Henry laughs. 'I got really into it when I was, like, ten. Whole Lego worlds and all the Technic stuff.'

'So a proper nerd then?' Lucie laughs quietly.

They carry on talking in low voices, remembering the games they played and then sharing details about the years since. It's easy. Natural. Like that summer thirteen years ago has connected them somehow.

'Were you still coming for tea when my dad left? Do you know where he was planning to go?'

The atmosphere between them changes. Lucie nods. 'You were right. I stopped coming for dinner the week after.' She stops herself from saying any more. She can't say the week after he left because it isn't true, but she doesn't want to tell him the truth now either. It's been nice to see Henry again, but once she tells him her suspicions, everything will be tainted.

'I knew it,' he says, his voice loud in the quiet of the library. The man by the philosophy section turns sharply to stare. Henry drops his voice to a whisper. 'That's why I wanted to track you down—'

'In case we'd run off together?' She means it as a joke, but it lands wrong like most of her jokes do.

'No,' he's quick to reply, horror pulling on his features. 'Nothing like that. But you were older. I thought you might remember something about why he left and where he was going. I've literally got no clue.'

'And you haven't asked your mum?'

He gives a furtive shake of his head. 'Can't.'

The ache returns to Lucie's chest. She wants to ask him why he feels he can't talk to his mum; she wants to coax his feelings out of him, but she is not his therapist. She's not even his friend.

'I only remembered you properly a few weeks ago when I was clearing out some old books and I found a little note in this old storybook.'

A distant memory sparks in the back of Lucie's mind. 'What did it say?'

'It said "Lucie Gilbert was here".'

'I remember that,' she says with a grin. 'You wouldn't let me say goodnight until I'd written something in the back of your book because you said I was the best storyteller. And then you drew a heart around it.'

The tips of Henry's ears turn pink and he pulls a face. 'Yeah. Saw that too.' There's a pause before he speaks again. 'Do you know anything that could help me find my dad?'

A silence draws out. Lucie feels herself torn.

'I'm sorry,' she says eventually, shaking her head.

Henry slumps in his chair, deflated, lost. His forehead creases; his eyes gaze into the distance. She wonders what he's thinking, what he's remembering. He turns back towards her, but before he can speak, his phone buzzes from the table beside his books. He jolts and snatches it up.

'It's my mum,' he says. 'I need to go. She's back from the supermarket. I've got to go.' He stands, pushing books into his rucksack, hurrying suddenly. 'I'm sorry I troubled you,' he says without looking up. 'Thanks for coming to find me.'

Lucie wants to ask if they can see each other again, but he's gone too fast, shoulders slumped forward, head down.

It's that image that stays with her as she boards a train back to London. That way he rushed to leave after just one text from Celia. Henry is seventeen, not seven. He should be out with his friends all weekend. A few hours in the library on a Saturday isn't living.

Poor Henry. Lucie can't help feeling responsible. If she'd only gone to the police or told a teacher of her suspicions, maybe Henry would've had a different kind of life. He was a sweet boy. He'd have found a loving home.

Their conversations repeat in Lucie's mind through Saturday night at the restaurant, then Sunday in the library.

She's aware of the sideways glances Jo gives her. Those gentle, 'Are you sure you're all right?' questions that she evades. She's not ready to talk about Henry or Celia and that part of her life, and Jo leaves her be in the end.

Monday is spent in the emergency department of King's College Hospital, helping the team assess incoming patients for mental health needs. It's her favourite team and she's usually buzzing by the end of the day, but on the walk home it is Henry that clouds her thoughts. She sees his face in her mind. That lightness when he laughed and how quickly it turned to worry at Celia's text.

A part of her knows she should leave it, but still, when she gets home that Monday night, she digs out her phone from her pocket, opens Messenger and begins to type.

FORTY-SIX

CELIA

At the sound of the front door shutting, I climb out of bed and step to the window. I watch Henry walk down the road, a bundle of reusable shopping bags under his arms. I wish I'd hugged him goodbye.

My heart stutters. I am unanchored, aimlessly drifting. No way back. There's so much he doesn't know.

On Saturdays, Henry wears his white knit jumper and dark-blue jeans. He goes to the library to revise until noon while I drive to Sainsbury's. But I do not stroll the aisles in my green ankle-length dress and matching green cardigan like Henry thinks I do.

I pre-order, collecting my shopping. Door-to-door in twenty minutes. I unpack the shopping and then I unlock the garage door again and I pull out the old laptop, finishing the book-keeping tasks from Friday while Martin hovers over my shoulder.

It's not fun. It's not what I want to be doing with my time, but it's the routine.

Anxiety rises inside me.

Henry will forget something or he'll buy the wrong brand

and I won't be able to cook the right dinners. Another disruption to a routine I desperately need to keep hold of. But then, it doesn't matter, does it? Because I won't be here when Henry gets home. I'll be in a prison cell.

'Finally stopped mollycoddling him, have ya?' Martin's gravelly voice makes me jump. I ignore it and walk to the bathroom.

Tears stream down my face as needles of hot water prick at my skin. I can't stop thinking about the shopping. Will Henry remember to get the organic milk? Will he get the fresh pasta or the dried? I grit my teeth, fighting the urge to stop the shower, pick up the new phone Henry has got for me and call him, rattling off my list, my fears.

I realise how ridiculous I'm being, but I don't know how to stop. Routines have been my salvation in the darkest of times with Martin. And before that, when my parents bounced me around from one school to another, never settling anywhere long enough for me to feel secure before moving to the next town, the next adventure, they used to say. I should have been a priority, but I was an afterthought. The only way to get through the day was to make a plan and stick to it.

A sob catches in my throat.

'You stupid bitch,' Martin says, laughing in that chuckling way he does. I picture him on the other side of the shower curtain and cower, wrapping my arms around my naked body.

'GO AWAY.' My voice is a shrill scream that scratches my throat and makes me cough.

This is where my routine has brought me.

I'm a murderer. A liar. A criminal.

I've tried to be a good mother, to protect Henry at all costs. I don't know anymore if I've achieved this. I don't recognise the person my son is becoming.

And this terror I feel in the deepest part of myself, which is keeping me awake at night, will not go away unless I smash my routine into smithereens – unless I do what is right.

With shaking hands, I finish my shower. I dress, pulling on a pair of jeans I only wear for gardening and a red jumper that used to be my Friday jumper until it got worn and pulled out of shape. I leave my hair in a ponytail and my face make-up free.

I hurry out into a grey wintry day with clouds sitting stodgy and low in the sky. Doubt creeps in, pricking at my resolve. Am I really going to leave Henry, the house, Martin, all my secrets behind? It isn't just what happened to Lucie that I'll have to confess; it's the last thirteen years.

Facebook Messenger, 8 days before

Lucie Gilbert

Hi, Henry, good to see you on Sat!
Can we meet again?
I think I know something about your dad.

Henry Watson

What is it?????

Henry Watson

Why didn't you tell me on Saturday?

Lucie Gilbert

It was all so long ago.
I'm not sure if I remember it right.

Henry Watson

Tell me! Please!

                                                  Lucie Gilbert

I'd rather talk in person.

Henry Watson

I can only do Saturday mornings.

                                                  Lucie Gilbert

Shall we meet in the park?

Henry Watson

It has to be the library.
My mum tracks my phone.
9.30

                                                  Lucie Gilbert

See you then.

FORTY-SEVEN

LUCIE

3 days before

'Explain to me why you're going to Hallford again?' Jo flops onto Lucie's bed, tying a folded bandana around her hair, pushing the curls away from her face. 'It's our first Saturday off in forever. We should do something. And I don't mean study,' she says quickly as if Lucie is about to suggest just that.

'I know. I'm sorry. I just need to go, all right?' Lucie glances at her friend in the mirror. She's wearing her favourite teddy bear fleece PJs and there's still a smudge of yesterday's mascara beneath her eyes. She wishes for a moment that she was in her PJs too and that they had the whole day ahead of them. She imagines how she would drag Jo to the university library in Camberwell, just for a little bit, before Jo took charge and took them to Greenwich Market to drink mulled wine and shop for early Christmas presents. It sounds so perfect. But Lucie can't let Henry down. The pull to Hallford is too great.

'Don't take this the wrong way,' Jo says, making a face that says there really is only one way to take whatever she's about to say, 'but you're doing that thing again.'

'What thing?' Lucie asks, switching on her hair straighteners and digging through her drawer for her comb because it always seems to fall right to the bottom.

'You know,' Jo replies, tone firm, 'where you get this tunnel vision for something and everything else drops away, including' – she pauses – 'your friends. And I don't normally mind because normally that tunnel vision is for studying, or when you need a break. Like that summer when you looked for your dad and didn't sleep for three days, and Christmas when Natalie convinced us both to download that fitness tracker and you started waking up at crazy hours to go walking. But this isn't the time, Luce. We're almost done. Just a little more pushing.'

Lucie swallows. She focuses on the pale face staring back at her in the mirror. She concentrates on sectioning out her hair and running her straighteners right to the ends. A memory surfaces. One she wishes wouldn't.

She sees her old shoe box of treasures. Celia's black ballpoint pen, the one she took from the careers office on their first meeting. The coaster from the living room. The little Lego girl she took from Henry's collection. The cheap jasmine air freshener she found in Wilkinson's that she used to spray in the flat sometimes. It was too sweet, too sickly, but she sprayed it anyway.

And the evenings after she left Celia's house, when she'd walk to the end of the road, perching on the road sign, just watching.

It was innocent – an infatuation of sorts; Lucie can see that now. This is not the same. She's trying to help Henry, to be there for him like she wasn't all those years ago.

'It's not that,' she says when she can't bear Jo's eyes on her for a second more. 'It's not a thing. I'm just trying to help someone, OK?'

Jo sighs. 'Fine. Just make sure that whatever you're doing, you're doing it for the right reasons.'

Lucie switches off her straighteners and lets Jo's comment sink in. It's such a Jo thing to say. But then determining the root cause of behaviour – the motivator – is key to understanding that behaviour. Didn't they learn that on day one of the doctorate? What is her reason for helping?

Guilt, she decides. For what she didn't do before. She'll help. She'll relieve her feelings. She'll move on. It's actually healthy what she's doing, she reasons.

'Honestly, Jo, you've got nothing to worry about.' Lucie turns, flashing her friend a reassuring smile.

'If you're sure,' Jo replies, sounding less than convinced. 'But the fact that you're not telling me everything is setting alarms bells off in my head,' she adds, tapping at her forehead before shuffling from the bed and following Lucie down the stairs. 'And that's OK. I know you'll tell me when you're ready, but be careful, Lucie. Think about your motives; think about what's right for you.'

Lucie nods, her face burning under Jo's comment. Lucie is a good psychologist. She knows the research, she knows the methods, but she is not intuitive like Jo, who sees beyond the words, the answers their patients give, into somewhere deeper. Jo will make a fantastic psychologist, but for a best friend, it's hard to keep things from her.

'Thanks,' Lucie says. 'I'll see you later.'

'Text me when you're on the train home,' Jo calls out as Lucie opens the front door. 'If I'm out, I'll let you know where and you can join us.'

'I will,' Lucie promises before stepping into a bright chilly day, pushing Jo's concerns to the back of her mind.

Thoughts of Henry – the little boy, and Henry the near adult, just as lost, just as scared as he was at five – clog her mind as the buildings of London rush by, replaced with fields and countryside and pockets of new housing estates, until she's back in Hall-ford, walking into the second floor of the library just before nine-thirty.

Henry is at the same table as before. There's a rucksack beside him but no books out this time. He's wearing the same white knitted jumper as last week and the expression on his face is nervous, edgy.

He smiles when he sees her, a quick flash of perfect teeth before his gaze moves past her to the door and then left and right. He's looking for Celia, Lucie thinks, glancing around her at the empty room. They are completely alone up here today.

'Thanks for meeting me,' he says, his voice fast. 'I've not got long. Mum wants me back in an hour. She didn't want me to come at all today. I think she might suspect something. But I told her I had to return some books.' He runs a hand through his hair, still a little damp from a shower. 'She said I could come but not to be long or she'd start to worry.'

Lucie frowns. 'That's pretty manipulative. You see that, right?'

He gives a slow nod, sadness drawing across his features. 'I'm starting to.' He fidgets in his seat before leaning across the table and dropping his voice as he asks, 'You said you knew something about my dad. What is it?'

Lucie pauses, the words sticking in her throat. Uncertainty twists in her stomach. She suddenly wishes she'd told Jo every-thing; she wishes they'd spent hours talking it through, picking at Lucie's memories and what she should do. 'Before I say anything,' she says, 'remember that I was only thirteen and might have misremembered stuff or got it completely wrong. This is only what I think I know. I was a pretty naive kid. I'm not sure—'

'Just tell me,' he pleads. 'I don't care what it is; I just want to know the truth.'

Lucie nods. 'Remember I said that I only met your dad once?'

'Yeah, when you were babysitting.'

'He came home early and I was scared because... Because I thought he was a bad man. There used to be locks on your bedroom door and on the cupboards in the kitchen. Do you remember them?'

There's a spark in Henry's eyes. 'I... don't know. There are these holes in the kitchen cupboards, like something used to be there but has been taken away. Anytime I look at them I get this weird feeling.' He presses a hand to his stomach. 'I sometimes wondered what they were from but I never asked. It's like I know it's something bad.'

'Locks,' she says.

'Are you saying my dad locked me in my room and locked up food?' Henry frowns, his eyes wide with surprise.

'That's what I thought was going on and so when he came home early, I was scared, but he didn't look mad, he looked sort of anxious and he told me not to trust Celia. But he was scary too. He had his hand on my shoulder and was standing really close. He told me Celia was crazy and that she'd end up killing me. I didn't know what to think or who to believe, only that I didn't want to be in your house anymore. And then—' Lucie falters again.

'What?'

The words stack up in her mind. Everything she wants to say about Celia and the nightmare and Martin being dead – murdered. A heat rushes through her veins. What is she doing? What is she thinking? She can't tell this boy that his father is buried in the garden. If it's true it will destroy him and if it's nothing but a figment of Lucie's imagination, then won't that be worse? To think his mum killed his dad but it not be true?

She thought not knowing was the worst thing, but maybe it's better this way. Henry will break free of his mum eventually, he'll become a doctor, he'll get his own life. She doesn't even know her father's name and she's done fine.

She stands so fast, the chair knocks back, toppling to the floor with a crash that echoes through the empty library.

'Lucie, what is it?' Henry is on his feet in a second, spinning around as though looking for the cause of Lucie's reaction.

'Nothing,' she says, shaking her head. 'You need to get back and so do I.'

'But my dad?'

'He left you,' Lucie lies, turning to walk away. 'Your mum was controlling him and you and me, and he had enough and he left.' She strides towards the stairs. She's been an idiot. This was never about Henry, or even about Celia; it was about her. It was about her past, her feelings.

'Lucie, wait,' Henry calls out, but she carries on, half jogging through the shelves of books to the main entrance, dodging a pushchair and a toddler in bright orange wellies walking in. The cold air hits her face and she gulps it in as she makes her way to the train station.

She walks quickly, passing the entrance to the shopping mall already decked out in blue and white Christmas lights, and a row of chain restaurants offering noodles and curries, sushi and Mexican.

'Lucie.' Henry catches up to her; a hand touches her arm. 'Please stop a second. I don't understand what's happening?' His voice is high and she can't stop herself from turning to look at him. There are tears swimming in his eyes. 'I have nightmares about him,' he half shouts.

Lucie stops suddenly and Henry almost trips over himself before spinning around to face her.

'I have nightmares about my dad. About him being dead.'

There's a bench to the side by a block of public toilets. Lucie catches the scent of urine and bleach, but she takes

Henry's arm and pulls him to the bench. 'Tell me about them,' she says.

Henry drops his elbows to his knees and buries his head in his hands as he talks, repeating nearly word for word that same nightmare from thirteen years ago. Then he sits up and looks at Lucie, his face pale and pleading. 'It's driving me half crazy. I keep getting this feeling when I'm in the house, like something bad has happened. Or I walk into a room and it feels like someone was just there when there's no one. I know it sounds stupid.'

She shakes her head. 'It doesn't sound crazy to me.'

'I just want to know the truth so I know if I'm going mad.'

'You're not,' she says, her own voice barely a whisper. 'You had that same nightmare the last time I was in your house. I thought it was just a bad dream but then I went down to the kitchen and I told Celia about it.'

'What did she say?'

'She laughed at first, a sort of forced humour. She did that when she wanted me to forget about something like the locks. But then... then I looked out at the garden and I—' Lucie pauses, drawing in a breath, the first in too long. 'I saw that the flower beds at the end had been dug over and cement had been put down. Celia said it was for a summer house.' She swallows. She looks at Henry, his eyes wide, hanging on her every word. 'And I remembered your nightmare and I asked her if she knew where Martin was and she didn't say anything, but she looked out the window to the exact place where the flower bed used to be.'

'Oh my God.' Henry drops his head back into his hands, rubbing at his face. 'It wasn't just a nightmare. I actually saw my dad on the kitchen floor, didn't I?'

'I don't know,' Lucie says. 'It's what I thought at the time.'

'It has to be that. It all makes sense.'

'What does?' Lucie asks.

'The summer house.' Henry stands up, pacing before her. 'She never goes in it. Never. It's just full of old bikes of mine and a few garden tools. She... She always asks me to get them out and put them away.'

'Henry,' Lucie starts, softening her voice, willing him to calm down.

He turns to look at her. 'She killed him. It's the only thing that makes sense.' He swoops down and grabs his backpack. 'I have to go. Thanks for telling me the truth.'

'Henry, wait,' she calls out. 'What are you going to do?'

'I don't know. I need to think.' He starts walking and doesn't look back. By the time Lucie gets to her feet to chase after him, he's gone, having disappeared into a crowd of shoppers.

FORTY-EIGHT

CELIA

Traffic picks up around me as I reach the edge of town. A line of cars queue to enter a car park – the first of the Saturday shoppers. I start to cross the road but ahead, on the other side, is a boy in a tracksuit, a black woollen hat pulled low.

My feet stop dead. I think of Sam – that moment when he jumped in my car and my heart seemed to stutter. The disbelief chased away by sheer terror.

'Hey,' the boy calls out at me and fear grabs me tight around the throat. What does he want from me?

He moves towards me and I go to step back, but my legs are sinking into quicksand. He's coming right at me. Has he got a knife?

'Hey,' he shouts again.

I cower away but a hand reaches me, grabbing, pulling. 'Watch out.'

I don't understand what's happening. His grip is tight on my arm. I can't find my voice to scream as I'm dragged across the road. Only when we're on the pavement again does he let go and I look up and see the bus hurtling by in the exact place where I was standing.

'Are you all right?' he asks. 'You almost got run over.'

I nod when really the answer is no.

'Look where you're going next time,' he says before walking away without a second glance.

I turn the corner and the police station looms ahead of me, the same grey as the sky above it. I reach the steps, one hand clasping the cold blue railings. And then I stop.

What have I done?

Images distort in my mind. Lucie alive, shouting. Lucie dead, silent. My breath comes in a wheezing gasp. The world spins. Tears fall hot on my skin.

I picture a funeral. A quiet affair in the crematorium opposite the far entrance to the park. Her mother will be crying. I can imagine the scene. A tight black dress, thick eyeliner; surrounded by the friends she put before Lucie again and again. I long to be there, but I have no right.

More tears slip easily down my cheeks. It feels as though I haven't stopped crying since it happened – that thud of the body against the car.

I didn't mean for her to die. I wasn't even driving.

The wound on my side throbs. The walk has been too much. I long to sit down, to collapse into a chair, and I will, just as soon as I climb the steps and walk through those glass doors.

But I can't seem to move. If I hand myself in then, everything I've done will be for nothing. Lucie's death will be for nothing. I don't want that. I have no right at all to want anything when it comes to Lucie, and yet I can't help it.

Yet how can I go back to the house? The fear clamps down on me – a bear trap with iron teeth biting into me. Henry dominates my thoughts. So like Martin with every passing day. I've lost control of him and Martin, who seems to wander out of his hiding place anytime it suits him. I can't stop him anymore.

I'm stuck.

From behind me, a man bounds up the steps and enters the

police station. He glances back at me, the door held open, an eyebrow raised in question, and I dip my head and ignore him.

Minutes pass. One. Two. Then a hand touches my arm. I wheel around, expecting DC Sató, but it's not. It's Henry. I gasp. My darling boy is here.

'Mum?' His voice is soft. He glances first at the entrance to the station and then at my face. 'What are you doing?'

'I just... I wanted to see how the investigation is going.' The lie flushes on my face. I've looked the two detectives straight in the eye and told them a fictional story as though it was real, but under Henry's gaze, my shell is crumbling. I feel his arm tighten around me and I lean against him.

'They'll call you if they have an update, won't they?' It's not really a question. 'You shouldn't be out. You look like you're about to collapse.'

'How did you know I was here?' I frown. The day has taken on a dream-like quality. I'm so tired.

Henry smiles and taps his phone. 'We're paired in Family Sharing, remember? You set it up so you could see me. And I can see you too.'

I nod. It's all I can do.

'Let's get you home to rest.'

The energy drains out of me then. I don't know how I made it home, only that it was with Henry guiding me. He leads me up to bed and tucks me under the covers as though I'm a child.

Then he leans against the door frame, staring at me for a long time and I find myself searching his face for a sign of my darling boy. He's there in the flick of hair that never stays in place and the pale rose of his lips. But still I struggle to recognise him beneath that stare.

'I had a nightmare last night,' he says, matter of fact. 'It woke me up in the middle of the night.'

'Oh.' I wonder if he heard me talking to Martin. 'The usual one?'

'Sort of. I went downstairs like I always do but it wasn't just anybody on the kitchen floor. It was you.' He frowns, his gaze looking somewhere off to the side.

I freeze, unable to form the words. Over the years, Henry's nightmare has morphed from the confused memory of a five-year-old boy seeing his father, to an unknown body. Sometimes it's a young girl that I think is Lucie, sometimes it's a strange man. But it's never been me.

Until now.

A sliver of fear traces its way across my body. What does he remember? What does it mean?

'I'll make you a cup of tea,' he says, and I turn away and cry silently into my pillow. I'm a coward.

I thought I could confess. I thought I could relieve myself of this burden – Lucie's death. Martin. But I was a fool to think I could leave Henry alone.

Facebook Messenger, 1 day before

Lucie Gilbert

Are you OK?

Henry Watson

Sorry for not replying sooner
and about how I left.
It was a lot to take in.

Henry Watson

I was going to confront Mum, but I couldn't.

Henry Watson

You're the only one who knows the truth.

Henry Watson

She watches my every move.
There is no one else I can turn to!
You see that, right?
You started this!
You have to help me.

                                                                Lucie Gilbert

                                                      I don't know what I can do!

Henry Watson

I'm a prisoner in this house.
I'm scared of what she's capable of.

Henry Watson

Do you believe me?

                                                                Lucie Gilbert

                                              I think we should go to the police!

Henry Watson

Can you meet me tomorrow?
I'm going to skip college! I couldn't
concentrate today.

Henry Watson

This is the only way!
I can't live like this anymore.

Henry Watson

I don't know how this will end for me!

Lucie Gilbert

I have lectures tomorrow. I can't.

Henry Watson

Skip them!!!
Please!!!!!!
You're the only one who can help me.

Lucie Gilbert

OK.

FORTY-NINE

LUCIE

The day she dies

A sick kind of anxiousness pulses through Lucie as she makes her way out of London for the second time in three days. It feels all wrong to be fighting against the tide of commuters and leaving the city on a Tuesday morning.

In her second year of studying, she caught scarlet fever and spent three days in bed and two on the sofa, pouncing on Jo as soon as she got home to ask her what she'd missed. Then last year, she'd developed food poisoning from using cream in a pasta bake that was one day past its use-by date. She missed two days of lectures. That's it. Seven days in nearly six years. She's struggled into classes through colds, sore throats, hangovers and a dozen other things, and never once did she skip a lecture or a day because she didn't fancy it or because she had something fun to do. Then lockdown happened and all that time at home, the online learning. She was lucky to have Jo to study with, Natalie to cook for them. She'd carried on studying every day, Zooming her lectures. Not missing a single one.

Until today.

The guilt turns inside her empty stomach – the spin cycle of a washing machine. She tries not to think about what she's missing – the patients she should be seeing under Dr Sheldon's watchful gaze – and instead keeps her thoughts on Henry. It's not hard. He's all she's thought about since that first message pinged onto her phone. When he asked her to come today, she found she couldn't say no.

What must he be going through? He came to her in search of a father he wanted to find, and she destroyed that dream and accused his mother of being a murderer.

Was she wrong to tell him? The question scratches at her insides as she boards the train to Hallford, finding a seat by a window and staring out into the vast curved top of the station, grey and grimy from decades of trains coming in and out.

She knows the answer Jo would give her right now. She'd tell Lucie she's interfering. She'd tell her that if she'd been sure of what she'd seen, if she'd felt any real morality or guilt over the past, she'd have gone to the nearest police station and explained everything. She'd have left it to them to break it to Henry.

As if on cue, Lucie's phone vibrates in her pocket and she knows without looking that it will be Jo.

Are you at the library? Swot ;-) See you in a bit xx

Lucie's shoulders slump. She left the house earlier than she needed to this morning, avoiding Jo and the questions she'd ask. A cowardly move, she knows that. She tries to reply, but no combination of words or excuses seem right. In the end, she stuffs her phone in her coat pocket. She'll meet Henry. They'll talk. She'll find a way to help him, and then she'll be back in London in time for afternoon assessments. And tonight, she'll explain everything to Jo.

· · ·

An hour later, the first spattering of rain hits the windows as the train pulls into Hallford station. By the time she's halfway to the library, the sky has opened, pouring in sheets that soak through her coat.

She hurries into the building, her fingers numb with cold, her hair soaked. The second floor is busier today. There's a group of men studying at one of the tables, and two librarians helping a woman in a wheelchair.

Lucie sits at an empty table and watches one of the librarians hand a cup of tea and a sandwich to a man in worn-out clothes, sitting alone in the corner with a newspaper. Lucie pulls out her phone, checking the time. It's gone nine. Jo will be sitting in the lecture room, wondering where she is.

Worry sweeps through her. She's sitting on an out-of-control rollercoaster, unable to get off, unsure if she wants to. Just a few hours, she tells herself, pushing damp strands of her hair behind her ears and reaching for her phone again. Before she can send a text to Jo, there's a movement in her peripheral vision. She turns and Henry is there, pulling up the seat beside her. His brown hair is two shades darker and just as wet as hers.

Already it's awkward. She feels connected to Henry, but a stranger too.

'Sorry I'm late. I had to walk to school first and then turn off my phone there so Mum couldn't track me.'

'You're in a school uniform,' she says as he shrugs off a sodden coat to reveal a burgundy blazer and white shirt.

'They make us wear it in the sixth form,' he says with an eye roll.

They fall silent for a moment. The uniform is a stark reminder of how young Henry is. It hits her then. The mistake she's made. Colossal. Undoable. What had she been thinking? Her throat tightens and she closes her eyes for a second. There is no going back. No time travel machine. She's made a terrible mistake telling Henry what she knows, and now she must own it – she must do what she can to fix it.

'I think I should go the police,' she says. 'And tell them what I remember. It's the right thing to do.'

He nods and falls silent. The library is quiet except for the occasional cough of the man in the corner, the soft murmur of the men at the table, the tap of the biro hitting the paper of the woman at the table beside them, peering intently at a textbook.

'You're right.' Henry says after a pause, his face paling, his expression so lost, so desperate that Lucie finds herself reaching out to touch his hand. His fingers are warm compared to her own.

'It will be OK,' she says, wishing she could believe it.

He shakes his head, swallowing hard. 'It won't. I hate my mum, Lucie.'

The venom in his words startles her. She moves to pull her hand away, but Henry wraps his fingers in hers. 'I'm sorry. I know I sound cruel, but you understand, don't you? You remember what she was like, how she picked at everything you did? And you weren't even her child. It's been a million times worse for me. You've no idea how hard it was to act normal with her this morning. I can't do it anymore.'

Lucie nods slowly. Henry is right and yet another thought is tugging at her mind. Her own mother wasn't manipulative; she didn't care what Lucie did with her time. She was an absent kind of mother. Lucie looks back now and it feels as though she was a penance for her mother to endure. But Celia cared. Whatever else she did, she cared.

Henry continues and Lucie loses the strand of her thought and where it was taking her. 'But she's all I've got. If we go to the police and they arrest her, I'll have nothing. I'm supposed to be finishing my A levels and going to university to study medicine. I've worked so hard.' His voice cracks and Lucie feels a sharp stab of understanding.

'You can still do that,' she says.

'How?' Henry pulls his hand away, raking it through his hair. 'Where will I live? Who'll pay my university fees? It's all I've been thinking about. Mum's been saving for years for me to go to university, but all that money will be needed for a court case, won't it? If we report her? And even if it's not, she's hardly likely to give it to me if I'm the reason she's spending the rest of her life in prison.'

'I'll be the reason,' Lucie says. 'Celia never has to know you were involved.'

'And where will I live?' Henry asks, already shaking his head.

'Social services will give you somewhere to stay.'

'I'm not exactly foster material here. I'm not a cute little five-year-old anymore, Lucie, despite what you might think.'

'I know that.'

'If Mum is arrested, if my dad is dead, then where does that leave me and my life, my future?'

'I don't know.' Lucie bites down on her lower lip. She recognises Henry's desperation, that desire to succeed that she feels in herself too. She's saved every penny she's earned since she was thirteen. As soon as she turned fifteen, she worked in a café on the high street at the weekends, picking up shifts in a clothes shop during the holidays. Then collecting glasses and being a pot wash in The Blue Lion. After A levels, she took on temp work as a secretary for two years. She was offered all kinds of full-time work and career opportunities, but she turned them all down, never losing track of her goal.

Without those savings, and a huge student loan, she'd never have been able to manage. And here is Henry, about to find himself in exactly the same position. Except without the savings, and based on what he's told her, no life experience either. Celia has sheltered him from the world.

Lucie doesn't know what to say. Henry could be all right.

He could find a room in a group home, he could defer his place at university and get a job like she did, but Henry is... he's softer that she ever was. She's not sure how he'd cope.

If Mum is arrested, if my dad is dead.

Henry's words swim in her thoughts. If. If Martin is dead. Doubt washes over her. What do they really know? What evidence do they have?

'What are you thinking?' Henry asks.

Lucie shakes her head. 'I'm just wondering... what if we're wrong. What if I go to the police and they don't believe me or they do but I get it wrong and your mum finds out that we've been talking and I ruin everything for you.'

Will the police even take her seriously? A young woman waltzing in from nowhere to tell them about a murder she thinks happened when she was thirteen years old. She didn't see the murder take place; she didn't see a body. They'll ask what evidence she has, and she'll have to tell them nothing but the nightmare of a five-year-old boy and the gut instinct of her teenage self.

'OK, so now I'm even more worried,' Henry says, his face turning dark, troubled.

'Sorry.'

'It's OK. It's not your fault,' he says.

Although Lucie thinks it might be. She walked away thirteen years ago. She turned her back on Henry then. She can't make the same mistake now.

'It doesn't matter,' she says with more conviction than she feels. 'Going to the police is the right thing to do.'

'We could speak to her first, couldn't we? To... Celia, I mean,' he says, stumbling a little over the use of her name.

'What?' Lucie sits back in the chair. The woman at the next table looks across at them, a pinch between her brows. 'What do you mean?' she asks, lowering her voice.

'You could talk to her, couldn't you?' Henry says, his words a fast whisper. 'You could ask her about my dad. You're a psychologist, right? You could ask her outright if she killed him and you'd be able to tell if she was lying.'

Lucie shakes her head. 'Psychology doesn't work that way. I'm not a mind-reader. This is crazy, Henry. I'm going to talk to the police. It's the right thing to do. Besides, all they need to do is dig up the garden, right?'

'But they'll need evidence first. The police don't go around digging holes randomly.'

Lucie senses a tension radiating from Henry as he thrusts his hand through his hair again, pushing the still-damp strands back from his face. 'I don't know what to do.' His voice is soft, reminding Lucie again of the little boy she remembers.

'Do you wish I hadn't told you?' she asks, holding her breath as she waits for him to consider the question.

'I don't know,' he says, and then, 'No. I'm glad you did. I've always felt this... this darkness in the house. I'm glad you told me. I just... I know this is selfish because my dad is probably dead, and I know we should do something, but I don't want to throw my life away.'

'I can leave it,' Lucie says, taking his hand again. It's clammy now. 'Go back to London and do nothing. You can carry on studying. Another year and you'll be at university and away from her control anyway.' Even as the words form, she knows she doesn't mean it. She can't let this go now. Every minute that passes, she feels more tangled in Henry and Celia's lives again. She needs to do the right thing. Correct the mistake she made thirteen years ago.

She holds her breath again, waiting for Henry's reply.

FIFTY

CELIA

Noises drag me from sleep. There's a strange humming I can't place and then a bang that pulls me back to consciousness. In and out I flit. Sleep then wake then sleep again.

After so many nights unable to sleep, I can't seem to stay awake. I've lost all sense of time. Days could have passed or minutes since Henry helped me up the stairs to bed and I cried myself to sleep.

Another bang. Then something else.

Is that a drill? It can't be.

I peel open my eyes. The bedroom is in gloom – that strange light of curtains drawn in daytime. Not light, but not dark either. There's an undrunk cup of tea sitting on the nightstand.

I turn onto my back, the movement releasing the smell of stale sleep. My covers need changing. I should have done it yesterday. Henry's too. The thought brings another wave of tiredness with it.

There's an ache stretching out of my stomach, from the wound on my side and right into every muscle in my body. The walk into town was too much, I realise, before remembering what propelled me to do it.

The police station. My confession. Would I have gone through with it if Henry hadn't turned up? Did Henry guess my plans? He's been listening in on my conversations with the detectives, I'm sure of it, knowing more than he's let on.

More noises drift into my bedroom. Henry is in the kitchen now. I can hear the clattering of a pan, the purr of the kettle.

'It's my turn to look after you now.'

My sweet darling Henry. So grown-up. Tears fill my eyes again, the emotion threatening to overwhelm me. It's all gone so horribly wrong, but I must get a hold of myself. Decisions need to be made.

Confess and go to prison. Stay quiet and live with this guilt and the fear of that knock at the door, of being found out. Stay and carry on. My routine. I picture the fridge and my colourful plans – evening meals, revision, a gardening schedule for each Sunday of the month.

There are other plans I keep hidden beneath my tights in the top drawer of my dresser. Clothes schedules. My lunch plans for each day.

Every hour of the day mapped out, keeping me anchored, but also... trapped.

I never meant to get so stuck in my ways. I never meant to push them onto Henry either.

In a year, Henry will leave for university and then it will just be me and these awful stuck habits. And Martin coming uninvited into my house, my bedroom, my thoughts. The air seems to suck away from the room. I can't bear it.

And then a third option appears – mystical and mirage-like in the haze of my exhaustion.

I could leave. I could run away.

I could go now. Go far. Never look back.

The idea races through me, pulsing and giddy, bringing with it a whoosh of energy.

I could go to Cornwall, to that little village I visited with

Henry when he was just a sweet boy. I could get a job as a cleaner. Scrubbing and tidying and being that kindly listening ear for my clients. I take a breath and fill my lungs for what feels like the first time in days.

But even as the idea takes hold, another voice is asking, *What about Henry? You can't leave him now.*

I can, I can, I want to say. Just look at who he has become. He doesn't need me. I'll leave him my savings and a note telling him I'll love him always. It's all he needs from me now.

The trilling of the phone snaps the thought away. There's a handset downstairs in the hallway and another by the bed, and I snatch up the receiver before Henry can answer.

'Hello?' I say.

'Celia, it's DC Sató.'

My chest tightens at the sound of her voice although I note that I'm Celia again not Mrs Watson. There's a pause on the line. I don't breathe. For a horrifying second I wonder if she saw me this morning outside the station. Was I caught on CCTV?

There's a click on the line. It's faint, but I imagine Henry picking up the hall phone and my body tenses another notch.

'Celia? Are you there?' Sató asks.

'Yes,' I say quickly. 'Sorry. I was sleeping. I'm still a bit...' My voice trails off and I don't bother to find the word.

'I'm sorry to have woken you. I have an update for you. Would it be convenient to pop over?' Her voice is clipped as though every word is taking a gargantuan effort. I have a sudden image of handcuffs and that grip on my arm again, leading me to a prison cell.

'Of course,' I say too fast. 'Is everything OK?'

'Let's talk later. I have some other items to attend to. I will be with you when I can.'

She hangs up without a goodbye, leaving me seized with panic and indecision. A nausea rises in the back of my throat, caustic and hot, but I can't seem to swallow, to push it back.

Henry moves in the kitchen below me. I catch the clink of cutlery. He'll know I'm awake now. He'll expect me to join him, but I can't. I can't pretend everything is normal.

Run.

Go now. Before DC Sató knocks on the door. Before Henry... I can't finish the thought.

With fumbled movements, I pull out a small suitcase from the back of my wardrobe and lay it on the bed. It still has the airline tags from our holiday to Crete last year. It feels like a different lifetime, a different world to the one I'm living in now.

Carefully, neatly, I pack underwear and socks, tops and trousers. One outfit for each day of the week. I zip up my make-up bag and tuck my toiletries into the waterproof compartment. The order of packing soothes me a little. That is how I will escape. Lucie's death, and Martin. And Henry. This world I've tried so hard to keep safe for him. I don't want to be part of it anymore. And I must escape this time. I thought I'd done it thirteen years ago with the frying pan and the rage, but I'm right back there living a life that isn't my own, feeling terrified every minute of the day, fearing what new horror will happen next.

Be quick, be quick, a voice shouts in my head. *Stop thinking. Time for that later.*

I keep a little cash in my bottom drawer – a few hundred pounds just in case. Of what? I don't know – this, I suppose.

When I'm packed, I open my bedroom door as silently as I can and creep down the stairs. Henry is still in the kitchen. I haven't written him a note, but there's no time now. I can do it later. I can post it.

I move quietly but quickly, stepping over the middle stair that always creaks. In the hall, I open the coat cupboard and pull on an old rain mac. It will do nothing to stave off the cold, but I'll be dry at least. I slip on my favourite black shoes. And then I'm at the front door, a hand clutching the catch.

I hesitate, not daring to breathe or believe even that I'm

doing this – leaving Henry. Another awful thing to add to my list.

Silence fills the house. Is Henry stood as still as I am? Is he listening? Can he hear my gasping breath, my thudding heart?

I want so desperately to call out, to say goodbye. To hug my son one final time, and yet I know that if I do those things, I'll never be able to leave. Tears stream down my face as I turn back to the door, but something catches in the corner of my eye – a small black globe on the ceiling in the corner above the door that doesn't belong. I falter, my mind trying to make sense of it in my house.

'It's a CCTV camera,' Henry says from behind me.

I start, muscles jerking, pain shooting out from my side. I spin around, aware of the suitcase in my hand and what must be so obvious.

Henry is leaning against the door frame of the kitchen, a tea towel and a mug in his hands. He's wearing a blue fleece I've not seen before. And, despite everything, I want to ask him about that jumper. It's not his Saturday jumper. I grit my teeth, pushing the thought aside.

I stand perfectly still, unsure what to do. The suitcase feels like a dead weight in my hand. Henry's eyes flick towards it and then back to my face. He starts to move towards me and my muscles tense. It's an automatic reflex – something ingrained inside me. My fingers curl into a fist, digging my nails into my palms, feeling the needles of pain it brings. I crave the pain, the distraction from what is to come. He really does look so much like his father.

'Why are there cameras in the house?' There's a tremor to my voice that gives me away. I place the suitcase on the carpet.

'They're for your protection,' he says in that matter-of-fact tone I know so well. 'I thought about how scared you've been after that man kidnapped you and I wanted to help you feel safe again. I thought having cameras would make you feel better and then you'd be able to sleep. Here, look,' he says, holding up his phone and closing the distance between us.

The speed of his movements turns my stomach, but I can't step away. The front door is behind me. I'm blocked in – a dead end in so many ways. My eyes peer at his phone and I see four small boxes each with an image in it. The hall, the living room, the kitchen and the upstairs landing. He taps on one of the boxes and it fills the screen and I see Henry standing over a shadow just out of shot – me.

'I told you I was going to look after you now,' he says.

Before I can find the words to speak, there's a knock on the door behind me. Three sharp taps that make me jump.

'When the detective is gone,' Henry says in a low voice, 'I'd like to talk, if that's OK? About my father and about Lucie.'

My mouth drops open. I'm floundering. Drowning. No words come out.

It's too late, I realise, staring into the questions and truths that blaze in his eyes. Too late to confess to DC Sató, who is standing just inches away from me on the other side of the door. Too late to run. I cannot leave Henry. I was a fool and a coward to ever think I could. All I wanted to do was save him, to keep him safe from his father.

FIFTY-ONE

LUCIE

The day she dies

A minute passes. Lucie watches Henry chew at his bottom lip.
A frown pulls at his forehead. She wants to say something else,
but she doesn't know what that something is. She doesn't know
how she can make this all right again.

Lucie thinks of Jo's warning at the weekend. *'You get this
tunnel vision for something and everything else drops away.'* She
shivers a little. The dampness of her clothes seeps through to
her skin. Henry is important to her. She must make this right.
She must help him. And yet, she can picture Jo's questioning
eyebrow, her voice of reason, and wonders for a moment if this
right here – everything she's doing – is no different from the
fitness tracker Natalie convinced them to download that had
Lucie waking in the night to do more steps. Is this any different?
Lucie isn't sure anymore.

Henry gives a slow shake of his head. 'No, I can't pretend
that nothing has happened. I can't carry on living in her prison
of a life.' He taps a finger on his lip. 'If only there was a way to

get the money she's saved for my studies and still go to the police.'

From across the room, the man in the corner launches into a coughing fit. Heads turn. It's not concern but alarm. The lingering fear of the pandemic ever present in people's minds. Lucie hates that she has the same questions flying through her thoughts, and turns away, staring instead at the tall rectangular windows. Raindrops cling to the glass, but the grey day looks brighter. Her phone hums in her pocket but she doesn't reach to answer it. It will be Jo wondering where she is.

'She's got a lot of money saved,' Henry continues. 'I saw a bank statement once. What if...' His voice trails off.

'What?' she whispers.

'I was just thinking, what if you surprised Celia after work tonight? You could ask her outright about my dad. She won't be expecting it and she won't have time to think up her lies.' He starts to nod, as though agreeing with himself.

'And what do you think I'm going to say – oh hi, Celia, I know I've not seen you for thirteen years, but did you kill your husband?'

'You could... you could ask her for money.' He looks up, large brown puppy eyes, pleading and sweet, just how she remembers them.

'What?' Lucie sits forward in her chair and he drops his gaze.

'Like, you could blackmail her,' he says. 'Tell her you'll go to the police if she doesn't give you the money. If she says she'll pay then we'll know it's true, won't we? And... And I'll get the money from her so I can go to university and my life won't be over. It's win-win.'

'No way.' Lucie shakes her head. The woman at the next table glares over and gives a harsh 'Shhh!'

'Come on,' she says, tugging at Henry's arm. She suddenly

wants to be away from the stuffy heat, the four walls, the people. 'Let's walk.'

They don't talk as they pull on their damp coats and walk into the fresh air. The rain has left a biting cold to the day. Lucie walks towards the park and stops at a quiet bench away from the main path.

Henry sits down beside her, his eyes boring into her.

'Celia isn't going to stop loving you if she goes to prison, Henry,' she says, her tone soft, pleading with him to see sense. 'She'll still want the money she's saved to go to your education. It will be OK.'

'Stop saying that.' His voice is a loud bark that makes her jump. 'You don't know what she's like. She can be... she can be vindictive. If I do something wrong, she punishes me. Like, if I don't revise between these set hours every day at the kitchen table, she' – he drops his face in his hands, the final words muffled – 'she's nasty to me. She stopped my driving lessons. I only got to have three or four, not enough to pass and then she stopped them. She told me I wasn't ready. She'll find out I was involved. She'll punish me by not letting me go to university. If I could just get that money first—'

'We still have to go to the police,' Lucie says, feeling herself waver under the weight of his words.

'I know. You can. Just get the money first. Then you'll know she's guilty and I'll be OK.'

Lucie feels everything around her unravelling. This isn't how today was meant to go. She came here to talk to Henry, to comfort him and make a plan, not to blackmail Celia. 'I'm not sure,' she says again. Everything suddenly feels so muddled and grubby. 'What you're asking me to do is illegal.'

'Like she's going to tell the police about it,' he says, sullen now.

Three children on scooters whizz by and they fall silent as

two mums jog to keep up. When they're alone again, Henry twists his body towards her. 'It's sixty thousand pounds.'

Lucie can't stop herself from gasping. 'Sixty thousand?' The amount catches on Lucie's breath. It's so much money.

'It's win-win, Lucie,' Henry says again. 'Surely you see that? I get the money I need for my future, and then you go to the police and tell them what you know.' Henry leans towards her, animated now. 'I'll have no one. I need that money.'

Lucie wants to tell him that he'll have her, but the words lodge in her throat. She's not sure if they're true. The connection between them feels as though it's a knot about to pull loose.

'Please, Lucie.' There's something intense in Henry's gaze and Lucie finds herself pulling back, standing suddenly, wanting to run away. It's wrong to blackmail someone, and yet, doesn't Henry deserve that money? Celia is not a nice person. She's mean and controlling. She's a murderer.

Lucie feels herself waver, and maybe Henry senses it too. He stands up, stepping close to her and taking her hand. 'You're all I've got, Lucie. Please help me,' he says, his eyes soft and puppy-like.

The pause between them grows. Lucie doesn't want to do this, but she's in so deep. She can't just walk away either. She made this mess, she told Henry the truth. Doesn't she owe it to him to makes things right?

'OK,' she says eventually. 'I'll ask for money first. If she says she'll pay it, then we know she's guilty. But I'm going to the police, Henry. Regardless of what happens tonight, I'm going to report what I remember.'

'Yes, of course. Thank you. Thanks,' he says, a little breathless. He leans forward, hugging her towards him and she catches the scent of fabric softener and, just beyond it, the smell of jasmine.

Her phone vibrates in her pocket. It'll be Jo again. Lucie

thinks of what she's missing now. And the assessment with Doctor Sheldon she promised herself she'd be back for.

'I can't do it tonight,' she says, biting her lip again.

'But you have to.'

'I've got to be back in London.'

'Call in sick. Please, Lucie,' Henry says, begging her now. 'You're already here, and Mum senses there's something going on. She knows I'm not myself. If she finds out... I don't know what she'll do. It has to be tonight.'

Lucie sighs and nods again. Better to get it done. It's not like she'll be able to concentrate on anything else until it's over. 'Give me Celia's number,' she says.

As Henry digs in his bag for his phone, a tightness wraps itself around her.

Later, when Henry heads home to change out of his uniform, Lucie huddles at the back of the M&S café next door to Citizens Advice. There's an unopened sandwich beside her, a mug of tea, cupped in her hands, staving off the cold of the day. She can't believe she's still in Hallford, that she's really doing this. She came to help Henry and now she's confronting Celia, blackmailing her. It's all got so muddled.

Is she really going to do it? Ask for money? Lucie isn't sure. She'll talk to Celia. She owes Henry that much, but she's not sure she can blackmail her. It's so extreme.

When her tea is gone and her fingers are warm, she picks up her phone and calls Jo. She answers on the first ring, her voice tainted with concern.

'At last,' Jo says. 'Where are you, Luce?'

'In Hallford.'

'Again? You've already missed the morning meeting.'

'I know.'

'Why didn't you tell me you were going? I've been worried.'

'I'm sorry, Jo. It was a last-minute thing.'

'Tell me what's going on,' Jo says, half command, half plea, and still Lucie can't find the words.

She sighs. 'It's a long story. I don't have time to explain it all now, but I will tonight. Can you do me a favour and tell Doctor Sheldon I'm sick?'

'Really?' Disbelief rings in Jo's voice. 'I mean, sure, of course I can but, Luce, I don't want to. We've only got a few months left. These assessments count for a lot. You know that more than anyone. Now is not the time to go off the rails.'

'I'm not,' Lucie says, forcing a firmness to her voice that she wishes she could pull out of the air and wrap around herself like a cloak, a cape. 'I'll make up the time next week. I have something I have to do here first. It's important.'

'Important enough to throw your career away?'

Lucie rubs at her forehead. 'It's not like that. I'll be back tonight, I promise.'

'I'm worried about you.'

'Don't. I've got myself in a mess, but I'm going to fix it and tell you everything later and you can tell me what an idiot I've been.'

Jo laughs. 'All right. Do you want me to come down there?'

A sudden warmth radiates through Lucie's body. She smiles. 'No. I'll be fine. I'll see you tonight.'

They say their goodbyes and Lucie drops the phone from her ear. Talking to Jo has slowed the rollercoaster. Lucie sits back in the chair and takes a long breath. For the first time in what feels like days, she thinks properly of her life, London, King's, Jo. Everything she has. Everything she has to lose.

Fear flutters through her. What is she doing here?

Memories surface. The bruise on Henry's arm that she thought was Martin's doing. Was it really Celia? That fear Lucie felt standing in their house; Celia lunging for her, the desperation in her eyes.

What will Celia do when Lucie asks her for money to keep quiet?

Her phone is still in her hand and before she can talk herself out of it, she types a message to Jo:

If anything happens to me, it was Celia! xx

A reply pings back a few seconds later.

What does this mean? Who is Celia? Lucie, I'm worried!!! Are you sure you don't want me to come down there? xx

Yes, Lucie thinks. More than anything, she wishes her friend was with her right now, but then Jo would talk her out of everything; she'd make her see sense, Lucie is sure of it, and she can't do that. She owes Henry this.

Facebook Messenger, the day Lucie dies

Henry Watson

I'm home!
Tell me everything that happens!!!

FIFTY-TWO

LUCIE

The day she dies

The car park is not the big open, well-lit space with lots of cars Lucie imagined it would be. This isn't so much a car park as an empty space behind two buildings, swathed in darkness. There are no lights, no thick white lines drawn on the tarmac.

The night has drawn in, dark and menacing, making her shiver inside her jacket. The ground is damp from the recent rain, and the sky above her head is a gaping blackness. Out of the town, somewhere, there will be stars, but not here.

Lucie checks the time. It's nearly five.

Unease travels through her. Away from the shops, away from the last of the shoppers, the stragglers, the early diners, the teenagers hanging out, it is eerily quiet. Horror-movie quiet.

Goosebumps prickle her skin. Cold, and something else, like she's being watched, like there are eyes on her from somewhere in the shadows. She scans the darkness then turns to gaze out to the road and the streetlights, but there's no one there. No one she can see. She wishes Henry was here, but they'd both agreed it would be better if he stayed home, waiting for Celia to return as though everything is normal.

A fan starts to hum from one of the buildings and she jumps, spinning back to the noise and catching the stink of fried food in the air – that clogging smell of fat. It's blasting out from the back of a fast-food restaurant. The smell feels as though it's clinging to her, like it's being absorbed into her skin. Her stomach turns.

There's a drizzle in the air. A dampness that makes her shiver inside her coat. She longs suddenly to be in the hospital. The bustle of staff, the intensity of her work, of patients who need her help. Or to be in the library with Jo, poring over books, eating chocolate bars in companionable silence that one of them will break every so often for a quick chat and giggle before dipping their heads into work again.

5 p.m.

A door clangs. A group of people exit the building in front of her. There are 'See ya tomorrow' and 'Have a good evening' shouts and the cars start and follow each other out.

Lucie pulls out her phone and, with a shaking finger, taps on Celia's number.

Celia answers fast, a surprised 'Hello?'

Lucie freezes, unable to respond. Celia's soft tone, that 'How can I help you?' question conveyed in one word, transports Lucie straight back to the little cupboard office in the school and the rows of careers binders, but most of all it takes her back to a time when she felt seen, like she mattered.

She swallows, surprised by the emotion Celia's voice unleashes in her, that tearing nostalgia, of wanting something that never really was. 'It's Lucie,' she says at last.

'Lucie, how wonderful to hear from you.' Celia's voice is treacle-sweet and yet Lucie thinks she can detect a note of guarded concern beneath it. 'How are you? How have you been? Gosh, it must have been... a long time.'

'I need to ask you something,' Lucie says, her voice shaking a little.

'Oh well, I'm just leaving work. Why don't we arrange to meet at the weekend?'

'It has to be now. It's life or death, Celia.' The words sound dramatic even to Lucie, but she has to make Celia see how important it is that they talk. And it is life or death. Life *and* death really. Henry's life. Martin's death.

A pause on the line and then, 'Right. OK. Are you in trouble? Do you need some money? How much do you need? Where are you?' The questions, the concern in Celia's voice push Lucie off-balance somehow.

Lucie has built this woman into a monster in her head, and perhaps she is one, but she is also kind. She has forgotten that. Suddenly, she remembers the revision books Celia bought her, the clothes, the shampoo. She remembers sitting at Celia's table, Celia listening rapt, to whatever Lucie had to say – that teenage angst. Making her feel special, important – seen.

'Lucie?' Celia says in Lucie's ear. 'Where are you?'

'In the car park behind your building.'

Another pause and Lucie can hear the sound of rustling. She imagines Celia grabbing her coat. 'I'll be right down.'

There is no goodbye, just the beep of a call ending, and then the ping of a message notification. It's Henry. Anxious now. She feels it too, that sense of a change coming.

She stares at the words and the unsteadiness returns. He was so sure today that this was the right path for them, coaxing and pleading. Lucie has allowed herself to be dragged along and now she's not sure what she's doing here.

The desire to turn and walk away thrums inside her, but before she gets the chance, a door in the far corner opens again with another clang. Lucie spots a silhouette of a woman, a shadow really, the tap-tap of heels on the pavement.

'Lucie?' Celia calls out, stepping into the puddle of yellow from the security light above the door.

She steps forward, holding a hand out in a wave and feeling stupid for it.

'Lucie, it's so good to see you.' Celia's face lights up, her smile genuine, unnerving. There is a moment of awkwardness where Lucie thinks Celia might step forward to hug her, and she shuffles back a little. 'You look so different with your hair blonde. It suits you.'

'Yeah.' She touches the edges of her hair, remembering Celia's insistence that she wore it back. That control. It spurs Lucie on. She thinks of Henry and everything he must go through day after day.

'I need your help, Celia. I need you to tell me what happened to Martin.'

'Martin? Whatever are you talking about? I haven't seen him for years. You remember he left.' Celia's eyes are wide with surprise, but there is fear in her voice too. Lucie is sure of it.

She shakes her head. She takes a breath, the words coming out in a rush. 'I think Martin is dead. I think you killed him and buried him in your garden.'

'What?' Celia's head jerks up, her mouth agape. 'That's ridiculous. I don't know what's going on in your life, Lucie, that's made you suddenly turn up here, accusing me of this, but I can help you.'

'I don't need your help. I want the truth. I remember the locks on the doors upstairs and the kitchen cupboards. Did Martin finally have enough and threaten to leave you? Did he get sick of your controlling ways? Is that why you killed him and buried him under the summer house you put in and never use —' Lucie stops. She's said too much.

Celia's face contorts, eyes widening then narrowing. 'Henry.' She whispers his name. 'You've spoken to him. He knows?'

Lucie says nothing. Her heart pounds in her chest. She's

landed Henry in a whole world of trouble. There's no going back now. Tension crackles in the air, but Lucie won't run away this time.

The silence drags out. From somewhere nearby, Lucie hears the distant beep of a lorry reversing and from somewhere closer she thinks she catches the sound of footsteps, although there's no one in sight.

Celia takes a deep breath and sighs loudly. Something shifts in the atmosphere between them as though a decision has been made. She looks at Lucie, tears building in her eyes.

'Martin was going to leave me,' Celia says. 'He was going to take Henry with him. He said I'd never see either of them again. I couldn't let that happen. I had to protect Henry. I couldn't let him live with that vile man. He was... violent and mean, Lucie. I tried to keep it from you. I made sure you were never at the house when he was there. But you were smart. You were figuring it out, weren't you? I could tell by the way you looked at me.'

Forgotten memories seep into Lucie's thoughts. She remembers Celia standing by the front door, practically pushing Lucie out of it. She remembers the shake in Celia's hand, the glance down the road, the fear.

These memories are as real as all the others, but they don't fit. A seed of doubt grows in her thoughts. Has she got this all wrong?

Lucie shakes her head, dislodging the question before it can take hold. She thinks instead of Henry, of what's he told her about Celia. 'You are the horrible one,' Lucie says. 'You are evil. Not Martin. It was you that had to have everything your own way. I remember how pushy you were for me to put my hair back or wear certain clothes—'

'What?' Celia's face is aghast. 'That was because you were clueless, Lucie. Your own mother wasn't giving you any help or support. It was down to me.'

'And the locks on the food cupboards, that was all part of your need to control, wasn't it? Funny how there was always food when I was there.'

'I... you've got this all wrong, Lucie. Yes, I like my routines, but I would never lock food away. I would never deprive Henry. There was food when you visited because I bought things without Martin knowing. I hid food from him, I... bought discounted items and took the stickers off. I made sure to be the good wife he wanted me to be so he'd leave the keys. He didn't always take them with him to work. It was normally at the weekends when he was there all the time that he'd keep hold of them and I'd have to go and ask him for them when it was time for breakfast.' Tears well in Celia's eyes before streaking in two perfect lines down her face.

She looks haggard in the glow of the security light. Tormented.

'He punished us all the time. Henry running in the house, or one of us laughing too loudly. Some nights he would make me cook him dinner, standing over me the entire time, making sure I didn't have so much as a nibble. Then he'd eat it all himself, leaving Henry and me to go to bed with empty stomachs.'

'No.' Lucie shakes her head, her own stomach knotting. Nothing Celia says is making sense. 'It was you who did that.' The conviction has gone from her voice now.

'Lucie, I'd never do that. I love Henry. I'd never have starved him. Never.'

'Stop lying.' Lucie shakes her head. 'Admit it – you killed Martin.'

There's a pause. A silence that stretches out for one, two, three seconds. Celia glances over her shoulder, eyes scanning the empty car park before turning back to Lucie. 'Yes,' she says at last, the single word a whisper. 'You're right.'

Lucie watches Celia swallow hard, wrestling with the emotions, an internal fight.

'I did kill Martin,' Celia says. 'I had to. And I'd do it again in a heartbeat. He was a bad man, Lucie. And maybe it makes me bad that I did it but believe me when I say that it has haunted me every day since. He has haunted me.'

Something changes in Celia's expression. Her face pales, her shoulders hunch.

'If he was so bad, why didn't you go to the police or leave him?'

'I should have done. But it wasn't that simple. I felt stuck. I didn't earn enough money on my own to support Henry. I didn't want to uproot his life either. So I stayed and I hoped it would get better, but it didn't.' Celia reaches into her pocket, pulling out a tissue and dabbing her nose. Her hands are shaking.

'And before you ask, I couldn't go to the police afterwards because it wasn't an accident and it wasn't self-defence either,' she says, her voice barely a whisper. 'Martin threatened to take Henry away from me and I lost it. I knocked him out with a frying pan, but he didn't die. So I... I finished him off. I couldn't risk going to prison and leaving Henry all alone in the world, so I dug a hole at the back of the garden. It took hours – most of the night. I dragged his body out and buried him, and then the next day, I went to a DIY shop and learned about cement and how to mix it. I went to a garden centre and bought a summer house to be delivered the following week.' The words tumble out so fast Lucie can barely take them in.

She steps back, unbalanced again. Celia's confession – it's everything Lucie suspected – and yet it's also not.

'I know I'm not perfect,' Celia continues, breathless with an emotion Lucie can hear blocking her throat. 'I know I'm bossy and I like things the way I like them. I know I'm a murderer. But I'm a mother who loves her son,' she cries out. 'Lucie, I would do anything to protect him. And that boy... he needs protecting.'

Lucie shakes her head, another step back. She doesn't want to be here anymore. She wants to turn and run, but she can't. She's stepped into a spider's web and now she's stuck, tangled in memories and lies and truths, and she's not sure anymore. Not sure of anything.

'I want sixty thousand or I'm going to the police.' The words blurt out of her, surprising her as much as Celia, she's sure. She doesn't even mean it now. She wants this all to be over.

'I'm sorry, Lucie,' Celia says, crying now. Sobbing. 'I'm sorry for whatever is going wrong in your life that means you need money, and sorry if what happened all those years ago is eating you up inside like it is me. You don't deserve it like I do. I'm so sorry I dragged you into my mess. I really was just trying to help you. I thought I was doing the right thing.'

'Why did you help me? There were loads of kids at that school in a worse position than I was.'

Celia shakes her head, lips pursed.

'Tell me,' Lucie shouts.

'You were special, Lucie. And not just because of your ambition,' she adds before Lucie can interrupt her. 'But because... because of who you were. Who you are. You were special to me because... you're Henry's half-sister.'

The words hang between them, sharp and unyielding. It takes Lucie a moment to understand. Then her head is moving from side to side. 'No,' she says. Her chest is aching so much, she feels sick, scared. 'My dad worked at the fair.'

'I'm sorry, Lucie. That's not true. Your mother lied to you. It was one of the only good things she ever did. I don't know exactly what happened between her and Martin, but I can imagine. She never claimed child maintenance despite money being tight. She wanted nothing to do with him and she wanted you to have nothing to do with him.'

'How do you know then?'

Celia huffs. 'You look just like him, Lucie. If you'd seen his childhood photos... And I'd known there'd been some kind of trouble a few years before I met him. We worked in the same accountancy firm together for a while, although I always wanted to do more to help people, which is why I became a careers adviser after Henry was born.

'At the time, when I was madly in love with Martin, I thought it was office gossip until you walked into my room that day. I could see you were lost,' Celia says, the words coming out in a rush. 'It wasn't fair that you had no one who loved you, who was looking out for you. I was trying to help.'

'I don't believe you,' Lucie says, although she's not sure if that's true either. 'You just don't want me going to the police.'

'Go,' Celia half shouts. 'Go to the police. Tell them everything. Haven't I already told you to do it? Don't let it ruin your life the way it has ruined mine.'

'What about Henry?' Lucie's voice is small now. She feels like that lost and lonely teenager who first walked into Celia's office. Nothing is making sense.

'He's older now. He'll have to cope on his own. He probably should've learned to do it a long time ago, but... I... I've kept him close to me.' She dabs a tear from her face. 'I guess I've worried he'd turn out like Martin if I didn't. That's a terrible thing for a mother to think, I know, but he's just like him in so many ways.'

A nagging sense of dread begins to creep over Lucie's thoughts. The same just-out-of-sight feeling she had when she was little, convinced there was a monster beneath her bed but too scared to look. It doesn't make sense. Celia is the monster...

They fall silent. Lucie is shivering all over. She wants so badly to go home. To flop on the sofa, bury herself in blankets, Jo sat beside her. Reassuring. Cracking jokes to make Lucie laugh.

'Why don't we go for a cup of tea, Lucie, and talk properly? It's starting to rain and you look freezing.'

Celia takes a step, but Lucie jerks away. 'No. Stay back.' She moves again, two long strides. 'I'm going. I need to think. But that doesn't mean I won't do it. I'll go to the police.'

'OK.' Celia holds up her hands. 'I'm sorry. I'm sure this has all come as a big shock. Take your time. Call me if you need me or if you have any questions. Do what you think is right.'

Lucie stands rooted, watching Celia turn and walk towards a silver car at the back of the car park, then Celia stops and turns. 'Lucie, wait,' she calls out.

But there's a throbbing in Lucie's head. It feels like a part of her has fractured, never to be the same again. She turns and walks away, glancing back at Celia a final time and shaking her head. How could she have got everything so wrong?

Martin is her dad. Was her dad.

Does she believe it?

She sucks in her bottom lip, remembering the way Martin had stared at her, disbelief morphing into narrowed eyes. Then something else strikes her. Martin didn't ask who she was that time in the bathroom. Lucie – a complete stranger in his house, looking after his son, and he asked what she was doing there, not who she was. And then there was Henry and his freckles, just like Lucie's. That connection she feels to him that she couldn't explain.

Yes, she believes it.

She believes everything Celia has said.

Lucie's legs are shaking, making it hard to walk. Slowly she moves towards the barriers. She has finally found her father. Years of searching. Of wondering. And now she knows. Her father is Martin Watson. An accountant who lived ten minutes from her flat for her entire childhood. Who didn't want anything to do with her or her mother. Who wasn't a very nice man. But he was still her father. And she'll never get to know him now.

The knowledge feels as though it's hollowing her out. She is empty. Lost. She doesn't know what to do. About Henry. About Martin. About Celia. About her own life.

Does she still want to go to the police? No. Not yet. She wants to talk to her mum. Lucie always thought her mum didn't care enough about her to bother to tell her about her father. Now she understands her mum was protecting her.

Lucie needs time, she realises. To process everything, including Celia's confession. Because even though Lucie believes her, it doesn't mean she's a good person. She might have killed Martin for a good reason, and her logic in keeping Henry close makes some kind of sense, but she is still manipulative. Still controlling. Still a murderer. Maybe she's trying to manipulate Lucie now too.

She rubs at her eyes, longing to be home. She wants to talk to Jo. Things will feel better once she's talked things through. She sighs, her breath puffing smoke into the cold silent night. She has lost her way. Again. Allowed her obsessions to lead her down a twisting path without stopping to think.

She's been a fool.

She keeps walking, the only sound the tap of her shoes on the wet tarmac. And then there's another sound. A car door banging, the start of an engine. The car draws closer. There's something in the sound that makes Lucie turn towards it, and even before her eyes register what she's seeing, she knows it's Celia's car. She knows it's moving too fast.

Her breath catches in her throat.

The car hurtles nearer. She sees Celia's face, filled with anguish, but she's not behind the wheel – she's running towards Lucie from the side, towards her car.

No, no, no. It doesn't make sense.

There is no time, no split second to jump out of the way. A

scream starts in Lucie's throat, but the jolt of impact knocks it right out of her. Pain explodes from everywhere. Her hip, her ribs, her chest, her arm, her legs. Something inside her crunches in a way it shouldn't.

Someone is screaming now. But it's not her.

Her feet lift from the ground and there is no space for thinking beyond the pain and the knowledge that she is still alive. Pain means she's still alive. Then she's falling, down and down.

A final pounding crash of her body, a flash of pain, white hot.

FIFTY-THREE

CELIA

I've always wondered what Henry remembered from the night I hit Martin with that frying pan. The same night he came home early to find Lucie – his daughter – in our house. The night he placed his sweaty hand on Lucie and whispered in her ear, turning her against me, planting that mistrust of me that in many ways led to her death. Why I blame him for it, as well as myself for dragging her into this family.

Martin and I had been fighting in the kitchen as usual. One of those fights that starts as one thing and morphs into everything. It started with Lucie.

'What was she doing here?' His voice was sharp, spittle flying from his mouth with each word.

'Lucie has been coming for dinner sometimes.' I tried to keep my voice even, reasonable, but I failed. The hatred for this man ran through me, thick like blood. 'I'm helping her. She's a lost child, Martin—'

'Helping yourself more like. Another little puppet for you to control, just like you try to do our son with all his clothes and your ridiculous meal schedule. You're making him into a freak, you know. What does Lucie's mother think to you doing all this?' The sneer on his face told me everything I needed to know about what Martin thought about Lucie's mum.

'I've not told her and I don't think Lucie has either. She doesn't pay much attention to her daughter. She's a good kid. Smart. You should be proud.' The last four words pushed him too far. The hand came from nowhere – a sharp sting on my cheek, the jerk of my head. He didn't follow it with a gut punch though, and I was glad.

'She's nothing to do with me.'

'She's your daughter, Martin,' I said, clutching a hand to my face, cowering but defiant for Lucie's sake. 'I knew it the moment I set eyes on her. Those freckles, that hair. She looks just like you as a child. And I remembered the gossip in the kitchens in the office when I worked at the accountants too. About a teenage girl that came in one day and accused one of the accountants of getting her pregnant, and I remember you talking about a relationship that went all wrong. "A lying bitch", I think you called her.'

'She was.'

'No. She wasn't. Lucie is Henry's half-sister. You should see them—'

'Shut up,' he shouted, grabbing the vase of flowers on the table and flinging it at me. I dodged and it hit the tiled wall an inch to my left, falling to the floor in a pool of water and a dozen pieces of china.

'You're not to see her again.' His voice was a booming command. I thought of Henry asleep upstairs and wished I'd locked his door. I hardly ever did that. It was Martin who used the locks, trapping us and thinking it was punishment. And it was for Henry. It was so very cruel, but it was a relief for me to hear that bolt, to get a break from such a pathetic excuse for a man.

He turned away from me, yanking a set of keys from his pocket.

'What are you doing?' I asked, though the answer was obvious.

He sighed, a heavy exhale. 'You need to learn your lesson, Celia.'

I thought of tomorrow and the breakfast and lunch I would miss. Dinner too, probably. I didn't care about the hunger. I needed to stay slim for Martin's weigh-in on Friday. There's a part of me that had grown to like the starvation – the power over my body, the only power I had. But it wasn't just me. It was Henry too.

'What about Henry?'

'He'll have to learn his mother's an interfering bitch.'

'Martin, you can't,' I said, desperation leaking into my voice. 'Henry is getting older. He'll tell a teacher. And he needs food.'

A padlock clicked into place and he moved on to the next one. 'You're a fucking self-righteous bitch, Celia.' He paused, head tilted to the side, a smile pulling at the corners of his lips. 'And do you know what? I've had enough of it. I'm leaving you and I'm taking Henry with me. You'll never see him again.' His grin was almost manic as he turned to fasten another lock.

The panic was blinding, a rage that came from nowhere, from everywhere. The next thing I knew, he was on the floor. Silent and unmoving. And Henry was standing in the doorway, pale-faced.

My mouth was dry. My heart racing so fast I couldn't think straight.

'He's sleeping,' I stutter, but Henry was already fleeing into the hall and up the stairs.

The world tilted on its axis in that moment. I was torn – split in two. One half chasing after Henry, collecting him into my arms and telling him there was nothing to fear anymore; the other half staying, rooted, dealing with an unconscious Martin in the kitchen.

I thought about running then; packing hurried bags for me

and Henry, but where would we go? What if Martin found us? I would never sleep again. Besides, I couldn't leave Lucie. So I lifted both of Martin's feet from the floor and dragged him into the garage. I found the plastic zip ties he used for DIY and I wrapped one around his wrists and one around his feet, pulling them tight.

Then I sat on one of the storge boxes and waited. It didn't take long.

'Celia?' His voice was groggy, a notch higher than I'd heard it before. 'What the f—?'

'Don't swear.' I sounded calmer than I felt inside – the raging storm.

'What are you doing?' he asked. His eyes were wide but his left eyelid was drooping slightly and I wondered how much damage the blow to the head had done.

'I won't let you take Henry from me.'

'I won't,' he cried out. 'Celia, come on. I was joking. What the hell would I do with that lad, hey?' He offered a smile, still hoping he would talk his way out of it. The fool. 'I'm sorry,' he said then and I almost fell off the box I was sitting on. How many times had he apologised before? Zero was the answer.

We stared at each other for a long moment. Something shifted in his face. Hope to panic. 'I can change,' he said, sounding desperate at last. The reality sinking in. He launched into a long speech, painting a different life for us. I let him talk, and for a moment I listened, I believed his words. But I couldn't forget what he'd said in the kitchen. He'd threatened to take my darling boy away from me. There was no coming back from that.

Martin paused for a second when I stood and walked over to the hooks where the tools hang. The words kept coming, growing more desperate and fractured as I lifted the mallet, a heavy weight in my hands.

Still, he pleaded. Even as I swung, he pleaded. And then he

stopped and the only sound was the huff of my breath as the weight landed and the blood pooled on the concrete floor. It was the point of no return and I'd crossed it gladly.

The plan formed so easily in my mind, almost as though it had always been there. The garden wasn't overlooked. Martin had made sure of that, growing trees and bushes that kept our house hidden. There was no one to see me dig the hole at the back. I checked Henry was asleep and I took one of Martin's shovels and I dug and dug, and thought.

I fretted over the details, of course, the lies I would tell Henry and everyone else. But there weren't many people to tell. The colleagues at the office and Martin's sister in Canada who he rarely spoke to. One story – he ran away.

I worried about the foxes and how deep to bury his body. In the end I decided concrete was the safest way. I'd put a summer house on top. Somewhere to store the gardening tools.

It was the wrong decision. A stupid thing to do.

I didn't anticipate a teenage girl being the one person to guess. I did it, in part, for Lucie, and yet I couldn't chase after her. I couldn't call her back and risk dragging her deeper into my lies, making her complicit. I had to protect myself and Henry.

I didn't expect Martin to come back. A ghostly monster in my dreams and my thoughts, haunting me from the grave of the garden, with strange noises in the garage I could never fully believe were birds. And always with that last smell I caught as I pushed his body into the hole – blood and dirt and his stink.

But I learned to live with those awful moments with Martin in my thoughts. I learned to push him back, keep him hidden in my mind, only allowing him out on the occasions I was alone in the house. It was worth it because we were safe – Henry and me. No more arms squeezed, faces slapped. No more locks, apart from the one on the garage door. I still needed that. The blood on the concrete never washed away, despite how many times I cleaned. Always it stayed – a rusty splodge I couldn't bring myself to look at and one I could never let Henry see. So I kept the garage locked always and put Martin's laptop in there when I decided to start a company and pretend to be an accountant, to be Martin, growing a nest-egg of money for Henry's education.

I clung to my routines to get me through the day and I watched Henry, I kept him close. Closer than a mother should have. Making him follow the rules, work hard, keep the routines. Even as a sweet little boy I caught glimpses of a monster lurking inside him, just like his father. I thought if I loved him enough, watched him enough, kept him safe, I could destroy that part of him.

All I wanted was to keep him safe from Martin and from himself.

FIFTY-FOUR

CELIA

'Celia?' DC Sató's voice carries through the door. 'Are you all right?'

Henry steps back out of sight of the door, tucking his phone in his pocket, my suitcase in his hand, and I spin around and open the door.

'Detective Sató, I'm sorry about that. I couldn't find the key to unlock the front door.' My voice is shrill, causing the detective to raise a disbelieving eyebrow.

My gaze pulls automatically to the small red Micra parked on the drive, searching for DC McLachlan, but Sató is alone today.

'Would you like to come in?' I ask, keeping the door close to me as Henry hovers just behind.

'No, thank you. This won't take long.'

It's then that I notice the cane in her left hand, a rainbow stripe running up its length like the sticks of rock sold at the seaside. Sató catches my stare.

'I only use it on my days off. Helps with the pain.' There is no more explanation and I don't ask. My assumption about a netball injury seems stupid now. Suddenly the sharp suits, the outward perfection of hair and make-up make sense. I am not the only one hiding something.

'I wanted to update you on your case,' DC Sató continues.

'On your day off?'

She nods but doesn't explain. 'Sam pleaded guilty to all charges last night, including the manslaughter of Lucie Gilbert.'

Sató's words hit me and I wait for relief. This is what I wanted. What I planned in the madness of that car journey. But all I feel is plummeting despair. It's over. It's just me and Henry now. No one to get in our way.

'Oh... that's... good. Will I need to be a witness in court?' I ask.

'There won't be a trial. A judge will decide the number of years he'll serve.'

'I see,' I say at last, fighting back tears, wishing I could drop to my knees and tell her everything. But Henry is right behind me, listening. Waiting.

Sató purses her lips. 'I'm sure he realised that it was his word against yours and he didn't stand much of a chance.'

'I don't—'

'Sam is not innocent,' she says, her voice sharp now. 'But I don't believe he killed Lucie.' Her gaze on me is fierce.

I stand frozen. I say nothing. What can I say?

'The CPS don't want to know about my theories,' she continues after a pause. 'They have someone in custody pleading guilty, so why would they? With no trial, there will be no gathering of evidence, which means technically my hands are tied to investigate your story and the evidence further. You're free to go on with your life.'

'I... er... thank you for coming to tell me this on your day off. I appreciate it.' My voice shakes. Sató suspects something. The truth? Half of it maybe, and yet there is nothing she can do about it.

'Technically, I can't investigate,' she says again, lowering her voice a fraction. 'But don't make the mistake of thinking that this is over for me. Sam doesn't deserve to go to prison for manslaughter. It is not justice, and I won't rest until that changes. Whatever game you're playing here, I'm on to you. I may not be able to continue digging into Lucie's death, but I will keep looking for your husband and I will find him. In the meantime, I'm going to keep my eye on you, and when you slip up, which you will do one day, I will be there.'

She doesn't wait for a reply. She turns away and walks back to her car, leaning heavily on her cane and leaving me clutching at the door frame, barely able to keep myself upright. Inside, I'm crumbling. A lifetime stretches out ahead of me, waiting once more for that knock on the door, for the tower of lies I've constructed to come tumbling down.

For a moment the madness inside me feels like it might break free, explode from my chest. I want to call Sató back, to tell her everything. To beg her forgiveness and make her understand that everything I did, I did for Henry.

He is safe now. I've protected him from the truth, from what he's done, but I've not protected him from the one thing I've always tried to – himself.

My breath comes in short gasping breaths. The truth – the real truth. Not what I've told myself, not the picture I've painted for the police, but what really happened that night – it thrums through my body and I want to scream at Sató to stop, to listen.

To tell her how Lucie had turned towards the sound of the engine coming right at her that night, surprise and fear on her face as her eyes darted to me, running across the car park, the same shock on my face as my car raced towards her.

Oh, Henry. What did you do?

Anger rushed through me at Henry and Lucie and what pushed them to this moment. If only I'd known he'd been there, lurking in the shadows, listening like he always does. Maybe I could've stopped it.

Lucie saw him behind the wheel. I'm sure of it. The way her eyes widened in the sickening second of disbelief before he ploughed right into her, only stopping as her body flew through the air.

I ran to Lucie, but it was too late. She was dead. Henry had killed her, and it was my fault. I brought her into the rotten core of our family. I thought I could help her. It was the least I could do after the way Martin had treated her mother, showing the real version of himself, I've no doubt.

'She's dead,' I cried out, the sob catching in my throat.

'Good.' Henry's voice was deep and harsh and sent a bolt of terror straight through me.

He kneeled down, his body shaking as much as my own. When he spoke, there was no anger, just fear. 'She... was going to tell the police about Dad. You'd have gone to prison. I had to protect you.'

'Protect me?' The words flew from my mouth. 'You've just killed an innocent girl, Henry. That isn't protecting anyone. She was your half-sister. How could you do that?'

'What?' His features contorted. Surprise. Horror.

'I thought you'd been listening?' I cried.

'I was.' The words rush out in an exhale of emotion. 'But then you told her to go to the police if she wanted to. You told her I'd be OK. I thought that was what I wanted too, but I realised I didn't want to be on my own, Mummy. So I rushed to your car and I did it. I stopped her.'

His words sank in with sickening clarity. Then something else occurred to me. 'Where did you get my car key from?'

He looked sheepish, eyes downcast. 'I took the spare from the drawer in the kitchen. Just in case.'

'Just in case what?' I asked, but he doesn't answer. He doesn't need to. It was intent. Premeditation. He came to the car park knowing he might try to kill Lucie. Nausea burned in the back of my throat. I stood suddenly, letting the cold air fill my lungs.

After everything I'd done. After watching him so carefully. Keeping him so safe, away from the world as much as I could, he still did this. I tried to stop him becoming the man I could see just beneath the surface, but I failed him. I failed Lucie. This was all my fault.

Something in Henry's posture changed, a softening, as though he'd woken up from one of his bad dreams. 'I didn't want her to go to the police,' he said, his voice whiny. He reached a hand towards her body as though to brush the hair from her eyes, but I shot forward, slapping him away.

'Don't touch her.' My voice was somewhere between a whisper and a scream, hoarse, harsh, making Henry jump back. 'Your DNA,' I said. 'You can't be here. Go now. I'll sort this. I'll fix it. She was in trouble. She needed money for something. God knows what.'

I closed my eyes for a second, blinking back the tears. How wrong I was. I held up my hand and Henry's voice trailed off. 'You need to go. You can't be here.'

'But, Mummy—'

'Don't say another word. We never speak of this again. Ever! Do you understand? I will save us.'

He dropped his head, still the little boy I remembered, and my heart broke in two and mended itself again all in one beat. I loved him so much. There was still good in there. If I could fix this, maybe I could still save him.

'I need you to say it, Henry,' I said.

He waited a beat, and then: 'We never speak of this again.'

'Good. It didn't happen. You have to forget about it. Now go home and revise. I'll be there soon.'

I made a plan as I struggled with Lucie's body, my own shaking with silent sobs. And then Sam jumped in my car and everything changed again. When I finally made it home the next day, Henry kept to his promise and didn't mention Lucie, and I didn't know how to tell him that I'd pinned her death on someone else.

And even though we carried on as best as we could, I knew everything had changed. He had changed.

Now, from outside the house, DC Sató's car starts and she pulls away. Still, I stand with the door open as though I can delay what is coming next.

Henry's hand reaches over my head, pushing the door out of my hands. It shuts with a firm click and he locks it before slipping the key into his pocket.

The air around me stills, the silence ringing in my ears.

'Henry,' I whisper. 'Please—'

'It's all sorted now,' he says, like he's talking about his schoolwork or a plan for the weekend. 'You and I, we fixed it all. I was so worried about you that night. I kept texting and calling and you didn't answer. I should have known you'd be OK. You always are.'

'She was your sister,' I say, tasting the salt of my tears running into my mouth.

'Half-sister, Mummy,' he corrects. 'Details matter, remember? I feel bad, OK? Really bad about what happened, but she was going to ruin everything and you were going to let her. All you had to do was agree to give her the money.'

'What?' I gape at him. 'What do you mean? I thought she wanted it for herself.' The words trail off. Understanding dawning.

'The money.' Henry swallows and his Adam's apple bobs up then down. 'It was for me,' he says in a strangled voice. 'She wanted to go to the police about... you and Dad,' he says and the flash of knowing in his eyes is ice cold in my chest. 'I asked her to get money from you first. What you'd saved for my studies. She didn't want to.'

The horror of his revelation sinks down inside me. It shouldn't make a difference now. I already knew from DC Sató that Lucie was following her dreams. Of course she wouldn't come to me for money. But somehow it matters. Another thing I got so wrong.

'If it makes you feel any better, I never meant for any of this to happen,' he says. 'I really was just looking for my dad when I first contacted her. But then Lucie helped me to see the truth about him and my childhood. And you, and the kind of person you are,' he says, calm, assured. 'I was upset and angry, which I think anyone would've been in my situation. I wanted you gone. I wanted you to pay for what you did.

'I convinced Lucie to confront you and went home to wait. And then I realised that even though I was angry, having you gone wasn't the answer. There was a better way for all of us. So I ran to the car park to tell Lucie not to talk to you, but I was too late.'

He reaches out to take my arm and I flinch away, pushing my body against the front door.

'I'm not going to hurt you,' he says, amusement ringing in his voice as though the very thought of my fear is something to laugh about. 'I know you think I'm like my father, but I'm not. I promise I won't hurt you. I just want to look after you and for you to look after me. I want everything to carry on the same as it's always done, just like you do.'

Nausea roils in my stomach as Henry's words sink in. He wants to keep everything the same. Just a few weeks ago, that's what I wanted too. Except now the veil of pretence I've lived behind all these years is gone and I can see our lives for what they are – a dark, nightmarish reality. It's a fight not to scream, to cry, to try to run again.

But after everything I've done – to Martin, to Lucie – I know I don't deserve an escape. I did it all for Henry. I really thought I could save my darling boy, but I was wrong – about so many things.

'Let's get you back to bed,' Henry says and this time when he reaches for my arm, I don't resist. 'I think we need a new routine now, Mum. I'm getting older, after all. I've got a lot of studying to do over the next few years and I'm going to need you right here looking after me.'

'What kind of routine?'

'No more trying to manipulate me with your emotional blac—'

'What do you mean?' I cry out.

He throws me an exasperated look. 'You really must try hard, Henry. There's only one of you, after all. You really must behave, Henry. You're all I've got. How do you think that made me feel all these years? All that pressure.'

'I... I didn't mean—' I stop talking. He's right. I never realised it before. Really, truly, I never meant those words to come out as they did. 'I'm sorry,' I say. 'I love you. I've always loved you.'

He gives a cautious nod and we carry on up the stairs.

On the top step, I freeze. I gasp.

The lock is back on my bedroom door. Same place. Same lock.

My eyes fly to Henry. 'I found them in the garage,' he says, pleased with himself now. 'To keep you safe,' he adds.

He opens my bedroom door and places my suitcase down on the carpet. 'Have a rest, and then you can make us dinner. Fajitas tonight, right?'

He steps out of the room, and I hear the thud of the bolt sliding into place.

A LETTER FROM LAUREN

Dear Reader,

Thank you so much for reading *My Word Against His*. If you want to keep up to date with my latest releases and offers, you can sign up for my newsletter at the following link. Your email address will never be shared, and you can unsubscribe at any time:

www.bookouture.com/lauren-north

The idea for *My Word Against His* came to me while I was driving home. It was a dark evening, but it wasn't late. I remember that. And I remember stopping at traffic lights on an empty road. Just me, alone in my car. It hit me in that moment just how vulnerable I was. We all have that fear when walking alone at night, but a car gives us a sense of safety, of being protected. And yet, anything can happen to us on a dark road alone. That became the first spark of the idea for Celia and Sam's story.

And of course, there is something intimate about sitting beside someone in a car. We're so close to them, but we can't get up and walk away. And when it's a stranger, that intimacy can be very uncomfortable, which makes for a great dynamic between two characters who are equally desperate to be somewhere else but are trapped together. It was such great fun to write those scenes.

For me, there is nothing better than having a 'WHAT?' moment when I'm reading a book. And I wanted to (and really hope I did) give you all a little shock at the end of Part I.

I always love to hear from readers, either with reviews, tags in posts, or messages. My social media links are below, and I can be found most days hanging out on Twitter and Instagram. If you enjoyed *My Word Against His* then I'd be super grateful if you would leave a review on either Amazon or Goodreads, or simply share the book love by telling a friend.

With much love and gratitude,

Lauren x

www.Lauren-North.com

 facebook.com/LaurenNorthAuthor
 twitter.com/Lauren_C_North
 instagram.com/Lauren_C_North

ACKNOWLEDGEMENTS

A massive thank you to you, lovely reader, for making it this far. I really hope you've loved Celia and Sam's story as much as I loved writing it!

A huge thanks to Christina Demosthenous for finding me a home at Bookouture, and to Christina and Lucy Frederick for being such fabulous editors and amazing cheerleaders of this book. Special thanks to the entire Bookouture team as well for all of your efforts. I know so much hard work goes on behind the scenes from lots of people and I'm very grateful!

To Tanera Simons, for being a massive champion of me and my books, and to Tanera and Laura Heathfield for the fabulous and insightful edits and support.

Laura Pearson, Nikki Smith and Zoe Lea – thank you for being such brilliant friends. There are no words to truly describe how much you brighten every day for me, which is saying something seeing as I'm supposed to be a writer.

Book people are the best people and I'm grateful to all of my social media friends for their support and cheering, along with the hard-working and dedicated book bloggers. Special thanks to Sarah Bennett for her motivational group, which got me through writing this book.

Thank you to my friends and family for understanding all the times I hide myself away in the writing cave. Special mention to Maggie and Mel Ewings for being on hand for chats and support. Mel, I forgot your birthday in the making of this book, and for that I'm truly sorry. I hope a HAPPY

BIRTHDAY in print will make up for it. And thank you to Tania Oxley for making my life infinitely easier.

This book would not have been possible without the wisdom and knowledge of Graham Bartlett, who is a brilliant crime fiction adviser. Any mistakes in police procedure in this book are my own.

To my husband, Andy, for your unwavering support and all the times you ask, 'What can I do?', 'How can I help?' when deadlines loom.

And to Tommy for brainstorming ideas with me – thank you so much! You're a hard sell, but a nod from you and I know the idea has legs. And Lottie, for always being ready to listen and chat, thank you. You are the best children!

A final mention to my writing companion, who is by my side for every early morning and late night I'm at my desk. Thank you, Rodney. You can't read because you're a dog, but I know it will make those who can read smile to see your name here.

Made in the USA
Las Vegas, NV
03 July 2023

74201696R00187